DEATH OF A
CHEERLEADER

CW01498470

MARINA EVANS

HODDER &
STOUGHTON

First published in Great Britain in 2025 by Hodder & Stoughton Limited
An Hachette UK company

The authorised representative in the EEA is Hachette Ireland,
8 Castlecourt Centre, Dublin 15, D15 XTP3, Ireland (email: info@hbgi.ie)

1

A CIP catalogue record for this title is available from the British Library

Paperback ISBN 9781399754262
ebook ISBN 9781399754279

Typeset in Sabon MT by Manipal Technologies Limited

Printed and bound in Great Britain by Clays Ltd, Elcograf S.p.A.

Hodder & Stoughton policy is to use papers that are natural, renewable
and recyclable products and made from wood grown in sustainable forests.
The logging and manufacturing processes are expected to conform
to the environmental regulations of the country of origin.

Hodder & Stoughton Limited
Carmelite House
50 Victoria Embankment
London EC4Y 0DZ

www.hodder.co.uk

DEATH OF A
CHEERLEADER

Marina Evans is a former Dallas Cowboys Cheerleader who graduated from Southern Methodist University with degrees in English Literature and Creative Writing. During her time with the Cowboys, she cheered under her maiden name/nickname, Rena Morelli. She lives in Arizona but thinks about her days in short-shorts often. *Death of a Cheerleader* is her debut thriller.

For women everywhere. I'm cheering you on.

PROLOGUE

~ OCTOBER 13 ~

On a crisp autumn game day, a wave of danger slithers up and over the rim of the Dallas Lonestars' football stadium. As it skitters to the center of the jam-packed arena, it begins to creep along the turfgrass like a deadly rattlesnake.

Jentry Rae Randall—the captain of the Dallas Lonestars Cheerleaders—is lined up with her teammates inside the stadium tunnel. About to perform, she feels her stomach knot and her lungs tighten. Today's matchup against the Philadelphia Condors will be broadcast to eighteen million viewers. She should be excited. Instead, the encroaching danger she senses is shredding her nerves like jagged glass.

Lips trembling into a smile, she explodes out of the tunnel like a sky-bound rocket. Ninety thousand fans in the stands leap to their feet when they see her and the other cheerleaders on the sidelines. Some spectators wave foam fingers, some

1

chomp on Touchdown Tater Tots, and others hold signs that read, SHIMMY AND SHAKE, JENTRY RAE! Or MARRY ME, J.R . . . YOU'RE HOTTER 'N HOT!!

The enthusiasm is ordinary.

Typical.

Familiar.

Not only is Jentry Rae the most popular dancer in the Federation Football League, but she is also a calendar cover girl and the Point—the star cheerleader who spearheads every triangular dance formation.

She should be over the moon with her life and her luck, but how can she be?

Vengeful eyes are fastened on her. She feels it in her bones.

Disguising her panic, she whirls her pom-poms and sashays to centerfield. Cameras flash. The crowd hoots. Her skin crawls.

Pregame routines don't normally make her anxious, but this afternoon she could barely put on her uniform. She isn't worried about another Lonestars' dismal season. Or a crazed fan. Or even remembering the dance steps. Her fear stems from what *she* has done. Guilt is a terrible thing, and it's squeezing her heart like a lasso.

Gulping, she assumes the opening pose. Once her teammates mimic her, a hush descends over the stadium.

"Ladies and gentlemen," an announcer booms on the PA system. "Here they are . . . America's Angels! Often copied, never surpassed, these are Your! Dallas! Lonestars! Cheerleaders!"

As the first bars of Shania Twain's "Giddy Up!" vibrate Jentry Rae's body, she snaps her head up and catches the beat. Twirling vivaciously, she exudes enthusiasm but, instead of connecting with the rowdy fans, her stare flits to the sidelines. There, she locks eyes with a Lonestars' football player. Anger reddens his face while he grinds his teeth. Is he wondering how she can pretend like nothing's wrong?

Sensing disapproval from the team owner's skybox, too, she squints up at the reflective glass. And when a fellow cheerleader flings Jentry Rae an icy glare, more worry freewheels in her veins.

She might be projecting confidence, but deep down she hates herself. She *deserves* to be scared. She used to be a simple country girl, but now she's drawn to complicated. And despite her capacity for compassion, she can be careless . . . even cavalier.

One thing Jentry Rae isn't, is stupid. Being a walking oxymoron is hardly a punishable sin. She is guilty of playing puppet master. And since people aren't toys to be manipulated, she's terrified that the puppets will come alive and exact revenge.

Moments ago, the field was deemed in-compliance, the players finished their warm-up, and touch tablets were activated. The preparations are standard football fare, but what isn't normal is the evil closing in on Jentry Rae. As she bats her blue eyes and flips her honey-blonde hair, she rallies the crowd into hysteria. Yet, the only noise she hears is trouble. And when it crescendos above the *whoosh* of her pom-poms and the *stomp* of her cowgirl boots, it blares in her ears like a penalty whistle.

PART I

As Texans say,
"That just ain't right."

CHAPTER ONE

THE FILMMAKER

~ OCTOBER 14 ~

Nikki Keegan clears her throat, turns on the microphone, and narrates.

"On October 13, 2024, a Dallas Lonestars Cheerleader named Jentry Rae Randall was savagely murdered inside the dance squad's locker room. Found in a pool of blood following a home game, the twenty-three-year-old veteran had been left alone by her teammates when they went to sign autographs in the parking lot. Reports confirm that the killer punched Jentry Rae so hard it sent her reeling backward into a knifelike corner of a locker. Sadly, she died from a massive brain hemorrhage.

"According to the stadium employee who discovered the beauty, horror and defeat marred her frozen expression."

Nikki's voice catches, and she covers the microphone. She is all for embellishing stories in the name of filmmaking, but she knew sunny Jentry Rae. At least she interviewed her for the football documentary she's directing. The effervescent dancer lit up the room.

Swallowing a lump of emotion, she continues. "The who-dunit homicide of a beloved American Angel has rippled shockwaves around the nation. Jentry Rae Randall kicked high and prayed deeply, and her leadership style was feisty but fair. As popular on social media as she was on the football field, she enjoyed being a member of the most prestigious cheerleading squad in the world.

"On the other side of the coin toss, the 'sexploitation' of the Dallas Lonestars Cheerleaders has been under debate for decades—showcased primarily on the cable series *Cheers and Tears*. The plug-and-play show drew heavy criticism for body-shaming and for promoting unrealistic societal standards.

"The show was recently canceled, but with that kind of controversy, the shocking murder of Jentry Rae begs two questions: Is there a dark side to the cheerleaders' razzmatazz? Or, did the Dallas Lonestars' four-season losing slump come into play on the day of the vicious killing?

"We begin our story by saying, 'Bless your heart, America's Angel. May you rest in peace.'"

Nikki shuts off the microphone and sits back. As she chews on the end of a pen, tension fills her rental apartment. What on earth is she doing? Her producer hasn't hired her to drag the Lonestars' name through the mud. And she isn't being paid to make a salacious tell-all about the team's cheerleaders.

What she *is* being paid to do is make a documentary about the Lonestars' potential comeback this season.

Period.

End of story.

But that's snooze-city, isn't it? How many floundering sports teams proclaim resurrection? Besides, unsolved murders—not football games—are Nikki's jam. She's an advocate for female victims; her first film covered that subject and, in her mind, Jentry Rae's death is ten times more important than the Lonestars having a new owner, new players, and a new director of the cheerleaders.

So far, none of those things are turning the team around.

Chugging an energy drink, Nikki focuses on a different reason she babbled out the narration. If she were to create a side hustle, reality-crime series featuring a murdered Dallas Lonestars Cheerleader, major streaming services might snatch it up.

A deal like that could earn her more than she's making for the sports documentary. God knows she needs money, especially since her unwell father started relying on her financially.

Chances are, creating a hit series would abolish Nikki's imposter syndrome, too. She comes from nothing, so she broke into the movie business through a back door. Her starter film about a cold case murder in the Kansas heartland *did* win an impressive award. *Pure luck, though, wasn't it?* Then, a Hollywood producer put her in touch with the Dallas Lonestars.

But Christ. What does she know about tackles and touchbacks?

Talk about self-doubt.

Frowning, she sets the drink can down and wipes her mouth. It'd be possible to assemble a top-notch, unauthorized miniseries if she doesn't eat or sleep much. And having a backup plan will be worth the stress. Botching this football documentary means her rivals in the male-dominated movie industry won't let her forget the failure.

Ugh. A lot is at stake. Damn it that she already signed an obligatory contract with the Lonestars.

Hit with a caffeine overdose, Nikki pushes to her feet. As she starts to pace, she hears the toilet flush.

Vince Whittle, her capable but talkative videographer, comes out of the bathroom scratching his full beard. "While I was taking a dump, Nik—you're out of toilet paper, by the way. Plus, there's nothing to read in there. Anywhoozit, I got to wondering why you're narrating already when we're still gathering footage. Oh, and ending the voiceover with 'Bless your heart' is a little much."

"Really?" She blinks. "I thought it was a sweet, Texan expression." She's a Californian who is still learning Southern culture. But the real issue is: did Vince hear the rest of her titillating narration? She hasn't shared the idea of a crime series with him yet.

"You don't get it." He takes off his thick glasses. "In Texas, the phrase 'Bless your heart' means only your mama thinks you're smart."

"Shit."

"Are we done now?" he asks. "We have been storyboarding since the crack of dawn, and I'm starving."

"I'm famished, too, so let's go for a bite. Put gas in the van then come back for me, okay?" Hopefully, her bank account isn't overdrawn.

After Vince disappears, Nikki immediately deadbolts the door. But what's with her paranoia? The Dallas rental the

Lonestars have set her up in is located in a safe neighborhood—safer than where she's from. Violent crime in Greater Los Angeles is rampant and survival is iffy.

Her father has worked two jobs his entire life. Then Covid hit. When Pop was laid off from both positions, he slipped into a deep depression. Nikki's mom died when she was a child, and if she thinks back, things started going downhill then.

Pop is her go-to best friend. His heart is always in the right place, but without his income, he might lose his mobile home soon. She had been staying there to keep him company, so she might be out on the street, too.

Jesus. Hollywood doesn't hire directors who live in their car.

Panic for herself and for her father circles her back to the idea of a lucrative crime series.

As Nikki waits for Vince's return, she considers calling her dad, except he'll have taken a sedative by now. Fueled by curiosity, she scrolls through her phone. The homicide of Jentry Rae Randall is splashed across every mainstream and social media site. No wonder; it aggrandizes all the juicy ingredients the public craves. Online sleuths have already conjured a conspiracy theory. That the cheerleader was killed by someone inside the Lonestars' organization. A jealous squad mate, maybe? Who else had access to the dancers' locker room?

Turning on the television, Nikki sees that CNN, FOX, and MSNB are exhibiting an identical crime scene photo: the blonde, damp-from-a-shower cheerleading captain spread across a tile floor. Jentry Rae's hair is fanned in all directions, and a gold infinity bracelet with a sapphire center is by her side. Those details are clear, but the majority of her body is pixelated out.

Nikki steps closer to the TV screen. Since the photograph has been fog-censored, it's impossible to tell if Jentry Rae was wearing a towel when she was assaulted. People are abuzz— speculating that if the star dancer died in the nude after a shower and a brain bash, it must have been a humiliating way to go.

Something else on the newscast catches Nikki's eye. As run-off shower water mixed with Jentry Rae's blood, eerie pink rivulets formed inside the tile grout. *Hell.* The photos are a little too graphic to be displayed on air, aren't they? Maybe somebody bribed a forensic photographer to release them.

"Jentry Rae Randall announced on social media that this football season was to be her last as a professional cheerleader," drones a television anchorman. "Unfortunately, somebody sped up that retirement decision."

Shuddering, Nikki watches the frame cut to Sonny Randall, Jentry Rae's elderly father. As the old man emerges from his Beaumont, Texas, farmhouse he is mobbed by reporters on his way to a dilapidated truck. "There's no kind 'a fury like a daddy who loses his baby girl!" he declares. "The killer will pay. I won't have my late wife turning over in 'er grave.'"

The crestfallen farmer tugs at Nikki's heartstrings. More so when she notices that his teary eyes are jaundiced and that his skin is pasty. He is obviously sick. During this tragedy? It makes her think of her father's own fight with health issues.

In her opinion, Sonny Randall's steadfast conviction points out the obvious question. Who hated his daughter enough to kill her? It took an incredibly strong person to propel Jentry Rae across the room and smash her against a locker. Two people might have done the job. Which is another hypothesis keyboard warriors are kicking around.

Going to her computer, Nikki watches the "Jentry Rae" interview she conducted weeks ago. On tape, she notices body language she missed. The superstar cheerleader couldn't sit still, and her lack of eye contact was evident. There was also the way the cheer captain rambled on and on—does this behavior indicate dishonesty? Or fright?

Guilt niggles at Nikki. She should have tuned in to the odd conduct sooner, but she was too busy being concerned with the Lonestars Cheerleaders' suggestiveness. The women might think winking for the camera and shaking their hips alluringly are harmless actions, but being in-your-face-sexy can attract weirdos. Cuckoos don't just prowl around Hollywood.

When Nikki clicks into Jentry Rae's Instagram account, she sees that each of the dancer's posts ring with a cute, Southern charm. Mainly, Jentry Rae spoke about wellness, her love of the DLC, the end of animal cruelty, and her day job as an administrative assistant.

Sure, a few judgy judgers commented *Lose the hair extensions, girl. Stop trying so hard.* And *Don't you believe in modesty?* But nobody seemed to have had a serious problem with the glamorous cheerleader.

Nikki taps her foot. Maybe she should forget playing detective. This murder could be good for her career, but it's shitty to think that. She should just wrap up the sports documentary, mind her own business, and return to California. Even though her brother is looking after Pop, Dave can't stay for long.

Coastal sunshine and lulling ocean waves might be beckoning her, but too bad she doesn't have a boyfriend to run back to. At twenty-nine years old, she is married to the fickle film industry. She's also consumed with taking care of her father while she fosters her fascination with justice. She'd probably hate a boyfriend breathing down her neck, anyway.

Nikki might have good intentions when it comes to her projects—who doesn't want to make a difference with crime journalism?—but her little secret is she's willing to sneak around protocol to make her work shine.

She is also willing to do anything for her down-and-out father.

With a mega-hit crime series under her belt, she could buy him a mansion.

CHAPTER TWO

THE DALLAS LONESTARS CHEERLEADER

~ OCTOBER 14 ~

The morning after the murder, Shaunette Simmons is crying buckets inside her car.

As she drives along State Highway 360, she keeps glancing at a glorious Texas sunrise in the rearview mirror. The sight is stoking her emotions. Jentry Rae, her best friend and teammate, loved daybreak. But she won't see another rising sun. Ever again.

Correction, Shaunette thinks.

Her *ex*-best friend won't.

Mercy! Thinking about their contentious falling-out brings on more crying.

Wiping away globs of runny mascara, Shaunette cannot believe Jentry Rae is dead. The two of them used to be super close. They were inseparable at the start of the season—like sisters! But then their toxic friendship ripped them apart. Shockingly, Jentry Rae expressed how much she despised Shaunette hours before she was killed.

Good gravy.

Shaunette really should bury that information in a deep hole.

Gripping the steering wheel tighter, she tries to reflect on some cheerful memories. Jentry Rae was a larger-than-life role model who hyped people up. She never spoke unkind words, and she always encouraged the cheerleaders to be their best selves. Because that is what she was. *The best.*

Few people can claim that title.

But still. Shaunette clenches her jaw.

Performers aren't always who they seem to be.

Shaunette is headed to church this morning to say a prayer for her deceased friend. As she drives faster, she assumes she will be one of many mourners. But isn't that another ironic factoid? Jentry Rae's fans can't know how infuriating the "real" Jentry Rae was. She acted like an irritating wind-up doll, cranking out inspirational advice nonstop. She could also be a five-star flirt . . . an enchantress of men who didn't know when to back off. Her demise has left behind scorched earth, so what monster despised her enough to kill her?

Taking an exit lane, Shaunette admits she is no angel, either. Piping-hot jealousy built inside her as she pivoted and paraded next to her ex-bestie during yesterday's performance. It made her screw up the DLC's famous kick-line.

Pulse racing, she flashes on the sequence.

1-2-3-4.
Head snap.
Bend knee.
Kick.
Repeat.

Even though she did her best to eclipse incandescent Jentry Rae, she just heaved and ho-ed breathlessly. She even flicked the wrong foot and bungled the final jump-split . . . *unacceptable!* But heck. Who could have competed with Jentry Rae's Colgate smile, Can-Can girl charisma, and Care Bear heart?

As the church appears on the horizon, Shaunette releases a sputtery breath. She needs to remind herself that she does possess looks, style, and spunkiness—all the requirements of a Dallas Lonestars Cheerleader.

Four months ago, she tried out for the squad because her mama—stage-mother Kaylene Simmons—was a proud DLC in the 1980s. When Shaunette was born, she was put in pricey kiddie pageants and endless gymnastics lessons in anticipation of becoming a DLC, too. It took her two tryouts, but now that she *is* a rookie cheerleader, her showbiz mother wants her to outmatch, outdo, outdance, and outdazzle everybody else.

Come hell or high water, she *will* do her mama proud. As if on cue, Mama's omnipresent voice echoes inside the car. *"Shaunette Lynn, if you want to BE the best, you have to BEAT the best!"*

It's unfortunate that the clock is racing for Shaunette to step up. She bites her bottom lip until it's raw because Mama's stage-four breast cancer diagnosis has been a horrible blow. But with Jentry Rae gone, can her mother hang in there until Shaunette reaches the top?

She has to!

Well—Shaunette muses as she pulls up to the church—Jentry Rae would *always* have been number one. Everybody knows it. Everyone except her mama, apparently. And that makes Shaunette wonder why her frenemy played with fire and risked getting booted off the DLC squad.

A heavy blanket of shame envelops her as she blows her nose in a tissue. Does anyone realize how relieved she is that Jentry Rae is dead? *Gracious.* The entire world is mourning the star frontwoman, but if Shaunette were to die, what would her passing look like?

Stop it, she chides herself. Thanks to beauty pageants, she ranks herself on a scale compared to others, but she doesn't have to compete with her biggest rival anymore.

Looking at the time on her phone, Shaunette knows she cannot be late for the DLC vigil honoring Jentry Rae later today. It's being held at the dancers' practice facility in Plano, and if she's late to anything *again*, Vana Lockwood, the director of the Dallas Lonestars Cheerleaders, will pitch a fit. Shaunette is a first-year newbie who can't afford to keep screwing up. So much is riding on how she measures up to her showstopping mother!

About to park at the church, she dries her tears and is grateful that at least Mama didn't have *murder* to deal with when she was a Lonestars Cheerleader. It's unfathomable that Jentry Rae died inside the squad's dressing room . . . the dancers' sanctuary . . . where they go to escape enthusiastic fans and bright spotlights. And since it's a high security area, *land sakes.* Did one of the girls take Jentry Rae's life?

No way, Shaunette thinks. The cheerleaders might have minor spats, but they aren't killers.

Fingers crossed that the group will be safe from intruders in the future. Except, will the scandal stop her from achieving what her mother wants her to?

Picturing her friend in a pool of blood makes Shaunette weep all over again. However, she isn't bawling from grief this time. Things don't look good for her. She was alone with Jentry Rae in the locker room minutes before the football game started. *She* initiated a screaming match. And—*Holy Moses!* She won't think about the rest.

As worry and fear thicken Shaunette's throat, she U-turns her car in the direction of the Americana Memorial Stadium. A plan is forming. If she can get into the crime scene and find Jentry Rae's phone, it might delay the police discovering something incriminating on it. By any stroke of luck, the bedazzled device was kicked into an unseen corner. Which might be a silly thought but worth a try. After all, Shaunette will do anything to keep Jentry Rae's secrets and her own from being revealed.

CHAPTER THREE

THE FILMMAKER

~ OCTOBER 14 ~

Nikki is in the driver's seat of the equipment van, waiting for Vince who's picking up their order at a juice bar. Peering out at the threat of rain, she hates how lousy the weather is this morning. Agitation sparks inside her because if Vince doesn't hurry up, they might waste a day of filming.

Then again, who is she fooling? Weather has nothing to do with her foul mood.

A phone call from her brother minutes ago deepened her concern for Pop. Her dad isn't running the heat to save money, so he and Dave are freezing inside the mobile home. Plus, the City of San Bernadino will be shutting Pop's water off next week.

Shit. She can't keep getting credit card advances.

And she won't receive the balance of her payment from the Lonestars until she finishes the sports documentary. *God.* Her poor father. She's letting him down.

Inadequacy pins her like a needle in a voodoo doll.

Pinching the tension between her eyes, Nikki wishes Dave was more help financially. But in his defense, her brother does have his own family, and he *is* staying with Pop until she returns. Their father is so despondent that he can't be left alone.

She introspectively returns to the idea of creating a crime series. Should she do it? She wants to, but with her luck there'll be consequences for acting without permission. Her career might never recover.

The chime of Nikki's cell phone breaks into her thoughts. Goose bumps fan across her skin when a text message from an unknown number appears.

Someone on the Lonestars' roster is breaking rules.

What the hell?

Who is being so weird and mysterious? And *which* football player is breaking rules?

Her stomach gnarls tightly. Then alarm pounds through her as she glances around. The only people who have her number are family members, Vince, her producer, and Lonestars' associates.

With fright blaring in her ears like a bullhorn, she crouches down in her seat. The next second, she realizes that the strange text might be an omen from above—telling her she'd be on the right track if she made a true-crime show.

Her phone pings again, only this time she breathes easier. It's a Google alert about the murder. Clicking into it, she watches a news blip.

"Our top story remains yesterday's tragic homicide of a Dallas Lonestars Cheerleader. The image we are about to show you is disturbing, so viewers be advised."

Nikki leans forward. The photo is a different fog-censored picture than the one she saw before. Snapped from a reverse angle, it shows Jentry Rae's blurred head and torso, but what's visible now is that the cheerleader's arm is outstretched and her shoulder is raised—as if she was reaching for something in death.

Reaching for what, though?

Jentry Rae's gold infinity bracelet is lying on the other side of her body.

Nikki presses her lips together. The explanation might be simple; the dancer could have just fallen with her arm out. In addition, police procedure dictates that evidence is bagged and tagged on site. But if that's the case, why is the infinity bracelet there, unbagged?

The reel continues. "Investigators haven't revealed possible leads in Miss Randall's murder yet," the newscaster says. "However, field correspondent Mason Boone may have a development. What can you tell us, Mason?"

"Hello, Candice. I'm at Jentry Rae Randall's Highland Park apartment complex where it's a frenzied scene. Police officers are trying to maintain order, but neighbors and restless mourners are demanding answers in this merciless slaying."

The camera pans across a large crowd to a sea of bluebonnets—the official state flower of Texas. Beyond the commemorative flowers are stuffed animals and framed photos of Jentry Rae set against a tree. As a uniformed officer emerges from the apartment building, he carries a box with a laptop protruding from it.

"I spoke with law enforcement officials earlier," the reporter says once he's in the shot again. "They have come to collect evidence, but what will they discover? And will it be of any importance? Back to you, Candice."

Just then, Sonny Randall, Jentry Rae's grieving father, barges into camera-range. Scowling, he pushes past reporters, ducks under a band of police tape, and barrels his way to the front door of the complex. Two cops stop him from going further.

"Please back up, sir," one of the officers commands. "We are still collecting—"

"See here; I'm Jentry Rae's papa. T'aint no one gonna invade her privacy without my consent. Let me in 'er unit."

"Sir—"

The old man blazes forward, reciting his amendment rights. Seconds later, he is wrestled to his knees, and in the scuffle, his tattered cowboy hat gets misshapen.

The crowd gasps.

Onlookers seem upset.

As terrible as it is, though, the police are following standard procedure.

Nikki cups a hand over her mouth. Tears fill her eyes because she thinks of her own vulnerable father.

What the news blip shows next shocks her a second time. Good-looking, twenty-eight-year-old Royce Holt—the second-string quarterback for the Dallas Lonestars—is nestled among the bystanders. His muscular bod and square jaw are distinctive; they certainly made an impression on Nikki when she interviewed him for the documentary. Only, what she remembers most about him was the way he kept mentioning his social media star wife and his darling toddler while he laid on the charm with her.

She didn't react to Royce's flirtations, of course. A man can be handsome, but in her book, he needs a brain and a sense of humor, too.

Seeing him in the crowd shifts her mind into overdrive. What is married Royce doing outside Jentry Rae's building? Paying his respects to a fellow member of the Lonestars' tribe? Carrying out a publicity stunt, maybe?

Judging from the football player's dark sunglasses and pulled-low beanie, Nikki doubts either explanation. Royce is hiding his face. So, why make the trip if he won't be acknowledged for a photo op?

A decision jolts her like a lightning strike. She'll go ahead with the crime series. Yes, her dad needs central heating. And yes, the anonymous text message she received is spurring her on. But Jentry Rae has become a spectacle in the wrong sort of way. What would she think of this circus, or of going down in history as a victim?

There must've been more to her than being a beautiful Barbie doll. Maybe no one knew the real her.

With Nikki's access to the DL Cheerleaders, she owes it to Jentry Rae to find her killer.

CHAPTER FOUR

THE DALLAS LONESTARS CHEERLEADER

~ OCTOBER 14 ~

Shaunette reaches the Americana Memorial Stadium, wiping her brow and nervously smoothing her long brown hair. The venue is still swarming with police vehicles, so she parks far away and debates about going in. A memory fills her head. She would carpool here with Jentry Rae, and in her friend's Mustang, they'd sing to Taylor Swift, munch on Jack Link's beef sticks, and giggle about guys. The good ole days.

Other fond memories involved weekend trips to Jentry Rae's family farm. The girls would sit in porch rocking chairs and gab like two old ladies. It's just what Shaunette needed. She never had a sister growing up, and friendships tend to evade her.

Fortunately, she and Jentry Rae got along from the get-go. They were the same age, and both of them were raised by single parents in small Texas towns. Shaunette felt lucky when Jentry Rae was assigned to mentor her. They'd practice routines late into the night, followed by giddy, two a.m. junk-food runs. Everything was great. That is, until the cheer captain dove into trouble and stopped taking Shaunette's advice.

Deciding to go ahead with her mission, Shaunette enters the stadium by flashing her ID at a familiar security guard. Then, doing her best to be invisible, she makes her way to the DLC wing layered in shades of gold and royal blue. Lonestars' colors.

As her heart booms like a ticking bomb, she positions herself behind the half-open dressing room door. Thankfully, police personnel don't notice her there. Without meaning to, she envisions Jentry Rae in every corner of the place. Leading a group prayer. Stretching her long legs before a game. And urging the squad to rock performances. But the moment you thought you had her figured out, she surprised you.

Bristling, Shaunette enters the dressing room and scurries to the edge of the locker room. Evidence placards outline a body shape on the bloodied tile floor. And a dented locker nearby shows a razor-sharp, blood-covered corner. Devastating sights.

"Miss?" A uniformed cop approaches her. "How did you get back here? This is an active crime scene."

"I'm a Dallas Lonestars Cheerleader, sir. I need something from my locker." She presents her lanyard ID.

"Honey, believe me when I say you don't want to see this. You should leave."

"Yes, sir." Sweat beads her upper lip as she glances around. Jentry Rae's phone isn't in sight, and panic torches her like a flamethrower.

Quickly, she looks up at the life-sized posters of her team-mates hanging above the dressing room cubbies. They display come-hither smiles, slung-to-the-side hips, and creamy cleavage, but Jentry Rae's poster is the standout. She had the curviest figure, the glossiest hair, and the most alluring grin. However, her image exudes a spine-tingling quality now. Like a spooky oil portrait with a shifting stare.

Lordy! The girl can make Shaunette feel inferior even in death.

Surveying her own poster, she acknowledges that she looked her best the day her cameo photo was taken. A trick is the cheerleaders knot the tassels of their cropped tops tightly around the center of their bras to pump up their cleavage. But she wishes her legs were longer, and her cheekbones were higher like Jentry Rae's.

The cop who told her to leave comes over again. Maybe he's noticing her jittery nerves. When he starts to chide her, she feels the color drain from her face in a slow fade-out.

"I'll go this time," she promises.

"Let me escort you out," somebody offers behind her.

Shaunette turns and sees Dante Marconi, the chief security guard who allowed her into the stadium. Seeing his teddy-bear physique and sensitive brown eyes fills her with fleeting comfort.

They share a moment of despondency before she sags against him.

"Whoa there." Dante steadies her by the shoulders. "I guess we're both missing Miss Jentry Rae something awful, huh?"

She nods.

After the guard releases her, he wipes tears away. He seems sweet—but to an extreme degree. He would do anything for the Dallas Lonestars and their cheerleaders. In particular, he panted after Jentry Rae like a puppy dog.

"This is unreal, don't you think?" Shaunette whispers.

"Sure is. But, um, can I ask you something? Did Miss Jentry Rae seem 'off' to you lately?"

She answers yes, although "off" is an understatement. Her friend was acting like a mouse at the end of a maze in her final days. Desperation wasn't Jentry Rae's style.

More curiosity chills Shaunette's skin as Dante escorts her away from the dressing room. Maybe the surveillance camera aimed at the cheerleaders' entrance door captured something suspicious. Does the guard know anything? "I heard you found Jentry Rae's body. Is that right?" she asks him.

"Yes, ma'am. Worst day ever."

"Did you see or hear anything odd *before* she died?"

He thinks for a minute. "I walked past the door and heard two tinkling sounds. Like somebody dropped jewelry, maybe."

Perspiration drips down Shaunette's back. *If Dante was by the door prior to that, did he hear me argue with Jentry Rae before the game? And why didn't he hear the murder occur?*

"There was a fan fight, so I left to take care of it." He shrugs.

His words don't sit right with her. He runs the stadium. Wouldn't he send other staff members to break up tussles?

But why lie?

As Shaunette reaches her beat-up Honda in the parking lot, she can't wait to leave the disturbing crime scene behind. Frazzled, she'll go to her apartment and redo her hair and makeup before the DLC vigil. What is it Mama always says? *"The higher the hair, the closer to God."*

Pulling out of the stadium parking lot, she wonders if police detectives will construct a character profile of Jentry Rae. The Dallas Lonestars Cheerleaders are coached to say that being on the squad is enough for them—that they aren't using the experience as a springboard to bigger fame.

But Shaunette knew better when it came to glittery Jentry Rae. Worse, Shaunette is hiding her own selfish motives.

PHOTO: Rays of sunshine catch the sapphire on Jentry Rae's gold infinity bracelet. A bouquet of flowers is visible in the background.

401k followers / 38,990 likes

#RandomActsOfKindness

My co-workers @HiedemanLaw are the best, y'all! They pooled their money together and bought me roses for my work-a-versary. I feel like a queen!

I'm also psyched that my boyfriend had this incredible bracelet made for me. He Who Shall Not Be Named is thoughtful and considerate. Sorry for keeping his identity a secret. Hopefully I can reveal it later! ☺

Death of a Cheerleader

Let us be kind to one another every day—not just on special occasions. Aggression is appropriate during football games only. Am I right? 💀📯

Watch the Lonestars eat the Condors for lunch on October 13.

Cheers and Godspeed xx

CHAPTER FIVE

THE FILMMAKER

~ OCTOBER 14 ~

In the equipment van, Nikki replays the newsreel showing quarterback Royce Holt outside Jentry Rae's apartment complex. Just then, Vince opens the van's passenger door with a clatter. The noise makes her jump, jostle her phone, and come out of her thoughts.

"Finally, right?" Grinning, her six-foot-four, bony videographer hands over a fruit smoothie and avocado toast in a container.

She sips the cold drink while Vince settles in the seat beside her. He is an awkward guy with no filter, but he's also a skilled, amiable co-worker. Overall, she's grateful for their easy rapport.

"*Brr*, Nik! Turn on the heat!" Shivering, he bundles his coat around his neck.

"Nah. Cold weather clears my mind." She smiles.

Rolling his eyes, he slurps his smoothie loudly through a straw. "'Preciate you treating me today."

"You're welcome. Did they punch my Yonder Free Card?"

"Yep." He passes it to her.

"Why does everything in Texas have to reference *being* a Texan?" Nikki cocks her head.

"Huh?"

"Yonder Juice Bar. As in 'over yonder.' That's a typical Texan phrase, right?"

"I reckon so, little lady, but I haven't lived in these here parts for long." Eventually, Vince drops his jovial expression. "Dang, I'm getting colder by the minute. Let's head back to your place before I freeze my nuts off—"

"What if we switch gears?" *Desperate times call for desperate measures.*

"Pardon?"

"Please don't freak out," she entreats. "Okay, listen. I'm going to level with you. I've decided to create a limited, true-crime series on the side. About the murder of Jentry Rae Randall."

His silence is chillier than the van's interior. "Are you crazy, Nik? Our producer won't like that. You and I are being paid to make a documentary about the new faces of the Lonestars. They're on Comeback Road with no detours."

"The project is a yawn fest."

"But you're a bottomless cup of creative solutions," Vince argues. "And you're fearless. If anyone can make a football film interesting, it's you."

"Thanks. I'm not totally fearless, but I am tempted to take an off-ramp. High profile murders go unsolved too often."

"Ah, can we stop making road analogies now?" He inhales a breath. "Believe me, I'd love to get up close with the hot cheerleaders. Hairy linebackers are disgusting, but we have bills to pay. Let's not break our contract on a whim."

His reasoning resonates with her. But not enough to change her mind. "You're right about us having bills. So, hear me out. There is a loophole in our contract allowing us to create side projects."

"Are you serious?"

"Yeah. I was just reading over the clauses. But if you're worried, we can crank out this bone-dry documentary about the fight for the Supreme Bowl, and that's all."

"Um, not so fast." Vince crosses his arms.

Let's do this because, what if I'm not crazy? she's tempted to say. *What if there is more to Jentry Rae's murder than meets the eye? Like an epidemic of wrongdoing in the cheerleaders' ranks. If somebody eradicated the cheer captain to that end, we need to prove it.*

Not giving up, Nikki hands over her phone. "Indulge me and look at this. See the odd angle and outstretch of Jentry Rae's arm?"

Vince nods.

Next, she shows him the snippet of Sonny Randall at his daughter's apartment complex with Royce Holt in the background. "What do you think?"

The videographer arches a brow as he hands her phone back. "I'll admit that's bizarre. Especially Royce Holt. I didn't take him for a creeper. I mean, I'm a guy, and even I think the cheerleaders are ogled too much. How do they stand it?"

"I'm rarely ogled," she replies. "But obviously the cheerleaders don't mind wearing skimpy outfits. Exploitation can be dangerous, though, don't you think? Hollywood sings that tune all the time."

"For sure."

Keeping the anonymous text she received a secret for the time being, Nikki starts the van's engine. "I suggest we head to the Lonestars' headquarters and keep our eyes open. Who knows what footage we'll capture with our all-access pass? Maybe it'll help the cops out. Do you agree?"

Vince's breath frosts. "Yes. Mainly because I'm crystalizing like Jack Nicholson at the end of *The Shining*. Let's go!"

As Nikki pulls out of the parking lot, she promises herself that when she pitches a true murder series, it will be killer. Especially with Vince's help. *Whew.* Her worry and anxiety are lifting.

CHAPTER SIX

THE DALLAS LONESTARS CHEERLEADER

~ OCTOBER 14 ~

Shaunette arrives at the Lonestars' world headquarters ten minutes late.

Known as The Depot, the enormous, ninety-acre compound in Plano resembles a sprawling space station. Painted a galactic white and shaped like a giant decagon, it boasts ten dining options, four merchandise boutiques, and an impressive 12,000-seat practice field. It also has a members' only fitness center called Lonestars' Club. Where the cheerleaders rehearse.

Shaunette tiptoes into the dance studio. Her throat is drier than dust because tardiness is a DLC sin. Why did she stop for gas on the way? More importantly, why did she visit the crime scene earlier this morning?

The trip wasn't worth it.

It left her mentally spent.

It probably raised eyebrows, too.

Sniffling back her worry, she hears strains of somber, new-age music in the hallway. Once she rounds the corner, she sees the cheerleading squad on the floor while the DLC directors are in chairs, dabbing their wet eyes.

It feels odd for Shaunette to be here in the daytime. Rehearsals are usually held at night. But these are unusual circumstances.

As she approaches the group, the atmosphere of death contrasts the usual bubbliness of the squad. The dancers are beyond frightened, as exemplified by the messages flying back and forth between them. Concern is being expressed about the security level at the upcoming memorial for Jentry Rae. In other words, the girls can't shake off a heavy shroud of paranoia.

I'm sure the outpouring of grief at the memorial will be volcanic, Shaunette thinks. Her personal grief runs deeper than that, however. Jentry Rae's photos in the press are inescapable, but she mainly sees her friend's face in a guilty recess of her mind.

Her teammates fling her disapproving glances as she sits down. She stiffens. It's true that her envy brewed and festered for a spell, and that's out in the "DLC" open. But hopefully nobody knows that her jealousy of Jentry Rae reached epic proportions.

While she settles crisscross on the floor, Vana Lockwood, the new DLC director, and Tammie Turner, the new DLC choreographer, seem angry with her, too.

Shaunette gets it. She is the skunk at the garden party.

"This isn't the right way to get attention, young lady," Vana tells her crisply. "We'll talk about your tardiness later."

"Yes, ma'am." She braids her fingers in her lap. Vana could be nicer, maybe even cut her some slack in light of her legacy status. Shaunette's mom cheered on the same DLC squad as Vana in 1986—when the dancers wore Frederick's of Hollywood push-up bras, vinyl go-go boots, and shook pom-poms the size of tractor tires.

It was a righteous, tubular era.

Shaunette's mother's words. Not hers.

One time, Kaylene Simmons relayed a story about a DLC who broke the organization's central rule: cheerleaders cannot be around, date, or sleep with the football players.

The doomed romance forced the girl off the squad.

"Jentry Rae was guilty of the same thing, y'all!" Shaunette is tempted to shout during the vigil. Instead, she chews the inside of her cheek and attempts a humble look.

Weeks ago, she dog-sat for Jentry Rae and that's when she snooped around her friend's apartment. A diary entry told her that Miss Perfect wasn't so perfect. Jentry Rae was hooking up with a Lonestars' player! Shaunette confronted her about it on the day of the murder, and all hell broke loose.

What's really bad is that Jentry Rae captured their heated exchange on her cell phone. Now, the info is dangling on a reachable iCloud.

As soon as the police mention the phone, Shaunette will need to contend that the nasty squabble didn't turn violent. Except, it did.

Shit on a shingle. Noises echo in the hollow locker room— louder than screams in an empty cave.

Jentry Rae's favorite song plays during the vigil. Some of the cheerleaders cry openly. A few use their shirt-sleeves to wipe their eyes. Others bury their faces in their gel-mani-cured hands.

A pretty, East Indian veteran named Priya leans toward Shaunette. "Thanks for your text," she whispers. "Sorry I've been too busy to reply."

"No worries." Rookie Shaunette might not be super influ-ential to the squad, but she *was* Jentry Rae's bestie for a few months. Her teammates respect that. However, she wants more. She longs to fit in, become a group leader, and be appointed a DLC goodwill ambassador, even. She was, after all, kind enough to locate Jentry Rae's bulldog and take the pet in.

Unfortunately, Sonny Randall is in no shape to be a dog owner. The devastated, ailing farmer has end-stage liver dis-ease—a condition Jentry Rae had informed Shaunette of.

Mercy! Shaunette's heart aches for the old man the way it aches for her mama. Watching her mother whittle away from breast cancer is something she wouldn't wish on her worst enemy. *Wait.* She doesn't have a worst enemy anymore.

Jentry Rae's favorite song ends. Vana gestures for the dancers to listen up. "All righty, ladies. Tammie and me want to say that we're in this with the thirty-six of y'all. Although each of us is coping with the loss of Jentry Rae in our own way, y'all need to be strong for the fans. Our Jentry Rae was a show-woman; remember that. So, if we want to make her proud, the show must go on." She clears her throat. "Ladies, what's our battle cry before every game?"

"We love us some football!" the entire squad shouts in unison.

"Amen . . . on and off the field," Vana concludes. Swiping tears from her dark-blue eyes, she scrubs anxiously at her short, caramel-colored hair.

Brunette, thirty-something Tammie Turner doesn't say a word. Her mouth is shut tighter than a casket.

It's a known fact that Tammie auditioned for the Dallas Lonestars Cheerleaders multiple times but was never selected. She might have mad dance skills and an incredible figure, but she also has a lazy eye and a weak chin.

At least she is an expert choreographer for the cheerleaders now.

Shaunette's mind wanders to a question often asked of her. Why be a DLC? The pay is low. The practices are grueling. And you can't even date the football players. The reason lies in honor. To be chosen to represent the 'Stars means you are part of history. And Shaunette *was* proud to have been selected for the squad. It's the hardest job application ever. Plus, she didn't do judgmental beauty pageants and withstand tough gymnastic lessons for nothing.

Once the cheerleaders form a big circle, they take turns discussing Jentry Rae's ripped-from-the-headlines absence. Shaunette will be last, and she's glad. She is also relieved that the dancers aren't seated in two groups today—how rookies and veterans stay separated from each other. A vigil is no time for hierarchy.

When it's her turn to speak, she sits up straighter. "Y'all know that me and Jentry Rae were close. She was compassionate and motivating. I mean, she was the top diva, right? I would have done anything for her. I felt totally honored that she befriended me and confided in me."

"You always make things about you, Shaunette!" Ashleigh, the leader of her dance group, sneers. "And if Jentry Rae had secrets, you should tell them to Vana and to the police."

Secrets? Shaunette frowns. *Uh-oh. The ones I'm keeping could put* me *on the police's radar.*

"What were you and Jentry Rae bickering about the day she died?" Problematic, redheaded Ashleigh asks.

"Excuse me?"

"The walls are thin. Everyone knows y'all got into it. Tell us why."

Shaunette's hands grow clammy.

Vana clucks her tongue. "Stop being a tattletale, Ashleigh. Emotions are high today but act respectfully. This is an observance."

Too bad it *is* a solemn occasion because Shaunette would love to call her teammate a choice name. She won't, though. Unladylike profanity is forbidden within the DLC.

Forcing godawful words down her windpipe, she tries to put things in perspective. The biggest positive is that no one knows what made her friendship with Jentry Rae fall apart. Plus, Jentry Rae died before she could throw anyone under the bus. But how long before Vana and the other dancers figure out what really happened prior to yesterday's game?

Shaunette tunes out what the other cheerleaders are saying; she's commanding herself to stop being a screw-up. Maybe then her teammates will like her. The Dallas Lonestars Cheerleaders are a sisterhood—a group that offers the opportunity for strong camaraderie. What brings them together is the challenge of being ultra-feminine performers on a worldwide stage. In spite of that, competitiveness oozes off Shaunette like slippery body oil. Can anybody blame her, though? She was made to fake-tan, walk in heels, and dye her eyebrows at age seven.

Another group prayer closes the vigil. As the cheerleaders gather their things, some complain about how they need to be at work early in the morning. Shaunette does, too. She's a personal trainer with very few clients, and since her competitive nature drives people too hard, she really needs to look for a second job. Pro cheerleaders are paid peanuts, compared to what pro football players make. Astonishingly, the dancers' compensation hovers in minimum-wage range.

While the other dancers filter out of the studio, Shaunette stays behind at Vana's request. The tongue-lashing she receives isn't pretty. "You're making lots of performance mistakes," Vana tells her. "Also, you are habitually late while in combat mode. Do better. You're a phenomenal dancer, young lady."

It feels like forever before Vana excuses her with a warning. She is about to exit the studio when she hears distressed voices. Quietly, she returns to Vana's closed office door and puts her ear to it.

"This is unbelievable!" Choreographer Tammie cries. "Poor little Jentry Rae!"

"Such a tragedy," Vana agrees. "I hate the word 'homicide.' Even more, I hate how salaciousness is gonna taint this year's squad. Our hard work . . . I mean, we hand-picked these girls! I'm the new director so I need to show out."

"Wow, Vana," Tammie says. "I'm new and affected, too."

Shaunette crosses her arms. Maybe she figured Vana wrong in the compassion department. The woman is certainly accomplished, though. Her bio boasts "Texas Rangerette", "Dallas Lonestars Cheerleader", and "Broadway dancer." Photos of Vana in *Rent* and *Mamma Mia!* reveal that she was a stunning headliner, so it could be that she's having trouble putting fame on the back burner now.

"I have a game plan," Vana speaks up again. "It's a strategy that could put this trolley back on track. A new opportunity has presented itself, so we should mix it up when we appoint a new squad captain."

"Staying relevant is important," Tammie replies. "Who are you thinkin' of featuring?"

"A rookie would be unprecedented. But let's discuss it tomorrow."

Heart hammering, Shaunette steps away from the door. She is a coordinated, nationally ranked dancer—a far cry from the chubby kid she used to be. And *she* is a rookie—hello! But what are Vana and Tammie looking for, exactly?

The cogs in her mind turn as she exits the studio. If Mama wants her to remain a DLC and crush it next season as the Point and as a member of Show Troupe, she'll do whatever it takes to increase her chances. Her path is clear. She needs to find a brand-new way to get on Vana's good side.

THIRTEEN DAYS BEFORE HER MURDER

INSTAGRAM POST

@JENTRYRAE_DLC

PHOTO: Jentry Rae is cuddling a bulldog puppy with a red bow around its neck

401k followers / 36,765 likes

#endanimalcruelty #adoptapet

The world is a complicated and chaotic place. We could lash out. Or bury our heads in the sand. But we are stronger than that, sisters! My advice is: be grateful for the good in your life. If you haven't talked to your loved ones lately, call them up. It doesn't matter if they're in the wrong. And if you are dating somebody special, treat them extra-nice.

I'm lucky that *my* somebody special surprised me with this rescue pooch! Beau Dog isn't a diamond engagement ring. 💍 And neither is a gold infinity bracelet. 💍 💍 But this new puppy tugs at my heartstrings like a romance novel. Eep—pinch me!!

Remember: life is too short NOT to be a Lonestars fan. Or a fan of love. Adopt a pet today.

Cheers and Godspeed xx

CHAPTER SEVEN

THE FILMMAKER

~ OCTOBER 14 ~

Nikki is at The Depot, waiting for the Dallas Lonestars Cheerleaders to emerge from their vigil. As she stands outside the fitness center, a cold breeze flutters over her, causing goose bumps. Shuddering and then zipping her worn army jacket, she glances at Vince who's curled up in the van. His thick glasses reflect his phone screen while he slowly scrolls through it.

He seems grateful that the heat is on.

Nikki begins to pace in the brisk afternoon. Not to keep warm. Out of nervousness. She really should have told a Lonestars' administrator about Jentry Rae's odd behavior during their sit-down interview. If she had, the organization might have kept closer tabs on the star dancer.

Guilt is walloping her on that account. Distress over her dad's situation is plaguing her, too. Her pop's psychiatrist doesn't take their insurance anymore, so it's *Everybody aboard the anxiety train*. Preventing her father's derailment is consuming her.

Stay focused, Nikki thinks to herself as she pulls out her vape pen. Being this close to a murder investigation is a rare event. She has to make the most of it. As it happens, her pop's favorite motto is *Opportunity comes to pass, not to pause*.

Glancing at the Dallas Lonestars' insignia plastered on a nearby building—a bursting letter "L" lassoed with a rope—she can't help but speculate that the football team's crashing-down universe might be sending her a sign, too. Is it her job to set Jentry Rae's part in it to rights?

When she turns her attention to the door of the cheerleaders' practice facility, none of the usual thumping music can be heard. The silence feels odd. DLC rehearsals have been postponed until further notice is what a guard told Nikki as she pulled through the security gate.

She knows she can't enter Lonestars' Club without consent from the director of the cheerleaders. But as soon as the dancers emerge, she'll ask them about Jentry Rae's behavior prior to her death. Did anybody else notice how "off" the cheerleading captain was acting?

On the surface, the Dallas Lonestars Cheerleaders seem to be a cohesive unit. It's just, inquiring minds want to know if they in-fight behind the scenes. Nikki has her Dictaphone and trusty notepad on hand in case anybody wants to make a revealing statement.

To her way of thinking, the DLC's restrictive rules can use a little shaking up.

Thumbing through the pad, she finds the list:

- Avoid the football players at all times. No fraternizing.
- Cheerleaders may have tattoos, although they can't be visible in uniform.
- Weight must be managed. No exceptions.
- Tardiness is unacceptable.
- No opinions or complaints shall be verbalized regarding the organization.
- Profane language is prohibited.
- Cheerleaders cannot chew gum or appear in photographs with alcohol and/or smoking paraphernalia.
- Posting inappropriate photos or content on social media is forbidden. May be grounds for dismissal.

Shoving the notepad back in her pocket, Nikki acknowledges that she has personally violated three of the rules. Fortunately, nobody is keeping tabs on her.

Minutes pass. The security guard who let her into the parking lot comes out of his tiny booth. He has a flirtatious look on his face, so she averts her eyes and hides behind her mass of dark, curly hair. After the decent-looking guard reaches her, he makes a joke. Surprisingly, Nikki finds it funny.

The moment the guard asks her for her number, his walkie-talkie bleeps. *Thank God.* Feeling cornered, she is relieved when he returns to his booth. Just then, the cheerleaders emerge from the practice building. Some are in tears. Others are stone-faced. The rest are chatting excitedly.

Nikki hangs back undetected while the dancers drive away.

She intends to speak to Shaunette Simmons first—Jentry Rae's best friend.

Fifteen minutes go by, and Shaunette finally comes out. She has a pretty, heart-shaped face and full bow lips, but distress clouds her features as she stops at her Honda. Brown eyes troubled, she crouches down and touches the side of her car. When she retracts her fingertips, she stares at them wide-eyed. They're layered with red paint.

Nikki cranes her neck and is able to read the message slashed across the passenger door.

Stay in your lane, or else.

What the actual fuck?

Shock rifles through her. The vandalism must have happened before she arrived with Vince.

Visibly frightened, Shaunette begins to cry. While the cheerleader darts her attention about, the same security guard who approached Nikki moves toward her. Even though Nikki is unable to hear the conversation, she sees Shaunette point to the threat on her car. The guard shakes his head, like he's playing dumb. Why didn't he notice the vandalism on his shift? Is he acting clueless on purpose? Nikki files that little detail away.

As the guard goes to make a call, flustered Shaunette gets on her phone, too.

Nikki signals at Vince to film by waving her arm wildly. Nodding, he grabs his camera and a parabolic microphone—a sophisticated sound-level data logger that amplifies volume. She inches into the van with him, and they lower the windows then slide down on the front bench.

Shaunette's phone conversation is mysterious. Startling, even. An unknown male can be heard saying, *"I told the cops I didn't know her." ". . . her death will ruin what I've worked for."* And *"Best friends don't turn on each other, Shaunette."*

Hanging up with a grimace, Shaunette gets in her car and starts to drive away.

Nikki and Vince sit up.

"The audio was crackly and a little spotty, boss. Sorry," Vince gripes.

"We were far away. You did your best."

"I'll try and refine the sound file later."

"Okay. But you captured the *entire* call, right?"

"Yep," he replies as he snaps a photo of the threat on Shaunette Simmons' car. "Except, spying on people feels a little slimy."

"We didn't plan for this to happen." Her heart beats fiercely. "Besides, we might protect other people by filming. Maybe even catch a killer. You agree that something is happening, right, Vince? What if Shaunette is in danger?"

"Seems that way."

Nikki exhales. "Okay. Buy whatever enhancing equipment you need. And when you're ready, let's replay that recording— with the volume way up."

JENTRY RAE'S DIARY ENTRY

OCTOBER 9

As much as I enjoy posting on social media, I'm unable to mention certain things. Like how I have broken DLC rules. Or how I'm in love with the wrong person. Thank goodness for recording secrets in a journal!

The truth is I'm willing to marry my soul mate. But there's a snag: he says time and circumstance aren't on our side. It's a rat-bad excuse, if you ask me. When you love somebody, you want to be with them, don't you? End of story. Timing doesn't matter.

My daddy says some cowboys have too much tumbleweed in their blood to settle down. Sonny Marlowe Randall is the smartest person I know. But I disagree with him on this one account. I think every man should care about two things: dedicating themselves to their partners and preventing pain. Not chasing fame.

Heaven help me! I might cease to exist without He Who Shall Not Be Named. (I'll keep his name in the dark even here. So much is at stake.)

If I gather enough courage, I'll beg him to propose. I wasn't kidding when I posted that a gold bracelet AIN'T a three-carat engagement ring.

Does my mystery man feel the same way I do about marriage? Or about having a family?

At any rate, I need to be careful. Pitting people against each other could lead all of us down a dangerous path. I'm locking my door tonight.

CHAPTER EIGHT

THE FILMMAKER

~ *OCTOBER 15* ~

The next day, Nikki and Vince present their access badges at The Depot's practice arena. They have come to film a Lonestars' training session—and so far, no one is stopping them. Either it means the football documentary hasn't been placed on hold, or nobody is mentioning anything different.

Given the strange vibe in the air, though, Vince has his small 35 mm camera in tow, instead of his bigger equipment. Discretion is best, he and Nikki have decided. The sports team is in the hot seat. Who knows what the mood will be?

A pulled-together woman in her thirties approaches them at the arena entrance. She extends her hand. "If it isn't the dynamic duo?"

Nikki accepts her handshake. Bethany Platt is the administrative assistant for Duke McCade, the team owner. All things "Lonestars" go through her.

"Let me know if I can help with anything," Bethany offers. "I understand you're making decent progress on the documentary, except you haven't interviewed all our players yet. Do you need a larger film crew?"

Vince grins. "We're the dynamic duo, remember? Anyway, Nikki filmed her first movie on an old GoPro and edited it herself."

Times have changed, Nikki thinks. *These are the big leagues.*

Nodding quickly, maybe to end the conversation, Bethany points to where they can sit. As Nikki settles in the stands with Vince, she makes a sweeping gesture. "See? We're welcome here."

He shoots her a dubious look.

Casting aside her own doubts, she spots Royce Holt on the sidelines. He is acting like he *wants* to be noticed this morning, as opposed to how he seemed at Jentry Rae's apartment complex. Exuding confidence, the second-string quarterback stretches, picks up a football, and rolls his shoulders back assertively. Is he ready to show off?

Nikki wonders how special Royce's athletic abilities are, so she leans forward.

Hustling forward a few steps, Royce pinwheels his arm and accurately whizzes the ball across the arena into the end zone. *Okay*, she thinks. *He has lots of talent.* But why was he a skulking voyeur at Jentry Rae's residence?

Sitting back in the hard seat, she concedes that the press has made no mention of Royce being there. So, did anyone besides her spot him that night? More to the point, did he know the dead cheerleader well, if at all?

Royce described how excruciating it is to wait in the quarterback queue during the interview Nikki conducted with him. His catchphrase is: "Keep moving forward like a Texas tornado." *Cute.* But being an FFL player can't be the only thing that drives him.

When Nikki looks to her left, she notices Duke McCade, the ostentatious owner of the Dallas Lonestars, seated in the same row. Emanating importance, the man has one arm slung over the back of an adjacent seat while his boot is perched on the seat in front of him. Tall and in shape for sixty-two, Duke is garbed in a white Stetson and high-end European clothing. But what he can't dress up is the concern on his face.

As the tycoon glances at Nikki, he doesn't seem to recognize her even though they've met. However, she can't blame the man for being transfixed on the practice. Duke must want his team to succeed. Rumor has it that he purchased the Dallas Lonestars for nine billion dollars . . . a stretch for anyone.

"BOO-YAH! Winner-winner-chicken-dinner!" The magnate surges to his feet and claps his hands.

Nikki shifts her eyes to the field, trying to discern what's going on.

"I'll explain everything since you aren't a sports fan." Vince must sense her confusion. "Wide receiver Marcus Armando just caught a pass from starting quarterback Ryder Hutchinson. The offense gained five yards."

"Yay." She fakes interest.

"Now, the players are starting drills and wind sprints."

"You're supposed to be filming, Vince," she says, frowning.

"Right. Sorry."

In the middle of a drill, first-string quarterback Ryder Hutchinson falls to his knees and grabs his ankle. Once he removes his helmet with a frustrated tug, he reveals a ruddy, middle-aged face soaked with perspiration. The over-the-hill QB groans while the coaching staff shake their heads and grumble amongst themselves.

A sports therapist named Chase Campbell rushes over and massages Ryder's ankle. Nikki also interviewed Chase for the documentary. Not only is he Royce's best friend, but he could be Royce's twin—same coffee-colored hair streaked with gold, same fit bod, and same moss-green eyes. Only, Chase is a few inches shorter than Royce, and compared to his friend's heart-stopping smile, the sports therapist maintains a chronic scowl.

What stood out to Nikki during her interview with Chase was how he spoke about his childhood. He and Royce have been buds since they were twelve. "I didn't have what it took to be a ball player. But isn't it dope that we both work for the Dallas Lonestars now?" he asked her.

"Very 'dope'," Nikki replied. "Did you get the job through Royce?"

"Yeah. He owed me. For always doing his homework growing up. Ha! Nah . . . I'm just kidding."

She walked away disliking Chase Campbell's sarcasm and cockiness.

Vince's voice brings her back to reality. "So much for a comeback season. Player trades and bad injuries are screwing with the Lonestars. Hence their continued losing streak."

Nikki nods. She can't help but wonder if Royce Holt is willing to capitalize on those injuries in order to climb the QB ladder.

"McCade's having a conniption. See?" Vince raises his long arm and points at the team owner.

"This is bullshit!" Duke drops his toothy grin. "Get Hutchinson on his flimsy feet now!"

Wounded, aging Hutchinson tries to go on, but he performs like crap. Wide receiver Marcus Armando messes up, too, and all the while, Nikki sees why the Lonestars are on the blink. Armando isn't catching for shit, and shouldn't Ryder Hutchinson be able to work through his pain? Isn't that what pro athletes do?

"I'll get closer and film a little." Vince leaves his seat.

As he trots down the steps with his camera, Duke McCade looks irritated with him. But the billionaire has no say in what Nikki and Vince capture on film. Their contract allows them to document the ugly as well as the good.

Standing, Nikki acknowledges that Duke might be upset for another reason. Maybe he is feeling the heat of Jentry Rae's murder. Reportedly, he flirted with the cheerleader at the start of the season. And that ruffled the feathers of his beauty-queen wife, LeAnn.

Nikki would love the chance to interview Duke McCade about it. Except emperors on high horses are hard to reach.

Careful not to scuff his pricey boots, the tycoon picks his way down to the field. While he stands toe-to-toe with Head Coach Bob Phillips, the players scatter.

Nikki inches closer to better hear the conversation.

"Bad practice, boss. Sorry," the coach mutters.

"We're facing a storm, Bobby. But I won't be known as a laughingstock who bought a sinking ship. Start Royce Holt next week. Forty-year-old Hutchinson played like an enfeebled lamb today. Send him out to pasture!"

"I don't advise making changes at quarterback."

Duke flushes. "Royce is a big gun. I feel it down to the marrow." When the coach shoots him an insolent look, he adds, "Drop the grimace, Bobby. Fans will love Royce. We need a megastar now that we lost that sexy cheerleader."

What did he just say?

The flippant remark roils Nikki's stomach.

Duke's phone rings. As the team owner steps back and answers the call, annoyance pulsates in his sharp eyes. "Howdy, LeAnn. No. I won't be home for supper. Um, today's practice? Crap in a hat—nothing went our way. But don't worry. Your black AmEx won't be canceled yet."

Nikki makes a face. Does the mogul even care what happened to Jentry Rae? Is this how he treats women?

Yards away, a coaching assistant gets Royce off the bench. The eager player jogs on the field, making the sign of the cross. Soon, Royce proves that he *deserves* to move up in the quarterback lineup. He expertly dodges the guys coming at him, and he long-passes with style and consistency, too. It's a dazzling display of ability. Once he's finished, back-slaps and fist-bumps greet him on the sideline.

Nikki hurries over to Vince who's at the edge of the turf.

"Wowza," Vince says in an excited whisper. "What happened a minute ago with Ryder Hutchinson was insane."

"Tell me," she urges.

"I got him on tape saying some surprising shit. But I'll show you later."

"Can't wait."

Camera on, they approach Royce.

The tired football player takes off his helmet and looks at Nikki. "Hey, I know you from our sit-down interview, right?"

"Yeah. Nikki Keegan," she reminds him of her name. "Um, how did practice feel today?"

"Great."

Hating one-word answers and disliking Royce's cluelessness, she drops her smile. She has limited time before he hits the showers, so she blurts, "Can you tell me how you think the murder of a Dallas Lonestars Cheerleader will affect the team?"

Hot fury glows in his eyes like sirens. Balling his hands into fists, he grits his teeth. Then he manages to turn his frown upside down, probably because he's being filmed. "Don't worry your pretty head about the Lonestars. We're strong. We'll get through this."

"My pretty head? What kind of game strategy is flirting?"

His deep scowl returns.

Nikki is about to express more irritation with Royce when his wife appears. Sporting a dazzling smile, social media star Piper Dupree moves down the sideline like a bouncing doll. Her straight, shoulder-length bob glimmers with hues of chestnut and cinnamon, and she is dressed head-to-toe in designer clothes. Maternity designer clothes, which makes her expensive outfit more ludicrous. She's expecting their second baby soon.

The minute Piper notices Nikki standing by her husband, the woman's hazel eyes darken. Rubbing her belly and frowning, she asks, "Who are you?"

Nikki is speechless. Piper is wearing a gold, sapphire centered, infinity bracelet—identical to the one found beside Jentry Rae's dead body.

TV TRANSCRIPT

An episode of the cable sports show *Field Talk*—hosted by game analysts Barry Levin and Glen Paderowski. The studio carpeting is green Astroturf marked with white yard lines. As Barry and Glen sit behind an enormous desk emblazoned with the *Field Talk* insignia, replays of league games flash on wall monitors.

Barry: Greetings from the Gridiron! Now that football season is off to a fantastic start, the Kansas City Cyclones are dominating . . . no surprise there. But the Dallas Lonestars—*oof!* What do you make of their lousy season so far, Glen?

Glen: The Lonestars are hardly the same team our daddies watched. Where is their usual slam-to-the-ground action? I'm holding out hope because brand-new owner Duke McCade claims to have a secret weapon in Royce Holt.

Barry: (Laughs) You mean, recently traded from the Tennessee Renegades Royce Holt? *Hmm.* Let's clarify. We are talking about the backup quarterback whose wife is more popular than him?

Glen: Right. (Smiles) Maybe we should refer to Royce as "*Monsieur* Dupree." His wife does. *Bonne chance, Monsieur.*

CHAPTER NINE

THE DALLAS LONESTARS CHEERLEADER

~ OCTOBER 15 ~

Shaunette can hardly believe there is a DLC rehearsal tonight. So much for Vana and Tammie suspending practices indefinitely. Then again, the Lonestars Cheerleaders are a multimillion-dollar-a-year business. Dormant pom-poms don't equal profits.

Still, Shaunette's nerves are half-baked. She'd be the first squad member to vote for a long hiatus with no performing.

Her reasoning?

Taking time off would give whoever hates her time to calm down.

As scared as she is, though, she hasn't said anything to Vana about her car vandalism. Nor has she reported it to the police. She doesn't want to be known as the dramatic DLC—although

is it too late for that? Most importantly, she hasn't said anything because she has too much to hide.

This evening, Shaunette is dreading leaving her apartment.
She has grown more and more attached to Jentry Rae's puppy,
Beau Dog. The cuddly cutie has been sleeping in her bed and
keeping her company, and it's just what she needs. An animal
control shelter picked up the dog following the murder, and
that's where Shaunette claimed him.

"Come over for a little love," she coos at the pooch. "You
know, my mother never let me have pets growing up, and I think
I missed out." As she snuggles the puppy for a few seconds, she
hears her mama's voice echo, *"Animal dander makes eyes red.
We can't have that."*

Everything reminds Shaunette of her mother. Even the pair
of L'eggs Sheer Energy pantyhose she reaches for and tugs on
for practice. Mama wore the same shade back in the eighties . . .
an enduring classic.

I even look like Mama, Shaunette thinks as she curls her long
hair into waves. *Why can't I be a golden star on the squad like
she was?*

After spritzing her mane with setting spray, Shaunette
applies false eyelashes and shiny raspberry lip gloss. Full-on
zhuzh is required of the renowned Dallas Lonestars Cheerleaders . . . pageant perfectionism bumped up a notch—even for
rehearsals.

It's a whole lot of work.

Which creates a cloud of overwhelming pressure.

As Shaunette grabs her keys, she wonders if Vana and
Tammie feel incredible pressure, too. It's the directors' job to
uphold the standard of DLC excellence the squad is known for.

But if that's their goal, why are they acting like danger hasn't entered the mix?

Nervous, Shaunette tosses a desirous look at a bottle of Kentucky Bulleit on her way out. It's her favorite brand of bourbon, and even though nipping booze is a bad habit, she only drinks at home. Sometimes she overdoes it, sure, but she would never recklessly drive sloshed. Especially now. There are eyes on her wherever she goes. Is she being followed?

Approaching her car, she realizes that she didn't scrub the cryptic message **Stay in your lane, or else** completely off. She just smeared it. Maybe she ought to tape posterboard over the words to disguise them, because if her clunky Civic wasn't embarrassing before, it sure as heck is now!

As Shaunette drives out of her apartment complex, she's desperate to know what the warning means. The shocking secrets she's keeping locked away could be powerful ammunition against the Lonestars franchise. Does somebody know that?

Her stomach twists with regret. She and Jentry Rae should never have gotten themselves into what they did before the murder. But is it wise to reveal those things now?

On the way to dance rehearsal, Shaunette blasts country music and applies more lip gloss. All at once, a car approaches her rear bumper. Fastening one eye to the rearview mirror, she watches the car speed up and then drop back repeatedly. "What's your hurry, a-hole?" she murmurs under her breath.

The dark SUV surges forward and lightly taps her car. Heart thrumming, she shuts the music off then presses the gas.

What is this car doing? Gripping the steering wheel tighter, she changes lanes in the hopes that the impatient SUV will pass her by. But the vehicle becomes more aggravated. Roaring forward, it jerks into the new lane with her and smashes into her bumper.

Panicked, Shaunette cries out.

Her pulse quickens while her belly wrenches.

What does the driver want? Is it the same person who vandalized her car?

As the black SUV viciously rams her bumper again, her body trembles. *Holy God!* Although she floors her Honda, the car does the same, and when she loses control, she swings into a scary, willy-nilly wobble before hitting the brakes—just short of a guardrail. Hurtling through the barrier and landing in a gully would have been the end of her!

Good Lord. At least her air bag didn't deploy.

Feeling nauseous, she is relieved when the aggressive SUV drives away. If only she'd been able to see the driver or the license plate. Then she could peg who's ambushing her. The weird message painted on her passenger door and the car chase tell her she's being marked.

Taking a minute, she sits in her sputtering car and tries to calm down. A question flashes through her mind. What if the crazy attacker isn't just after her? Does somebody intend to eliminate Dallas Lonestars Cheerleaders one by one? Maybe she *should* file a police report. It'd be the sensible thing to do.

After Shaunette sobs off all her makeup, she drives again. She CANNOT be late for the seven p.m. dance rehearsal. When her mother phones, her heart rate speeds up again but she answers the call, anyway. "Hey, Mama," she greets unevenly.

"Howdy, Shaunette Lynn. You sound out of breath. Are you practicing like I told you?"

"Not right now."

"Don't you have rehearsal tonight?"

"Yes. I'm driving there now." Her voice breaks.

"Show those girls what you're made of, darlin'. You promised me you would when I got sick. Remember?"

Her mother's terminal cancer diagnosis still has her upended. "I'll try, Mama. Um, how are you feeling?"

"Not great. But let's not talk about me. You're in the spotlight, just the way we wanted."

Hmm, the way you *wanted, Mama. But I'm doing my best.* "Um, is Aunt Noleen taking good care of you?"

"She is. But what's important is that you seemed off during the last game, Shaunette. Did you get that foundation I recommended? Normally, the camera loves you, but your face looked cakey. Take better care of your skin; I won't be raising no raisin."

"Will do, Mama. Sorry, I gotta go now. Bye." Her emotions fully unravel as she hangs up. Crying and driving, driving and crying, she can't get to The Depot fast enough. She doesn't want to be alone another minute. Nearly careening into a steep ravine has her trembling like someone facing a firing squad, and she doesn't want to die.

A bright light in all this is Vana's and Tammie's secretive conversation. Are they really fixin' to select a new cheerleading captain? Traditionally, rookies aren't allowed to be head cheerleader or the Point or a "month" in the DLC wall calendar. Veterans only need apply. But being a standout DLC next season could alter Shaunette's life. Maybe then her mother will finally be proud of her.

CHAPTER TEN

THE FILMMAKER

~ OCTOBER 15 ~

Nikki is happy to say she stood her ground with Piper Dupree at The Depot earlier today. She calmly stated who she was: a film director from Hollywood . . . a professional with no desire to flirt with Piper's husband, Royce.

When Piper heard the word "Hollywood" the woman's whole demeanor changed. She boasted that she's a famous WAG—the trendy term for wives and girlfriends of popular sportsmen. But the moment she began asking questions about producers and talent agents, Nikki walked away.

Now that she and Vince are back at her rental apartment, Vince is about to show her the segment he recorded of middle-aged Ryder Hutchison at the Lonestars' practice session.

"I approached Ryder like a fan instead of a cameraman," he prefaces the scene. "He went ballistic on me. That's when I started to film. Wait 'til you see how he acted."

Nikki watches the footage, and Vince is right. A flushed Ryder swatted at the camera, screaming, "Get out of my face with that thing! The murder of Jentry Rae Randall is the real tragedy—not me hobbling around!"

The next minute, he broke down in tears.

What on earth? Who cries like that over a casual acquaintance?

Then again, Ryder could be acting emotional about his fading career. Given the brief snippet of tape, it's hard for Nikki to tell.

"Great job." She gives Vince a pat on the back.

He seems proud. "You know, Nik, I'm glad you found me on that job board. We make a solid team."

"I agree. I like having you as my partner in—"

"—crime shows?" He cracks a smile. "Speaking of which, I thought of a title. 'Give me an M for Murder.' Kinda cheerleading-related, huh?"

She makes a face. "Maybe. Um, but right now, I'm headed to the corner store to buy a vape cartridge. Need anything?"

"*Ooo* . . . grab me some double-rich, frozen fudge bars, will you? And take my umbrella. Dallas's weather fluctuates fast. I learned that after my Texadus from Minnesota."

Carrying the folded umbrella, Nikki goes outside and sees a mass of billowing, dark clouds. *Damn Vince's prediction.* She needs sunshine, not rain. Pop got another notice for his water shutdown, and now he's worried that the electricity will be next. Maybe it's time she sold her mother's necklace. Her eyes tear up at that.

As she hurries along the street, live music follows her. The blues melody is coming from a bar called Swindler's, located across from her place. Whiffs of beer, tequila, and peanuts fill her senses, too.

Nikki would love to duck inside the place right now and have a shot with the locals, but she needs mental clarity today. She plans to call Royce Holt and ask why he was loafing outside Jentry Rae's apartment building.

To prepare for the conversation, she enters the mini mart, takes out her phone, and clicks into the quarterback's Instagram account. Royce's feed displays team updates and stunning vacation photos featuring him and his wife in exotic locales. There are pics of their cherubic toddler, too.

Royce and Piper have an amazing life. They might be on constant public display, but do they really care what people say about them?

Nikki checks out Piper Dupree's socials next. According to the feed, the fashionista recently frequented an expensive LA dermatologist, a trendy New York fashion show, and a posh Paris boutique. She's an A-lister, for sure.

A Google alert interrupts Nikki's phone scrolling. She sees a live clip of Sonny Randall speaking with news reporters about his daughter. Instead of watching it on her phone, though, she dodges into Swindler's Bar next door and rushes up to a wall-mounted television. Curiosity spiking, she asks the bartender to turn up the volume.

"The police sumbitches are looking for the wrong thing at the wrong time," Sonny says as he pushes his tattered cowboy hat off his forehead. "They might'n do their jobs better."

"Do you have any idea who killed your daughter?" a reporter asks.

"None. Even though I'm battlin' a fatal illness, I intend to find out." Gesturing for the journalists to get the heck out of his path, the old farmer shuffles into a hotel . . . the Highland Park Luxe.

So that's where he's staying. Nikki makes a mental note.

An inkling tells her that Sonny Randall must have important knowledge about his child's death. If Jentry Rae confided things to him, that is. The father-daughter pair seemed close. At least the star cheerleader's social media posts show that Sonny reared her carefully, kept her grounded, and encouraged her to give back to the community.

"Hey." Nikki phones Vince from inside the bar. "I won't be back to the apartment for a while."

"Why? What about my fudge bars? And where are you? It sounds like a party. I love parties."

"I'll tell you later. Just keep working, okay?" She intends to Uber to Sonny Randall's hotel and, with any luck, she'll speak with him off the record. However, if she arrives with a cameraman, Sonny might slam the door in her face.

From the looks of it, the old man hates reporters.

Fortunately, Nikki likes bristly people.

"There is leftover pasta in the fridge if you get hungry, Vince," she says. "I'll call you later."

"Thanks, Mother. Roger and out."

Once she orders the Uber, she climbs into its back seat and watches Dallas's scenery flash by. The moment she winds the window down, raindrops splash in.

CHAPTER ELEVEN

THE DALLAS LONESTARS CHEERLEADER

~ OCTOBER 15 ~

As Shaunette enters the DLC dance studio, she does her best to compose herself. She *was* nearly run off the road, but she was also smearing on lip gloss. Maybe she simply irritated an innocent person with her distracted driving. At least that's what she's telling herself.

One look from Vana prompts her to fix her makeup.

Priya taps her on the shoulder. "Shaunette, girl, there is juicy gossip at the rumor mill."

"Tell me."

"Vana will name the new head cheerleader at the end of rehearsal. Isn't it exciting?"

Shaunette nods but not too eagerly. She's already aware.

Music starts up, so she drops to the floor and begins the dancers' customary warm-up segment. Lying flat on her back, she extends her leg in the air, grabs her ankle, and rolls over into the splits. Electricity crackles around her. She wonders if the dancers are thinking what she is. Are they Point material?

Most of her teammates are sweet and sincere, but the zinger is nobody can *show* ambition. All the cheerleaders have been instructed to bury personal aspirations beneath politeness and respectfulness.

Once the warm-up is over, the first bars of a hit pop song blare. Shaunette gets to her feet, plasters on a megawatt smile, and acts ready to dance.

"Five, six, seven, eight!" Tammie the choreographer counts the music in strident shouts. "All y'all need to show more energy!" she yells.

Shaunette catches on fine to the new routine. Perspiring, she spins, shimmies, and jetés. Then she leaps, kicks, and twerks—giving one hundred percent the entire time.

Tammie performs the steps along with the dancers, and she's incredible. In that moment, Shaunette feels sorry that the woman never realized her dream of becoming a Dallas Lonestars Cheerleader.

When the song ends, the squad strikes a fierce pose. Shaunette crushed the new routine, but so did everybody else.

Happy for a breather, she chugs water from a logoed bottle. The moment she bends over to catch her breath, the team members are told to break into their four designated dance groups . . . how they perform mini cheers at arena corners on game days. She excels at the short routines, too. All in all, her dance talent is in her favor.

"Whoo-wee!" Vana gives a cowgirl wallop. "Pat yourselves on the back, ladies! Y'all rock like an eighties band! All righty. Sit, veterans and rookies. I have an important announcement."

Exhausted, the cheerleaders do as they're instructed. Hardly pristine after the grueling workout, they wipe their brows.

"I'm not gonna lie." Vana expels a breath. "The loss of Jentry Rae is still tough for me and for everybody. Her memorial service is Saturday at nine a.m. *sharp*." She flings Shaunette a critical look.

Shaunette nods dutifully. She'll be first in line to honor Jentry Rae. It's the respectful thing to do. After all, she reacted badly when Jentry Rae divulged scandalous information to her. God—why wasn't her carefree friend more careful?

Shaunette tried to talk sense into Jentry Rae but was called "invasive."

All eyes turn to her, and she prays that her solemn expression is concealing what she doesn't want exposed.

"Ladies, we might be feeling Jentry Rae's absence in our hearts every day, but we can't go on this way. Y'all need a new leader," says Vana.

The dancers grip the handles of their pom-poms until their knuckles turn white.

"Tammie and I have given this a great deal of thought. And we've chosen Priya," the director declares.

Beautiful, black-haired Priya jets to her feet and squeals in delight. Chiding herself for thinking she had a chance, Shaunette stands, too. Rejection rips her to shreds as she fawns over and congratulates the veteran dancer. How will she explain this lost opportunity to her mother? She wants to be the best DLC legacy ever, except it's apparent that bloodlines count for zip.

She retreats to the dressing area of the studio where defeat stabs her deeper. When she looks in a mirror, she sees that her face is non-reactive thanks to her beauty pageant experience, but today is a bleak day.

Priya joins her, flushed with excitement. "Can you believe it, Shaunette? Me? The new Point? It's a dream!"

"I'm so happy for you." Shaunette forces a smile.

The other cheerleaders appear to gather their things. A second later, Priya drops her grin. "Something's bothering you. I can tell. Level up."

Shaunette shakes her head. She isn't ready to share anything. If she dares mention the word "stalker," Priya will tell Vana. And Vana might think Shaunette craves attention any way she can get it.

"Come on. What's wrong?" Priya prods.

Besides failure? Regret? Confusion? Terror? "I'm fine."

Her friend offers a smile. "Don't worry; you'll have your shot sometime. You're a great dancer." Priya pauses. "But, um, since you and Jentry Rae were close, some of us veterans are wondering if she told you anything that could help the police."

"It's none of your business if Jentry Rae confided things to me or not," Shaunette snaps.

Doubt coats the new cheerleading captain's expression as she walks away.

Exasperated and afraid, Shaunette leaves the studio with the group. She refuses to be a sitting duck alone in the parking lot. Once she reaches her car, she wonders who she can talk to about her stalker instead of the police. Nikki Keegan, the film-maker, maybe? Nikki might know something about the murder investigation. Didn't she make a crime film once? Then again, she and Shaunette got off on the wrong foot during Shaunette's interview for the football documentary. To put it mildly, they are opposites. Nikki likes to stick her nose where it doesn't belong while Shaunette prefers to guard the skeletons in her closet.

Surely, Shaunette acted suspicious during that interview. Does Nikki already think she's hiding something?

Then it dawns on Shaunette. The person who understood Jentry Rae most was Jentry Rae's father, Sonny. She'll call the ailing man once she gets home . . . if she makes it that far.

CHAPTER TWELVE

THE FILMMAKER

~ *OCTOBER 15* ~

Upon exiting the Uber at the Highland Park Luxe Hotel, Nikki's nerves ignite. She isn't sure why she's anxious to meet Sonny Randall. Maybe because she doesn't want to succumb to indelicacy while digging deeply.

A magazine on a lobby table catches her attention. Duke McCade's face is on the cover, so she picks it up. By perusing the article, she learns that the now-billionaire was born to dirt-poor farmers in Nacogdoches, Texas. After Duke put himself through the University of Texas, Austin, he made some risky investments that paid off. First, he amassed a fortune in crude oil. Then he used that capital to finance a rocketing clean-tech company—and it was that venture which hedged his main source of wealth: fossil fuels.

In the process of reinventing himself, the up-and-coming entrepreneur changed his name from Dennis Beauregard McNutt to Duke McCade. A man about town, he lives in a chic Dallas penthouse with his middle-aged, beauty-queen wife. He might have luxury homes in Majorca, Bermuda, and Bel Air, but he calls Big D home.

The article ends with an unappealing quote from Duke. He asserts that his wife's talent for Miss Teenage Texas may have been opera singing, but her *real* talent is being high maintenance.

Nikki sets the magazine facedown.

Striding farther into the hotel lobby, she hears an elevator ding. Sonny hobbles out of it, holding a coffee cup. As he passes the front desk, he gives the clerk a wave.

"Howdy, Mr. Randall," the clerk calls out kindly. "The public adored your daughter, by the way."

"Mighty kind of you to say, sugar. I'm headed to my usual chair now. Your bellhop always brings me the daily paper."

"You got it."

Nikki notices that Sonny's face is even pastier than it appears on screen. In fact, no one has ever looked so devastated. Losing a daughter in the violent way Jentry Rae was killed would rock anybody's boat. And if the lonely farmer is facing the end himself, he must be beyond seasick.

Sonny plops down in a lobby chair with a grunt. Soon, he accepts his newspaper and then sips his coffee, seemingly lost in thought. The paradox of the scene leaves its mark: the farmer's dusty blue jeans and dirty hat as opposed to the hotel's posh, pristine décor.

Summoning the courage to speak, Nikki steps forward. "Are you Sonny Randall, sir?"

"Who wants to know?"

"My name is Nikki Keegan. I'm filming a documentary about the Dallas Lonestars. I would like to talk to you about your daughter if you have a minute."

"Are you a reporter? Tell me the truth." His eyes squint.

"Not exactly."

"Good day, miss."

He tries to wave her aside, but she gently lays a hand on his arm. "All right, I'll be honest. My goal is to create a separate crime series featuring Jentry Rae's unsolved murder. Will you talk to me?" She inhales. If he says yes, *shit*. He'll be drawn into the unauthorized project, too.

"I'll only talk to you if you can help find my girl's killer," Sonny grouses.

"I *can* help. I'm all about seeking justice for female victims. When I was fifteen years old, a woman in Kansas was stabbed by an escaped convict. It made an impression on me because of how the press handled the tragedy. The murdered woman was blamed for gardening in her front yard while living near a maximum-security prison. Like she deserved to be killed, right? Her reputation was eviscerated, and I had to make a film about it."

The old man crosses his arms. "Are you fibbin'?"

"No, sir. Like I said, I have been hired to direct a film about the new faces of the Dallas Lonestars. Which means I've been given VIP access to rare footage, archives, and news within the organization. We might help each other."

He mashes his mouth in a straight line.

She shuts up, too. No need to oversell herself.

"Maybe we could team up," he replies in a thick drawl. "Give me yer phone number."

Nikki hands him her business card. "I'm very sorry about your daughter. She seemed pure and good when I interviewed her."

"*Somebody* got their hooks into her."

"I agree. Jentry Rae acted scared during our Q and A. I want to know why."

Sonny pauses. "Let me understand this correctly, young lady. The Lonestars want you sniffing around a murder investigation?"

"Not exactly. But they'll only get upset if they find out." She cracks a small smile.

"*Hmph.*"

"Be sure to contact me, Mr. Randall."

"Wait." His voice grows softer. "You need to know somethin', sugar. I'm dying 'a liver failure. I should be in the hospital, but I'm here instead—to find out what happened to my baby before I leave this earth. Promise me you won't quit until you uncover the truth."

Anxiousness tears through Nikki like a hurricane. Should she give this grieving man hope? Her instincts tell her it's the right thing to do, so she ekes out, "I promise."

Sonny sets his coffee down with a shaky hand. "My daughter . . . she was given a bulldog as a gift. Beau Dog is the animal's name. Start by discovering who gave it to her."

"Will do." Nikki turns to leave, anxious to tell Vince.

The moment she passes the glossy magazine on the entry table, she has another thought. If Duke McCade's real name is Dennis *Beau*regard McNutt, could it be any correlation to Beau Dog?

CHAPTER THIRTEEN

THE DALLAS LONESTARS CHEERLEADER

~ *OCTOBER 17* ~

Shaunette is having a heck of a time concentrating on her favorite wellness podcast. After yanking her earbuds out, she starts to unload the dishwasher in the stillness of her kitchen.

Good grief! She can't get Jentry Rae's fame and face and failed friendship out of her head.

And it's all because of guilt.

She really ought to spill the tea to Vana about the nasty argument she had with Jentry Rae in the locker room on the day of the murder. But is that smart? She's already in the DLC doghouse. It's best to refrain from making more waves. Right?

Ultimately, if she gets kicked off the squad she'll be forced to go back to Nacogdoches. Mama won't take kindly to the failure. In fact, it might put her mother over the edge.

However, the most important question is: can Shaunette continue to sweep her conflict with Jentry Rae under the rug? Cheerleader Ashleigh heard part of their contentious squabble in the locker room. Ashleigh said so herself, and the blabbermouth redhead isn't the type to stay quiet.

Shaunette's phone rings. To her surprise, Sonny Randall is calling. "Hey, Mr. Randall," she greets.

"Howdy, sugar. Sorry I missed your call earlier."

"No worries. I wanted to tell you I got Beau Dog in time. He was nearly adopted by someone else."

"Good. Thank you. My girl loved that puppy. But, ah, please call me Sonny." Mournfulness quavers the old man's voice. "Shaunette, do you know who gave the dog to Jentry Rae?"

"I don't. I'm sorry." She envisions the weather-worn farmer's marionette mouth lines, straw cowboy hat, and age-crinkled blue eyes. His personality is hard-shelled candy on the outside with a soft, gooey center. "How are you holding up, Sonny?"

"Not well t'all. Here's the thing. If somebody hated my girl enough to toss her around like a rag doll and end her life, then why? I can't stand that I didn't protect her."

"Don't beat yourself up."

"Can't help it. Failure is eating at me like a coyote on a carcass." He blows into a handkerchief. "I'm supposed to identify Jentry Rae's body this afternoon, right before her autopsy. But I'm not sure I'm up for it."

"Her autopsy is happening already?" Shaunette fights tears. "I haven't even processed that she's gone."

A long pause ensues.

"Today's dance rehearsal wasn't the same," she says to fill the silence. "We have a new Point now, but us cheerleaders are gonna miss Jentry Rae's leadership."

Sonny gives a half-hearted chuckle. "My baby was a great captain. Wasn't she?"

"The best. *Err*, excuse me for saying so, but I saw you on TV the other day. You've lost weight, Sonny. Terminal cirrhosis of the liver, right? Jentry Rae told me."

"Yep. My time is running short."

Her insides twist. "I'm sorry to hear that. Are you getting any treatment?"

"Just some ineffective pills. 'Cause I refuse to be hooked up to tubes when a murderer is on the loose."

"Right. But you should have a caregiver at your farmhouse. I loved going out there with Jentry Rae. She and I were close then." *Her happiness during those trips was infectious.*

"My girl was never the same after y'all's falling-out. What happened with the two of you?"

"I don't like to talk about it," Shaunette replies. "But maybe I can visit you when you go back to Vale View Farm. All those rolling hills and strawberry patches . . . the place puts my childhood apartment to shame." She can't stop her voice from shaking.

"Nonsense, sugar. And remember. Complaining is as worthless as chewing gum on a boot heel."

She absorbs that.

While the old man weeps in the background, Shaunette tries to stay positive. Her mama might demand the impossible, but at least she's still around. And during whatever time Sonny has left, Shaunette can share a bond with him. Her own father left home when she was an infant. Left her and Mama broke, was more like it. They managed to scrape by, but why didn't her mother save for college instead of spending a ton on pageants and performance-prep dance lessons?

"People tell me I should stay out of the press." Sonny's voice can be heard on the phone again. "I'm the lunatic who barreled into my child's apartment building in front of the whole world. You probably saw the debacle on Face-ta-gram."

She smiles at the misnomer. "When will you be leaving town?"

"As soon as I put this ugly business to bed. Dallas is too big a city. I'm trying to visualize Jentry Rae living here."

"She loved Dallas. Until—"

"Until what, sugar?"

"Nothing."

"Shaunette, honey, will you accompany me to the coroner's office this afternoon? I'm not sure how it all works, but I could use the support."

She hesitates. Is she prepared to see Jentry Rae's dead body? Will she even be allowed to?

She *is* free. And knowing she'll feel terrible if she lies, she answers, "Of course I'll come."

"Praise the Lord. Meet me at the coroner's office at three p.m."

Soaking up her tears with a tissue, Shaunette gets out of her Honda and glances at the coroner's office across the street. As afternoon shadows lengthen, hell's creatures seem to be dancing in and out of the building's eaves.

A sickening feeling climbs her throat when she heads inside. Not only is she dreading seeing her friend's lifeless body, but remorse is strangling her, too. To wish somebody dead and then they are, is unfathomable.

Minutes later, Sonny shuffles into the lobby from a different door. His rumpled clothes are hanging on him and his hat is misshapen. Nikki Keegan, the Lonestars' documentarian, trails behind him.

Surprise jingles through Shaunette. Why is the filmmaker here? She couldn't have known Jentry Rae well, and it seems intrusive. Will she snoop into Shaunette's business, too?

"Afternoon." Sonny gives Shaunette a hug. Stepping back, he says, "I want you to meet someone."

"We're familiar. Hi, Nikki." Shaunette inclines her head. "Are you here in a professional capacity?"

"Um, no. Just to show support."

The filmmaker could've fooled her. In fact, Nikki might as well have the adjective "ambitious" stamped on her forehead. Shaunette is tempted to voice her concerns but won't in front of Sonny.

The sickly farmer doesn't seem to notice the friction between the women as he pops a pill in his mouth. "This damned medication's gonna make me groggy, so let's get this show on the road. By the way, as much as I dislike lawyers, I ought ta talk to the district attorney. You think?"

"Good idea," Nikki answers.

Shaunette is tempted to run away. Maybe this was a mistake. If prosecutors show up and question her, who knows what she'll say? And what will her reaction be when she sees Jentry Rae's body? Will she guilt-word-purge about how badly she treated her best friend at the end?

Before she can decide what to do, Sonny shuffles up to the front desk and explains who he is.

"My condolences, sir," the clerk says. "May I see some ID?"

While the old man hands over a state-issued card, a lean Latino man with a close-cut goatee and an astute expression appears. Approaching Sonny, he offers his hand. "Sir, I am Brandon López, Dallas County's assistant district attorney."

"Ah, just the man I want to see."

A bald, burly detective materializes next. Shaunette recognizes him as Sergeant Wes Emerson—an investigator with Dallas PD to whom she gave her official statement. She found his gruff, assertive manner off-putting.

Sonny frowns at Emerson. "You again? Didn't ya grill me enough at the police station?"

"Just doing my job, sir," the sergeant replies tightly. "I'm ready to take you to the morgue. You, too, Mr. López. But . . . hold up. Who are these ladies?"

"They're my kinfolk," Sonny fibs.

"Even you, Miss Simmons?" Emerson locks eyes with Shaunette.

"Sonny considers me family," she replies breathlessly.

The sergeant doesn't seem convinced but allows her to walk with the group, anyway. Nerves aflame, Shaunette drops back. Astute prosecutors and suspicious detectives . . . no doubt "fear" is the word written across *her* forehead.

Once the group passes through a set of automatic doors, everybody enters the morgue attached to the coroner's office. Four metal dissection tables line one wall, and a corpse covered with a sheet fills the last slab.

Is Jentry Rae's battered body under the sheet?

Shaunette's fragile emotions splinter into tinier pieces.

How has it come to this?

"Lord in heaven," Sonny chokes out. "My Creator better put me straight in the ground when I die. No heart-wrenching autopsies for me."

Shaunette and Nikki steady him as he sways on his feet.

"They haven't cut my baby open yet, have they?" he asks the assistant DA.

"Not yet," Brandon López replies. "There will be an initial identification by you. Then an extensive postmortem will follow. You're aware of that, sir. Correct?"

"Yes, I'm not stupid."

López nods sincerely. "Please accept my sympathies on behalf of your daughter."

"Thanks, son. Yer young—your prom boutonnière might still be in the fridge—but I'm putting my faith in you. Do you have any potential suspects?"

López's answer is no. It's an ongoing investigation.

Just then, a geriatric, gray-haired man wearing a bow tie enters the autopsy room. Sonny waves at him. "This is Jentry Rae's lifelong doctor. He knows her health history." He lumbers over and shakes the physician's hand. "Thank you for coming at my request, Percy. I'm mighty grateful."

"Anything for you, my friend."

Shaunette watches their whispered conversation, thinking that maybe the doctor is allowed to attend because he represents the family.

A female coroner enters the room a minute later. As she washes her hands, she greets everybody in a professional manner. Next, she instructs all the attendees to don face masks. Once they do, she slips on green gloves and moves to the body on the dissection table. The group joins her there.

The second she lowers a white sheet, Sonny's knees buckle. "That's my girl, all right."

Shaunette goes numb. Once-vibrant Jentry Rae looks battered, traumatized, and freakishly wounded. Her skin is an unnatural shade of baby blue, as are her lips, and the deep gash on her forehead adds a shocking slash of red to her frosty coloring. She has never NOT been gorgeous.

"Clearly, the cause of death was homicide," the ME states.

Moaning, Sonny rushes to a trash can. After vomiting, he wipes his mouth, puts his mask back on, and returns to the group with an apology.

Shaunette is queasy and grief-stricken, too. She wishes more than anything that Jentry Rae would open her eyes. Maybe then she could retract all her hurtful words. On impulse, she reaches for her friend's stiff hand, but the ME intervenes with: "No touching the body, please. Any trace DNA must be preserved."

"My girl's Dallas Lonestars Cheerleaders pinkie ring is missing," Sonny points out. "She always wore it."

"No jewelry was found on her person," López explains.

"Speaking 'a jewelry, have you figured out who gave my daughter that gold infinity bracelet, son?"

"Not yet, sir."

"Well, what *have* you done?"

The assistant DA blinks calmly. He doesn't seem rattled.

"I'm about to start the autopsy," the medical examiner interrupts. "Family members outside, please. The police will relay my findings once I'm finished."

The bald detective approaches Sonny. "Allow me to escort you to the lobby, sir."

Shoulders slumped, Sonny pads out of the room. A tidal wave of despondency hits Shaunette as she follows the farmer and Nikki to the waiting area. Left alone, the trio settles in uncomfortable chairs, masks off. Then they start to watch the clock.

Time passes slowly. When the Randalls' family doctor finally appears, he sits down on unsteady legs. Pale-faced, he shakes his head. "I really shouldn't tell you what I saw, Sonny."

"It's why I brought you here, Percy!"

The elderly physician exhales. "Very well. But shall we have some privacy?"

Shaunette and Nikki frown at each other but then exchange a temporary truce. Getting to their feet, they only pretend to leave. Really, they hide around a wall with their ears peeled.

"I took it upon myself to secretly *record* the autopsy," the family doctor discloses. "My memory isn't what it was. But taping autopsies is highly illegal; you need to know that. I could lose my license. Good thing I'm retired, but I did it for you, Sonny . . . to relay precise information."

"Good God." Sonny grimaces. "Hurry up, man. I don't have much time left."

"Brace yourself." The doctor starts a little device. The medical examiner's dictation begins.

"This is a full autopsy on a Caucasian female victim. Her body is that of a normally developed twenty-three-year-old woman. Height is sixty-nine inches; weight is one hundred seventeen pounds. The deceased shows a severe bruise on her right wrist that left a handprint. A DNA sample will be collected from that handprint. Defense wounds are visible on the victim's hands, so plainly, she fought her attacker." The ME pauses. "The victim also shows a profuse contusion on her forehead, which measures five by two—along with a five by three depressed fracture at the back of her head. The rear wound is chief. It cratered her skull and caused a subarachnoid hemorrhage that seeped blood into her brain. Since the brain stem controls respiration and heart rate, non-treatment of this condition stopped the victim's breathing and heart function. Next, I will examine her vital organs."

"Your girl was left on the ground to die," Percy clarifies to Sonny.

When Shaunette peers around the corner, she sees Sonny cup his hand over his mouth. Her dismay swells, too.

"I am slicing into the victim's skin," the ME continues. "Now, I'm removing the uterus." Suddenly, she inhales. "This is surprising."

"What is?" the Randalls' family doctor asks on the recording.

"I'll backtrack a moment. The initials R.H. are tattooed on the victim's right hip. By my calculation, those letters have been there less than six months. A fresher tattoo reading D.M. is on the victim's other hip. Days old, maybe. Most significantly, Jentry Rae Randall was three months pregnant."

PART II

Tornado warning in Texas! Gather
at the Lonestars' Stadium.
No chance of a touchdown there.

CHAPTER FOURTEEN

THE FILMMAKER

~ OCTOBER 17 ~

Nikki emerges from the coroner's office in a daze. The scent of death follows her outside, and soon, her mouth begins to water—the first sign of nausea.

Jentry Rae was pregnant?

Which means the baby died along with her.

Shock zaps Nikki's spine like a stun gun.

She turns and sees that Sonny and Shaunette seem knocked for a loop, too.

"Holy Mother of God," Sonny bemoans. "My baby was going to *have* a baby? I don't believe it." He staggers to a nearby bench, sits, and practically hyperventilates.

Shaunette comforts him before she breaks down herself. In the meantime, Nikki's heart aches for the old man. He lost his daughter, and now he will never meet his grandchild. The degree of tragedy must be dizzying.

Tingling with questions, she joins Shaunette and Sonny on the bench. As she gives them a minute to calm down, she looks up and sees lightning flash against a dark sky. A murder of crows is silhouetted against a cluster of gray storm clouds, and the flock's name seems nothing short of an ominous symbol. Was Jentry Rae killed for the sole reason that she was pregnant? Labeling her murder premeditated?

A morose chill spreads over Nikki's skin. Perhaps she shouldn't have come today. Showing emotion and comforting people for their emotions aren't things she's used to. Except, she can't abandon Sonny now. She wouldn't want her father to be without support in a similar situation.

Empathy for the old farmer keeps her rooted to the bench seat—until rain pounds down in big splats. Gently, she takes Sonny's arm and steers him under a restaurant canopy. Shaunette follows them.

"Are you hurt that your daughter didn't tell you she was pregnant?" Nikki asks.

"Darn tootin' I'm hurt! Here I thought my girl told me everything. What was I missing about her life?"

"If it helps, I don't tell my dad everything," she jokes to lighten the mood.

Shaunette shoots her a disapproving stare. The cheerleader looks just as wrecked as the ailing man. Her face is colorless, her eye bags are dark, and her pupils are dilated. The anguish Shaunette is feeling makes sense, though. She was best friends with Jentry Rae—until she wasn't. Rivalry severed their relationship is what other cheerleaders have told Nikki. How guilty is Shaunette feeling?

Sonny wipes his eyes with a handkerchief. "I'll never have the chance to know my grandchild. Believe me, I would've loved that young 'un. Would've pushed him or her for hours on the swing set at home. I built it for Jentry Rae but never had the heart to tear it down."

Nikki swallows a hard lump. When it lands in her stomach, it burbles and fizzes like corrosive acid. She is more comfortable digging into murder cases that occurred in the past. It's mostly what true-crime junkies do. Jentry Rae's gruesome slaying is only four days old, so emotions are high and the danger is deep.

"At least you have nice memories of your daughter. Right, Sonny?" Shaunette asks. "I mean, your trove of family photos and mementoes at your house—they impressed me when I visited the farm. You loved Jentry Rae unconditionally."

"All I *have* are memories." He shoves his trembling hands inside his pockets. Although he has stopped crying, his pallor and unsteadiness are concerning. "Shaunette, do you know who the father was?"

Her bottom lip quivers. She seems uncomfortable. "I wish I did."

"Are you sure? Can you take a guess?"

"As far as I know, Jentry Rae dated casually."

Sonny winces. "You mean my daughter was going to have a child with a *nobody*?"

"I w-wouldn't put it that way," she stammers.

Nikki interjects. "Only a guy in an exclusive relationship would've given Jentry Rae a puppy and a jeweled bracelet."

Shaunette raises an eyebrow as if to retort *Have you met a lot of men? Some play the field.* "Jentry Rae never told me who gifted her those things," she says. "So we have to figure out who or what her tattoos mean. Maybe D.M. stands for Duke McCade. Or Direct Message. Or Doesn't Matter. That was Jentry Rae's favorite phrase. She'd always say it with an offhanded shrug."

"Dante Marconi, the stadium guard, has D.M. initials, too," says Nikki. Were the two of them close?

The old man draws himself up. "Hold on a doggone minute. Did you mention Duke McCade? That sneaky ball of cow dung is my nemesis. When he bought the Lonestars, I hated that he had re-entered my life. I even tried to persuade my girl to leave the cheerleaders."

"How do you know him?" Nikki asks.

"Years ago, he tried to buy my farm. Had plans to convert it into an enormous condominium complex. Can you imagine? When I refused, the bastard tried to slander me. Duke McCade is a conniving, pig-stinking blockhead who told people I was usin' dangerous pesticides. I took him to court, but he hid behind his corporation."

Shaunette takes a breath. "People can change, Sonny. Besides, I don't know why I mentioned Duke McCade. Jentry Rae was too smart to get mixed up with the team owner."

Nikki shoots her a look. Does the cheerleader know more than she is saying?

"What do *you* think, Nikki?" Sonny asks.

"All I know is your daughter wrote on Instagram that she was quitting the DLC after this season."

"I didn't believe it. Jentry Rae adored the limelight." Shaunette shakes her head. "She must have been quitting because she was pregnant."

The farmer whips his hat off in a defeated gesture. As the moderate rainfall turns into a forceful thunderstorm, he huddles and wheezes under the restaurant canopy.

"You should rest, Sonny," Nikki suggests.

"In a minute, sugar. Listen up, ladies. The medical examiner's report won't be released for a while, so please don't repeat that Jentry Rae was expecting."

The women concur, after which Nikki fidgets on her feet. Information like that can get leaked.

Shaunette clears her throat. "All right, I'll come clean. I *do* know something more, and I don't feel right keeping it to myself. But this is going to be shocking."

She waits several beats then blurts, "Jentry Rae was seeing two men at once."

"Two men? Pardon?" Sonny looks affronted.

"It wasn't like her," the cheerleader adds, "but she pitted one boyfriend against the other. I think that explains the set of tattoos on her hips."

The news blasts Nikki like a firehose. Sonny leans against the wall in horror. "Do you know the names of these men?" he asks.

"No."

"This gol-durned place poisoned my baby," the old man laments.

"Maybe. Maybe not." Shaunette starts to cry. "Jentry Rae became great at hiding things. It's possible you never knew her at all."

"What do you mean by that?" Sonny flings his eyes wide.

"Nothing. Forget I said anything. I apologize."

Nikki wonders why the cheerleader is acting more skittish than a cat on hot bricks. Is Shaunette just putting on a sad act? And was she faking "cheer"-i-ness during their previous interview? Acting is easier than people think. Nikki knows; she's in the film industry.

"Gracious. Look at the time." Shaunette inches away. "I'm off to feed Beau Dog, but what about the funeral, Sonny? The Lonestars organization is holding an elaborate memorial for your girl on Saturday, but I reckon you'll want a small, private burial afterward."

He grinds his teeth. "I can't put my baby six feet under yet. What if the answer to her death can be found on her broken body?"

Nerves churning, Nikki calls the old man a cab. She'll send him back to his hotel to lie down. She has something important to do.

As she watches Shaunette leave, she hopes the police will find a match for the foreign DNA on Jentry Rae's corpse. Those fragments under the cheerleader's fingernails and the chromosomes left on her wrist—who will they belong to? Given the level of security at the stadium, the only thing that makes sense is that Jentry Rae knew her attacker.

CHAPTER FIFTEEN

THE DALLAS LONESTARS CHEERLEADER

~ *OCTOBER 17* ~

Shaunette waves goodbye to Nikki and Sonny as she climbs in her Honda. The postmortem exhausted her, and she wasn't even inside the room for it.

While she drives away from the morgue, the shock of her friend's scandalous pregnancy mushrooms. Would Jentry Rae's baby bump have been obvious before the end of football season? Shaunette does the math. The answer is yes, and her hands shake with disbelief.

Jentry Rae might not have divulged the news to her personally, but she could've told another Dallas Lonestars Cheerleader about the pregnancy. Only, who did she trust more than Shaunette?

Heck and high water.

In Jentry Rae's own words—it doesn't matter.

She is dead. No one can protect her or her child now.

Needing a distraction, Shaunette pulls into a coffee shop drive-thru lane. As her car idles, however, her self-contempt doesn't go away. She failed to save her friend from two doomed relationships—a misstep that haunts her. What if she had exposed the romances? What then?

Jentry Rae confided the identity of Lover Number One to Shaunette, and Shaunette did nothing about it. Upsettingly, that boyfriend is married. A relationship that could cause devastation if revealed.

Gut gnarling, Shaunette wonders why Jentry Rae didn't share the identity of her second lover. Leaving that info out was unwise. More to the point, it ticked Shaunette off.

But she won't flap her lips about any of it yet. She's in protection mode. It's the least she can do for her former friend. Besides, she needs to devise a plan of action before divulging more secrets to Sonny and Nikki.

After she pays for her iced latte, more regret riddles her. She questions why she and Jentry Rae inserted themselves so deeply in each other's business. The goal was to be helpful, but toxicity took over. The final result was total friendship dismantlement.

Even now, Shaunette is keeping dirt in her pocket about Jentry Rae in case she needs it.

Mercy.

She is the worst friend ever.

Jealous foes deserve the way things backfire on them.

Turning onto Preston Road, Shaunette sets her coffee in a cupholder and gnaws on her bottom lip. It's clear that Jentry Rae couldn't tell her daddy she was pregnant, and when she needed a compassionate shoulder to cry on, Shaunette went missing in action. It's why she needs to find out who fathered Jentry Rae's baby. Sonny wants answers, too. In that regard, He Who Shall Not Be Named *will* be exposed. It's not too late for Shaunette to make amends.

The sound of the rain hypnotizes her as she drives. Losing herself in thought, she wonders how Jentry Rae could've maintained her gleaming smile and upbeat attitude knowing she was expecting. The luminous head cheerleader possessed two magical characteristics: luck and magnetism. Things that don't come naturally to Shaunette. She has to *work* at her luck. And she is constantly trying to *improve* her personality.

Yet, somehow, everything was effortless for Jentry Rae. She wanted a big life, and *presto*, she got it. Crushingly, she became the winged mythological creature who flew too close to the sun and caught fire.

Shaunette was selected as a DLC, yes. And yes, she won a few small-time beauty pageants like Miss Sippy Cup. But due to what? Her mama being a former cheerleader?

Somehow riding on the coattails of a parent doesn't feel right. Tons of deserving girls would kill to be a Dallas Lonestars Cheerleader, and Shaunette was fortunate enough to get her foot in the door. Shame on her for messing up a lucky break.

As she drives through an intersection, the driving rain makes it difficult to see. Suddenly, a car approaches hers from the rear.

At first, it hangs back, but then it hiccups forward. The frightening chase she endured two days ago ricochets back. Searing worry burns through Shaunette as she struggles to maneuver her car in the thick storm without applying the brakes. The car behind her is close enough to clash hers!

Unnerved, she jerks the wheel to the left. Switching to the adjacent lane did her no good before, but she doesn't have a choice right now.

She waits.

Thank goodness the innocent SUV paddles by and disappears.

Breaking out in sobs, she pulls into a grocery store lot and shoves her car into Park. Her paranoia is getting the best of her. As she drops her head against the steering wheel, she closes her eyes and urges herself to hold it together.

The bleep of her cell phone interrupts her meltdown.

Shaky, Shaunette looks at the device and recognizes the number. Her pulse throbs. Wondering if she should answer the call, she watches her finger twitch above the slide bar. Is she ready to talk to them? And are *they* ready to admit how they suffocated Jentry Rae sometimes?

The phone screen goes dark, and she blows out a relieved breath. They have been doing that lately . . . calling and hanging up before she answers. It seems childish. Then again, grief can take many forms.

When Shaunette's phone rings again, Nikki Keegan is on the other end. The women exchanged numbers at the coroner's office. Nervous about what the documentarian will uncover, Shaunette reluctantly picks up. "Hey, Nikki."

"Hi, Shaunette. I wanted to make sure you're okay. You seemed devastated at the morgue. Seeing Jentry Rae on that

cold dissection table and then learning she was pregnant—
Christ. It must have been a blow, right?"

"It *was* a lot to take in," she replies. "But I'm okay. Ah, I'm
kind of busy, so what do you want?"

"You don't sound all right. Did something just happen?
You're breathing fast."

Transferring the phone to her other ear, Shaunette cracks the
window for ventilation. About to burst, she needs to tell somebody—about a portion of what's happening, at least. "Nikki,
I'm being harassed. A vicious message was painted on my car,
and an SUV tried to plow me down the other day. I nearly died.
It's part of why I acted so emotional at the coroner's office."

"Oh my God. Are you scared?"

"I'm terrified."

"Okay. Take a deep breath. Are you someplace safe now?"

"Yes."

There's a pause.

"Look, if you have important information, you should
confide it to someone," the filmmaker suggests.

"What do you mean?"

"You know the identity of the two guys Jentry Rae was
dating, don't you, Shaunette?"

Her heart beats faster. Time stands still. Does she trust Nikki
Keegan enough to share what she's privy to? "I *think* I know
who one of the guys is. Royce Holt. But I'm not sure I should
tell the authorities."

"Royce Holt, the Lonestars' backup quarterback? Whoa.
You have to."

"But somebody wants to hurt me! In addition to being
hounded, I've been getting hang-up calls."

"From Royce?"

"No."

"Even so, shit. That's a lot," Nikki says. "You know, I got a strange text the other day informing me that a football player on the Lonestars' roster is breaking rules. Do you know anything about that?"

"No."

"Do you at least recognize the number of your hang-up caller?"

"Nope," Shaunette repeats. *Can Nikki sense that I'm lying?*

"*Hmm.* People with something to hide call and hang up," the filmmaker says. "Otherwise, they would just confront you. I think it's another form of stalking. So, if this creepiness becomes a real problem, I'm here to help. Women have to stick together. Right?"

"Right." Shaunette pushes her shoulders down. Maybe Nikki has good intentions, after all. Being friends would be nice. She doesn't have many.

Ending the call, she sits in her car to recalibrate herself. Grateful when the storm dissipates, she dabs at her swollen eyes and then drives. However, by the time she pulls up to her apartment complex, her guilt and worry return full force. Melding together, they squash her chest like a heavy suitcase full of secrets she can't unpack.

Did Jentry Rae feel the weight of her choices, too?

Ensuring that the coast is clear, Shaunette runs into her apartment unit. Her life has changed considerably these past few days. She used to be concerned about trivial things—how her hair looked and if she could master dance routines. But now, a psycho murderer is on the loose.

As she picks up Beau Dog, even he can't soothe her over-wrought condition. She isn't sure she'll get through this. The situation is critical.

A pregnant Dallas Lonestars Cheerleader was savagely massacred.

The Lonestars are suffering a horrible losing streak.

And a deadly assailant has set his sights on *her*.

If she was wearing a pageant sash, it would read *Miss Bullseye Target*.

CHAPTER SIXTEEN

THE FILMMAKER

~ *OCTOBER 17* ~

Nikki hasn't left the county coroner's office yet. She is still in the equipment van, having just ended a call with Shaunette. Concern over the conversation is thudding her heart.

Who's hounding the scared cheerleader?

Shaunette doesn't believe it's Royce Holt, but hearing his name blew Nikki away like a bazooka. The quarterback was at Jentry Rae's apartment complex the night after the murder—trying to blend in with the crowd. So, it's looking more and more like he was personally mourning her death.

Is Shaunette being tight-lipped about him on purpose?

Nikki gets on her phone again and calls Royce to see what he has to say for himself. No answer. She leaves a message. She has his number because she was given a players' roster for the documentary, but considering the unpleasant exchange she had with him at The Depot's practice field, she'll be surprised if he calls her back.

Wanting a fuller picture, she climbs out of the van and heads back inside the coroner's office. She intends to speak with Brandon López, Dallas's assistant DA. The prosecutor seems like a stand-up guy—someone who's dedicated to and focused on the case. Maybe he can offer some useful information.

After she scours the first floor for him, she hastens up the stairs to the second level. Damn it that López is nowhere to be found. Assuming he already left, she turns to go. About to descend the stairs, she catches him emerging from the men's room.

Crumpling a wet paper towel in his hands, he seems startled to see her. Once he throws the paper in a trash can, he comes closer. "Are you looking for me?"

"Yes. Hello."

"We haven't been properly introduced." He extends his hand.

"I'm Nikki Keegan." She accepts his handshake.

"Who are you in relation to Sonny Randall?"

"I'm his friend. He said we're 'kinfolk,' but he just needed support today."

"Got it. So, what do you do for a living, Miss Keegan?"

"I'm a documentarian. Currently, I'm directing something for the Dallas Lonestars."

López crosses his arms and studies her with warm brown eyes. "That's funny. I took you for a journalist, not a filmmaker. A journalist with a healthy curiosity, in fact."

She was right about him being dialed in. He sees right through her. Still, she won't admit anything just yet. "I'm working on a sports documentary; that's all." *Jesus.* If he quizzes her on football terminology, she's screwed.

"Interesting," he replies. "But is Jentry Rae Randall's murder something the football team can ignore? Are you including a segment about the homicide in your movie?"

"Not exactly."

He arches an eyebrow.

Flinching, Nikki's mind warbles as her imposter syndrome rears up. What does López see? A woman who is comfortable lying through her teeth? Or a caring friend who's here out of compassion for an old, grieving man?

Is there anything wrong with being both?

The prosecutor says nothing. He seems to be giving her a pass.

"I want to ask you something," she rushes on. "How long will the DNA results take?"

"It's hard to say. Could take weeks. A month, possibly."

"A month? Can't you use your authority to speed things up? Sonny doesn't have much time left."

"If I could don a lab coat and borrow a microscope, then maybe."

"That's too bad." Nikki taps her foot. "What about testing the fetal tissue for the father's DNA?"

"That could take even longer. And then we'd have to find the guy."

"I see." *The process might put Sonny through too much, anyway.*

"You're impatient for the results, Miss Keegan. I get that. But are you eager only because the victim's father is ill?"

"No. A crime must be solved."

"Exactly. Which has nothing to do with your sports documentary." López smiles at his own joke.

She feels herself blush. *Time to change the subject.* "Ah, so, this might seem out of line, but who do you think murdered Jentry Rae?"

"That's a conversation for another time." His voice changes as he starts to walk.

She hurries to keep in step.

He rolls his eyes. "Are you sure you weren't an investigative journalist in another life?"

"I did want to write a newspaper crime column early in my career."

"Why change to documentaries?"

"Words are great, but things only count when you get them on film."

The statement halts him in his tracks. "Should I be wary of you?"

"Only if you have skeletons in your closet." It's her turn to joke. When the jest falls flat, she clears her throat. "But seriously, I swear we're on the same team with the same goal."

"Your Californian dialect is obvious, Miss Keegan. And since you aren't from Texas, may I give you some advice?"

"Yes, please."

"I have lived in this state all my life. I roped longhorns on a cattle ranch when I was a kid, and I even worked an oil field. So, I'm well aware that Texans in small towns are kind and forgiving."

"I'm not sure I follow, Mr. López."

"This is Dallas. A big city. People here aren't that nice. If you're seen sticking your nose where it doesn't belong, you'll be zeroed in on. Then you will get no information from cops, detectives, or attorneys. I'm not making a veiled threat. I am suggesting that you be more discreet." He smiles.

"I hear you loud and clear. Thank you for that."

"You're welcome. And if we really are on the same team, maybe you can be my eyes outside my office."

"Thanks, but no thanks. I'm focused on my film, remember?" She shoves her hands in her pockets and closes herself off.

"Fair enough. But one more thing. Be careful who you trust. My favorite Southern saying is: *Salt and sugar look alike*." He passes her his card. "In case you change your mind."

It's a wonder he trusts *her*. She didn't belong at the morgue today. She's an interloper—not part of the Dallas Lonestars in an official capacity. She has temporary access, only. Like a spy in disguise.

To that point, she faked her credentials at the start of her career. She didn't attend a prestigious film school. Or intern with industry greats, the way her résumé claims. Lying has become second nature.

It's why Nikki will take López's advice. She'll do her best to be less straightforward . . . act like a quiet fly on the wall. Now to convince Vince that he needs to be quiet, too.

As she hurries back to the van, she is grateful to leave the morgue's scent of death behind a second time. By now, she assumes Sonny is back in his hotel room, sleeping off the news he received today. If that's possible.

The pitiful farmer wants her to find out who gifted Beau Dog to Jentry Rae. He believes that person impregnated his daughter.

Except, Nikki has a different intuition. She believes whoever gave Jentry Rae the infinity bracelet probably killed her.

Is the culprit one and the same person?

CHAPTER SEVENTEEN

THE DALLAS LONESTARS CHEERLEADER

~ *OCTOBER 18* ~

Shaunette parks at the Dallas Police Station, but in two quick shakes she regrets her decision to pay detectives a visit.

After forcing herself out of the car, she heads for the station's front door. She almost turns around, but then a thought strikes her. Realistically, she can't put off talking to investigators any longer. Although she gave them a statement already, chances are they'll come sniffing around with more questions. Questions about her rivalry with Jentry Rae. About the undiscovered details of Jentry Rae's life. And about Shaunette's argument with the cheerleading captain that got recorded on Jentry Rae's phone. The detectives have the phone, after all.

Isn't it best to get ahead of things?

Quaking in her sneakers, she pushes through the police station's door and approaches the desk. Bald, burly Sergeant Emerson greets her within minutes. As he guides her into an interrogation room, he reminds her of his name.

"How could I forget?" she murmurs under her breath. Every encounter with him has been unpleasant.

The instant he shuts the door, his cordial demeanor disappears. "Sit down, Miss Simmons. Let me guess why you're here."

Her heartbeat soars. *What does he think he knows?*

"You have important information about the death of Jentry Rae Randall. Correct?"

She nods.

As they sit at a small table, Emerson tosses a manila folder on the surface of it. She wonders what it contains. When the sergeant doesn't talk for a minute or open the folder, she gets more nervous. Urging herself to breathe, she looks around. Why are they alone? Aren't detectives assigned partners with whom they play good cop/bad cop? No doubt somebody is observing them from behind a two-way mirror.

"May I call you Shaunette?" Emerson's Western twang fills the small room.

"Sure."

"Okay. Begin with any information you want to share."

Anxiety seizes her by the throat. The sergeant is sizing her up. That much is obvious.

Distressing thoughts fill Shaunette's mind as she considers fleeing. Instead, she stammers out nonsense.

Blowing out an impatient breath, Emerson sits forward. "Allow me to make this easier. Do you know who killed Jentry Rae Randall?"

"No. I'm here to clear my conscience. I want to relay an argument she and I had minutes before the football game between the Lonestars and the Condors. On the day she was murdered."

The detective nods.

Her mouth grows cotton-dry. Once she gulps from a water bottle, she begins her tale. "Um, so Jentry Rae and I were alone in the cheerleaders' locker room . . . where the showers are located. While the rest of our teammates were primping in the dressing area, I mentioned to her that she'd been acting weird. I offered to help if she needed out of a crazy situation, but she denied being in trouble. That's when she accused me of being meddlesome." *Translation, I read Jentry Rae's diary.*

Sergeant Emerson frowns.

Shaunette sits on her hands to keep them from shaking.

"That's it?" he asks. "What kind of hot water was Jentry Rae in?"

"I won't speak ill of the dead."

"*Ookaay.* I guess you're being compassionate, but you're also wasting my time."

She waits a beat. "The thing is I knew my friend was seeing two men at once."

"And you're just revealing this now?"

"I told her to confide everything to the DLC director. I didn't want to get involved."

"But she didn't disclose a thing. So, you need to give me more details. Any and all information you can provide is crucial."

Shaunette's jaw practically locks. Can she get the words out? "Okay, here it is. I knew Jentry Rae was dating a Lonestars' player. I wasn't sure which one, but he was definitely one of the guys she was involved with."

The detective rubs his bald head. "Two boyfriends, eh? Fascinating. But for now, let's stick to the football player. Was it a casual thing?"

"Jentry Rae loved him, but sadly he didn't reciprocate her feelings. I threatened to tell the franchise bigwigs that she and her mystery guy were breaking FFL rules. I wanted to protect her." Tears spring to Shaunette's eyes. She knows the player was Royce but won't smear his name just yet. Making giant waves will get back to Vana. Then her spot on the squad might be jinxed.

Shaunette has left something else out, too. How she accused Jentry Rae over the phone of being with Royce just to get famous. Dating a pro football player is a straight line to that.

Feeling her knees bounce under the table, Shaunette reflects on that terrible September 23rd phone conversation and how it caused her falling-out with Jentry Rae. A few weeks later, she again voiced her strong disapproval about the affair with Royce—on the fateful afternoon of the murder.

That conversation went even worse.

"Mind your own business, Shaunette!" Jentry Rae snapped as she lifted her chin. "I'm not talking to you; don't you get that? I'm tired of you always comparin' and despairin'. And I can't believe you read my diary. What's wrong with you? I've tried and tried to help you. To mentor you. To be your friend. But it's clear you want to step into my life and be me."

The assertion stabbed Shaunette in the heart. "That's not true! I'm telling you things to help you. You're making a mistake with Royce! He sleeps around!"

"Enough! You're just jealous. Mercy. Stop being a negative vortex that sucks people in. If you don't keep my love for Royce a secret, I know certain things about you, too. Leave me alone!"

What Shaunette did next was unforgivable.

Sergeant Emerson picks up a pen and grips it tightly. "I think you're double-talking, Shaunette. You wanted to protect your friend. Or rat her out?"

"Jentry Rae needed a wake-up call."

"I'm still confused. If Jentry Rae had come forward about any of this, it would've placed her in trouble with the director of the cheerleaders. Right?"

"Yes. But her heart was about to be broken. I sensed it. The Lonestars player thought of her as a plaything. He needed to pay for stringing her along. Anyway, Jentry Rae shouted that I shouldn't tattletale."

"She was angry with you then?"

"Very," Shaunette replies. "But I swear I didn't hurt her!"

"We haven't been able to pinpoint who bought her an infinity bracelet with a sapphire center"—Emerson scowls—"but we did track down the name of the shop that custom-made it: Brookson Brothers. So, save me some work, Shaunette. Tell me who the boyfriends are. I know you know their names."

"I don't." *Jentry Rae didn't entrust me with all her secrets.*

Blotches of irritation bloom on his face. "Withholding information is morally wrong. Plus, I can subpoena access to your digital devices."

"I didn't come here to snitch! I'm in danger, too. My car was vandalized, and I'm being followed."

He looks at her blankly. As though he doesn't believe her.

Frustration shimmies up her spine. "Do you think I'm lying?"

"I don't have to believe everyone who comes in that door, young lady. And if you don't know who is stalking you, a restraining order is out of the question, too. Sorry."

"You've been real helpful." Sarcasm drips from Shaunette's voice as she pushes to her feet. "I'll leave now, if I'm free to. I just wanted to tell you that Jentry Rae and I had a tense argument. I think the other cheerleaders heard it." She pauses to control the tremor in her voice. "You have to believe that I didn't hurt my teammate. She and I used to be good friends. What would I gain from her death?"

Emerson's eyes go dark. Bolting out of his seat, he steps closer in the already-claustrophobic room. "I'd say you'd gain a lot. Maybe you like this secretive boyfriend of Jentry Rae's. *Really* like him—enough to want him for your own. We found DNA on your friend's body. Male or female, we don't know yet, but it's being tested. Did your altercation with Jentry Rae turn violent, Shaunette? Did you touch her? Harm her?"

Her blood boils. When will Emerson stop trying to entrap her? She blurts, "M-maybe I scratched her *accidentally*."

"Now we're getting someplace. Listen up. We retrieved a disturbing recording from Jentry Rae's phone."

Shaunette freezes. Can she please swap her soft hoodie for a bulletproof vest? Her voice on that recording is damning. It's why she needs to shut the heck up. Coming here equals a step into quicksand. Nothing she reveals from this point on will pull her out.

"I think you wanted Jentry Rae gone," the sergeant crows. "You have one mean competitive streak—at least that's how your teammates describe you. Here's also what I believe. Whenever Jentry Rae one-upped you, you grew angrier and angrier. She recorded the argument you two had to prove your temper. You wanted to destroy her. Stealing her boyfriend away was a start. Without a doubt, you want to be lead cheerleader."

"It wasn't like that!"

"Didn't you compete in cutthroat beauty pageants? Slippery baby oil smeared on the bottoms of shoes? Laxatives sprinkled into water bottles before the bathing suit portion—"

"Stop it!" The accusations curdle Shaunette's stomach. "Nobody died in the last beauty pageant I competed in."

"Very funny. But female catfights are all hiss and no makeup. I venture to say you hated Jentry Rae because she had everything you wanted." Shaking his head, Emerson opens the manila folder and withdraws crime scene photos. Jentry Rae's once-glorious hair is matted with sticky-looking, red-black blood, and her eyes are flung open in horror. Worst of all, the gash on her head is split wider than a sliced-open football.

Shaunette totters off-balance. At least Jentry Rae looked semi-peaceful on the autopsy slab.

"Somebody did this to that beautiful girl," the detective barks. Fuming, he extracts a flash drive from the folder. "This here's the memory stick that contains the sound file we retrieved off the phone. Do you want me to play it for you?"

"No!" She cannot relive the worst moment of her life.

"Okay. I'll summarize. You're heard on the recording saying, 'I'll kill you!'" He inhales. "*You* said that, Shaunette. You threatened to kill Jentry Rae Randall, and guess what? She is dead."

Shaunette flees the room. She refuses to hear another word. If she *had* stayed, she probably would've told the detective that wanting Jentry Rae dead wasn't a knee-jerk reaction. She'd been wanting it to happen all season long.

JENTRY RAE'S DIARY ENTRY

SEPTEMBER 28

I never thought I'd write this, but I am cheating on the man I love. I usually say that things don't matter, but two-timing is wrong.

What's happened to me? I used to be an open, loyal person, but life in the big leagues will gobble you up and spit you out if you don't protect yourself. As awful as it sounds, I have to play both sides. Hopefully, my backup game plan will pay off.

Still . . . I'm a horrible person! I hate thinking I've hurt anyone. And now I'm up a creek. I wish I could call Shaunette and ask her for advice. Although, I know she would say, "You're a homewrecker, Jentry Rae. Back off. Leave things alone!"

Shaunette believes that since I have already licked the spoon of fame, I want the whole bowl. She's wrong; I don't buy into my own fantasy of fame. All I want is the complete family unit I never had. My ma died having me, and because

I never knew her, it's always been me and Daddy . . . a lonely scenario sometimes.

Shaunette and I don't see eye to eye anymore, but we agree on one thing: the Dallas Lonestars Cheerleaders are sexy in a wholesome way. We aren't sluts. I'm not a slut; I'm one of America's Angels! The two guys I'm seeing are the only men I have ever been with. But do either of them truly want to be with me? I shouldn't require a man's love to make me whole, but there it is.

My heart is going in two directions—like a fork in a country road. I didn't plan to fall in love, but when Boyfriend Number One refused to say he was in love with me, somebody else professed THEIR love. I fell into HIS trap. Regrettably, I can't cut off my connection with my first love, because what if he changes his mind and chooses me in the end?

The scary thing about Boyfriend Number Two is that no man wants to lose a championship game.

CHAPTER EIGHTEEN

THE FILMMAKER

~ OCTOBER 19 ~

The memorial for Jentry Rae is a lavish, almost garish affair held in a gigantic performing arts center on the outskirts of Dallas. The venue is filled to capacity with friends, colleagues, the DLC squad, and the entire Lonestars football team. Nikki and Vince have been invited as a courtesy, only. Meaning they can't film.

There is an odd, excited buzz in the air, as opposed to a heavy cloak of grief. Maybe it's due to the fact that the cheerleaders and the football players rarely appear together at non-sports-related events.

Once Nikki and Vince show their Lonestars badges, they settle in the back row. Nikki reflects a little more on the "no filming" restriction relayed to her by Duke McCade's assistant. The tone the woman used wasn't exactly a nice one.

Frowning, she runs her fingertips over the program guide printed in Lonestars' colors. Then she glances at the stage. A foil, letter-by-letter DLC sign is hanging above a podium laden with flowers, and centering the stage is a blown-up photograph of Jentry Rae in her cheerleading uniform. Off to the side, a Grammy-winning country singer is strumming a sad ballad on his guitar.

Soon, Duke McCade ambles on stage. The audience goes quiet as he reads a statement that expresses Jentry Rae as caring, upbeat, naïve, and feisty. Nikki considers each adjective flattering except for "naïve." Next, the team owner dives into an earnest speech about how valuable the cheerleaders are to his organization.

While Nikki listens, she notices that rows of seats separate the Dallas Lonestars players from the cheerleading squad. The juvenile dynamic speaks of division between the boys and the girls. What's up with that? Didn't Duke McCade just say that the cheerleaders complement his football lineup?

Vince gestures discreetly at the hundreds of attendees. "So much for an intimate affair, huh?"

"Exactly." She cranes her neck to look for Royce Holt. There he is, in the seventh row. He is chatting quietly with a teammate while his shaggy brown hair practically drips from a recent shower. Obviously, he took two minutes to get ready. Do any of the football players really want to be here?

Nikki wads the program into a ball.

If Royce turns around, maybe he'll point at her and say, *"There is the pushy bitch who had the balls to call me out at practice."*

Let him. She doesn't freaking care what he thinks.

She did her best today, appearance-wise. But not for him. Her curly, shoulder-length hair is blow-dried straight, and she even pinned one side up and applied lipstick. Her black suit is ancient, however, and is baggy in all the wrong areas. However, she doesn't give a flip about her looks. Now that she's rubbing elbows with the big boys, she is focusing on what she does best: piecing things together.

Chase Campbell enters the venue. Attendees toss him irked looks for being late, but he acts like he doesn't give a flying fuck as he struts to the seats. Attractively dressed in a tailored sports jacket, he displays his customary scowl and is welcomed into Royce's row. The other athletic trainers are gathered in a different area, so Nikki figures Chase must have some clout.

Grim organ music begins to play.

Soft weeping can be heard.

The sounds echo throughout the enormous venue like something unholy.

While the affair grows more solemn, Chase and Royce keep their heads tilted together in private conversation. Nikki would love to know what they're talking about.

"I don't like that guy," Vince says under his breath.

"What guy?"

"Chase Campbell. He gives off a bad vibe . . . as opposed to his cool buddy Royce. But in Chase's defense, if I had a rich, famous friend, I'd be jealous, too." Vince crosses his arms. "Damn. I wish we could film the variety of looks on everyone's faces."

"Me, too. This is the weirdest memorial I've ever attended."

After a local pastor leads a prayer, Duke McCade cuts out early. Nikki figures that he probably wants to avoid questions about how a bubbly young cheerleader died on his watch. Sonny Randall is nowhere to be seen, either. She assumes he was invited but declined.

Taking Brandon López's advice, she quietly studies the gray faces of the cheerleaders as they come on stage one by one to share heartfelt stories about Jentry Rae. Their recollections move most of the attendees to tears. Tributes are always somber, but more so when the person being honored was struck down in the prime of life.

Nikki flicks away a tear, too. She might not be capturing this event on film, but in her opinion, memorials always have cinematic impact.

Once the gathering ends, weepy guests filter out of the auditorium. As Shaunette materializes, she nods at Nikki, and Nikki nods back. Judging from the cheerleader's smeared mascara and the clumps of tissue in her hand, she was among the mourners who cried the hardest.

"Let's get going." Vince eagerly directs Nikki to the equipment van. "I want to show you something back at your apartment."

CHAPTER NINETEEN

THE DALLAS LONESTARS CHEERLEADER

~ OCTOBER 19 ~

Shaunette decides to linger alone in the parking lot of the performing arts center. She has already said goodbye to her squad mates, and now she needs a minute to collect herself. Looking down at the celebratory program in her hands, she considers how touching Jentry Rae's elaborate memorial was . . . a true testament to what she meant to people. Shaunette feels insignificant by comparison.

Sniffling a little, she is about to climb into her Honda when somebody clasps her shoulder.

"Hey, you," a voice says behind her.

It's Chase Campbell; his deep timbre is familiar. Fear chills her blood as she spins around stiffly to face him. "Why are you creeping up on me, Chase? You and I shouldn't be talking."

"Why not?"

She wants to say, *"Because you're a buzzkill who has always spooked me. You spooked and smothered Jentry Rae sometimes, too."* Erring on the side of caution, she replies, "These entanglements all of us have formed . . . they're out of control. Things are getting too complicated."

"What's complicated?" He kicks at a stone that clatters loudly under her car. "Everything is pretty clear. You were jealous of your best friend, and now she's dead. Things have conveniently become *less* complicated for you, Shaunette. Am I right?"

"Stop with your insinuations! You're such a shit." Turning and clicking the car fob, she tries to ignore the half-truth of his words.

He grips her shoulder again, with more pressure.

She winces a little as her heart bangs against her ribcage. Chase uses his hands all day doing sports massages. They possess incredible strength, but *hell*. Is he literally holding her in place?

"Take your hand off me," she commands.

He does. When she pivots around again, she notices that his expression is more dire, less aggressive.

"Look, Shaunette. I know what it's like to have a best friend you hate. Royce and I aren't biological brothers, but we grew up together. Things are different between us now, though. Lately, he has bigger things in his life than our friendship. And the son of a bitch will always have more than me."

"Jealous much?"

"You should talk," he bites out.

Touché. Her cheeks burn.

"I don't get you or Royce," she confesses.

"Didn't Royce tell you about his dad driving him too hard? He has been trying to please hard-ass Warren Holt all his life. That's what inspires Royce more than anything. My problem is I had a screwed-up childhood."

Shaunette backs up against the car; Chase seems especially chatty and pushy today. "But isn't it true that Royce blows his problems out of proportion?" she asks.

"A hundred percent. The guy turns leaky boats into capsized ocean liners. I mean, shit . . . he's just as dramatic as his wife. They both love the limelight; it's why they get along. But weirdly, he lets her wear the pants at home. Anyway, to Royce's credit, he never rubs my rough background in my face. I'm the one who fixates on our inequalities. Is that how you felt about Jentry Rae?"

"I've already talked to you about this, Chase."

"Yeah, but it's been a while. You've been avoiding me."

She hugs her arms around her body. "Just tell me you're grateful that the Holt family took you in."

"I am, goddamn it."

She stops for a second. "Your rough background—I'm sorry. I didn't know."

"I went through foster care—a broken system that tossed me around like a hot potato. Boo-hoo, right? Then I met Royce at a girls and boys club. He felt sorry for me and convinced his family to take me in. And I *was* thankful." Chase hesitates. "But it's hard to watch everything your friend touches turn to gold."

The "gold" reference strikes Shaunette like a thunderbolt. Golden boy Royce was drawn to golden girl Jentry Rae. But did their relationship turn volatile and become the *Clash of the Titans*?

126

"I'm done being envious." She shakes her head. "Living that way is unhealthy."

"You're right. Jealousy can make a person do terrible things."

The statement ties her mid-section in a knot. Running away and never looking back feels tempting. "If you're finished trauma-dumping, I'll go. I'm in a hurry."

"Wait. Weeks ago, you told me you wished Jentry Rae would disappear, remember? Then I heard about the huge falling-out you two had. I also know about your other little secret. So, when I heard you were the last person to be with Jentry Rae alone, I connected the dots."

"What dots? I was alone with her before we marched out in front of millions of people. I wasn't alone with her *after* the football game."

"You claim to have an alibi for the time of her murder?" Chase asks.

"You aren't a detective! And how dare you make accusations like that. We're done here." Frightened, Shaunette makes a move to get into her car, but he steps closer.

Pain surfaces in Chase's green eyes. "You need to know this. My favorite thing was talking to Jentry Rae one-on-one. Like Duke McCade said at the memorial service, she was magnetic and feisty, but she could also be naïve. She thought life was fun and games, so she toyed carelessly with people. On the flip side, she hated that about herself. She also hated the way you called her out about it, Shaunette."

"You're lying."

"I'm not. Go ahead and run off. I won't stop you. But you have to admit that Jentry Rae was made of starlight. The sun rose and set with her in my opinion, and she didn't deserve to die.

So, if I find out who killed her, that person will suffer the way she did."

Fear and anger pound through Shaunette like a dopamine hit. Enough about Jentry Rae's brilliance! And enough obsession-ranting from Chase! She had no idea he was so focused on her friend. Maybe he wanted too much from the star cheerleader.

Icy tentacles squeeze Shaunette's body as she fumbles her way into her car. While her hands shake, she winds the window down. "I know it w-was you," she stutters.

"Me, what?"

"You have been calling me and hanging up like a schoolboy. Maybe you're using a burner phone, whatever, but I know it's you. Stop it. Go to the police if you know anything."

"Why? Because that's what you did?"

As Shaunette drives away, Chase's unnerving laughter echoes behind her in the hazy morning air.

CHAPTER TWENTY

THE FILMMAKER

~ OCTOBER 19 ~

Nikki puts two potatoes in the microwave and nukes them for six minutes per side. Baked potatoes and scrambled eggs are the extent of her culinary skills. Thank goodness her brother is a chef at Applebee's. It's a relief that he's feeding Pop.

"I'm ready!" Vince calls out.

Bringing the potatoes with her, she sits next to him at the computer screen. "What are we about to look at?"

He takes one bite of the potato then sets the plate aside. "Not look at. *Listen* to."

"Sorry. What are we about to listen to?"

"Prepare to be amazed." Vince's hands resemble an enthusiastic magician's as he punches some buttons on the keyboard. "I was able to enhance the audio of Shaunette Simmons's phone call to that mystery man. Remember how I recorded her on a parabolic mike in the parking lot of the cheerleader's practice studio?"

"Yes." Nikki's pulse quickens.

He starts the audio, and her blood runs cold.

"Hey, Shaunette," a male voice picks up the cheerleader's call.

"Hey, yourself. You heard about Jentry Rae, right?"

"Yeah. It's all over the news. I can't believe it!"

"Me, neither."

"It's a fucking tragedy." His voice catches. "I'm having a hell of a time concentrating. I mean, Jentry Rae was s-such a star. She w-was my world."

"Jeez. How come you never got this upset when she was alive?"

"Christ. Back off." He pauses. "Are the other cheerleaders freaking out?"

"You could say that."

"I'm sure this is tough for everyone. Okay. You're going to think I'm a dick, Shaunette, but as much as I miss Jentry Rae, I told the cops I didn't know her."

"I guess that's understandable," she replies after a hesitation. "I mean, you didn't have a choice. A murder investigation is happening. And there are those FFL rules. You weren't supposed to be anywhere near Jentry Rae in the first place."

"Exactly. So . . . hell. This is going to sound even worse, but I'm worried her death will ruin what I've worked for."

"That IS going too far! Have a heart!" Shaunette cries. "You and Jentry Rae—"

"She never understood me the way you do. You and I have pressuring parents. I can talk to you—"

"I'm not perfect. But I really like spending time with you."

The unknown male pauses. "You're right; you aren't perfect. Best friends don't turn on each other."

They share an awkward silence.

"Will you be at the memorial service?" Shaunette asks.

"Yeah. The entire Lonestars team will be there. It's optics."

She hesitates. "I'm scared because something else has happened. I'm in the parking lot of The Depot because my car—"

"Gotta go," he interrupts. "Don't call me for a while. It isn't a good idea."

Click.

Adrenaline courses through Nikki. The male voice—she recognizes it but wants confirmation about who it is from Vince.

He plunges into a soliloquy. "I splurged on a subscription to Audio File Comparator through Wave Lab. On a good day, spectral analysis software *is* highway robbery, but in this case, it was worth it. I was able to compare the guy's voice on this call to Royce Holt's acceptance speech on Draft Day." Vince pauses. "It's a match."

Her mind accelerates. "Shaunette was speaking with Royce Holt?"

"Yep. Shocking, right?"

"You're a genius."

Vince grins. "Thanks. I'm here all week."

She gets up, walks around a bit, and then settles on the couch. The voice on the audio exuded self-concern, so that much fits with Royce's MO. And having all of this on tape is great for the crime series. But why isn't Shaunette being honest with her? The rookie cheerleader said she *thought* Royce was dating Jentry Rae, but that sugarcoated the scenario. Plus, Shaunette never mentioned to Nikki how she and Royce are "chat on the phone" chummy.

Shaunette is keeping her share of secrets, and Nikki wants to know why. Not only is being in the dark eating away at her, but it's also amplifying her fury.

Vince joins her on the sofa. As he spreads his gangly, thin limbs over the cushions, he resembles a daddy longlegs. "What are you thinking, Nik?"

"This means Shaunette Simmons lied to me."

"When did she lie?"

"At the morgue."

"The morgue? What? I thought we were in this together. Snooping around by yourself could put you in danger."

"I'm all right. But listen. Shaunette told me that Jentry Rae was dating two men at the same time. Maybe Shaunette and Royce were close, too."

"As in, they were doing bedroom yoga?" Vince strokes his beard. "I suspected that from the audio. But the more I listened to it, the more it sounds like they're in a situation-ship."

"Maybe Shaunette wanted more. At any rate, she is the jealous type. She could be painting Jentry Rae's reputation in a bad light now that she's dead." There is only one way to find out. Nikki will call Shaunette right now and ask her.

As soon as the cheerleader picks up, Nikki dives into, "Why did you lie to me?"

"What?" Shaunette gasps.

"I audio-captured your phone conversation with Royce at The Depot. I happened to be sitting in the parking lot inside my van and overheard it. Why give me some cock-and-bull story about 'maybe he was dating Jentry Rae?' What else are you withholding, Shaunette?"

"Breathe, Nikki. I'll explain. I wasn't ready to say anything. You need to understand that Jentry Rae entrusted me with deep secrets. Coming clean about them is tricky. I feel loyal to her."

"I don't like being lied to," she insists.

The cheerleader exhales. Then, begging to get off the phone, she arranges for them to meet tomorrow.

Still keyed-up, Nikki texts quarterback Royce a message.

We need to clear the air, post awkward encounter on the practice field. What do you think?

Surprisingly, Royce texts back.

Meet me at a restaurant called Bogart's. In three hours.

CHAPTER TWENTY-ONE

THE DALLAS LONESTARS CHEERLEADER

~ OCTOBER 19 ~

Shaunette is at her apartment, trying to relax under her favorite quilted blanket. *Correction.* She's under the blanket hiding from her strained phone conversation with Nikki. And from her bizarre run-in with Chase.

The comfy, soft quilt happens to be a family heirloom. Decades old, it was made by one of Mama's fans back in the day. Seeing the old DLC logo sewn across it fills Shaunette with nostalgia. The emblem has evolved over the years from a cartoon image of boots and pom-poms to three, sleek, sparkling "DLC" letters.

The former logo was more fun.

Beau Dog jumps up and wants a cuddle. Smiling forlornly, Shaunette pulls him close and ruffles his ears. "Do you think I'm a bad friend, boy?"

The dog whines.

"You're right. I am."

As Chase's insinuations replay in her head, her apartment descends into stillness. Feeling lonely, she glances at a framed photograph of her mother on a shelf. Mama is wearing a special version of her Dallas Lonestars Cheerleaders' uniform: spangled hot pants and a red, white, and blue vest for a patriotic performance. Pure glee is spread across her fresh-off-the-farm face, and her gleaming brown hair is brushing her tiny waist. The picture was snapped at a play-off game while "Kaylene Simmons—star cheerleader" stood front and center on the sidelines, shaking her poms overhead.

No wonder Mama wants to relive her glory days through me, Shaunette thinks. *Look at the joy on her face. Too bad I'm a disappointment.*

Embarrassingly, Shaunette causes nothing but trouble on the DLC squad. As a result, Vana is peeved at her. And if she keeps this up, she will never be the star of the team.

Sliding deeper under the blanket, she avoids reaching for a bottle of liquor. She reckons abandonment issues are at the root of her problems. Her daddy left the family when she was little, and being rejected does something to a person. It robs you of worthiness. Then it keeps you from feeling accepted by anybody. That's when you begin to seek approval wherever you can get it.

In short, dealing with abandonment makes a person want to BE somebody else.

A gust of wind whistles outside Shaunette's apartment. She shudders to her core, despite the warmth of the blanket. Sadly, she can't call anyone and unload her troubles. As guilt rears up like a vicious monster, she clings fiercely to Beau Dog and wonders: Was Chase right? About jealousy making people do terrible things?

CHAPTER TWENTY-TWO

THE FILMMAKER

~ *OCTOBER 19* ~

Before Nikki goes to Bogart's Bistro, she drives to The Depot. She'll catch Ryder Hutchinson after practice outside the workout room if she has any luck. Everything about his emotional anger-spree that Vince captured on film is bothering her.

What exactly was Ryder's relationship with Jentry Rae? The initials the cheer captain had tattooed on one hip . . . "R.H." *Hmm.* Do the letters represent Royce Holt or Ryder Hutchinson?

Nikki might be able to distinguish between the two men if she can worm her way under Ryder's skin.

She quickly exits the van as soon as she sees the aging QB emerge from a side door. Fortunately, he's alone. "Excuse me," she says. "Do you have a minute? I'm Nikki Keeg—"

"I know who you are. What do you want?" Disheveled and unkempt, he slings an equipment bag over his shoulder.

"I heard what you said on the sideline the other day, describing Jentry Rae's death as the real tragedy and not your injury. Can you tell me what you meant by that? Were you friends with her?"

He rolls his eyes. "I heard you were nosy, ma'am. Ever try 'keep it professional'?"

"I'm just gathering facts for the documentary. Doing my job."

Ryder flares his nostrils. "Okay. But I won't give you a long, dish-the-dirt interview. Finally and absolutely for the record, I'm married. I love my wife. I didn't know Jentry Rae Randall from a hole in the ground. But I do know what it's like to be seen by the FFL as an object and not as a person. It's the way that cheerleader probably felt, and I can relate. I even heard she bought a gun because she sensed danger around her."

What? Nikki thinks. Nothing about that has come to light. And if it's true, how does Ryder know it?

His red-rimmed eyes fill with tears while his Adam's apple quivers up and down.

Before she can ask anything else, he hustles away. *The man is a mess*, she concludes. And while it must suck being a has-been, there seems to be more to his anguish.

As Nikki heads for the cheerleader's dance building, she mentally arranges the questions she'll ask the squad members next. But all she can think about is that Ryder Hutchinson is full of shit. *I CARED DEEPLY FOR JENTRY RAE* was written all over his face.

≈

Arriving at Bogart's Bistro, Nikki is shown to a table in the rear. She received little to no information from the cheerleaders today, but right now, she needs to focus. If only Vince was here to help tamp down her nerves, but it's best that she speaks to Royce alone.

While she waits for the quarterback, she wonders if she should bring up the audio of him conversing with Shaunette. The phone exchange alludes to his involvement with a murdered Lonestars' cheerleader, so if dinner goes well, she'll save that subject for the end of the meal.

Royce finally arrives. Clean-shaven, cheeks flushed, he charms the hostess as she escorts him to the table. Nikki's heart doesn't flutter, though. She refuses to be bowled over by a flirtatious married man. In fact, she hates how Royce's charm gets under her skin. She will definitely stick to her original goal. Obtaining information from him.

As he sits, an overhead lamp illuminates his appealing dimples and square jaw. "Thanks for meeting me," he greets in a friendly cadence.

"Of course. I mean, I think I ruffled your feathers a few days ago."

"You did . . . yeah. And I ruffled yours, too. Right?"

She smiles but doesn't elaborate.

He inhales. "I tend to shift into defensive mode too often. Sorry. It's something I've always done. But I swear I'm a likeable guy. I hate it when I think I've affronted someone."

She nods.

"This is my chance to make it up to you." Royce flashes a charismatic smile. "See? I just switched to persuasive mode."

"Ha, ha." Nikki laughs lightly. "But maybe you can help yourself, just this once."

That seems to break the ice.

They order drinks. A carafe of white wine for her. A non-alcoholic beer for him.

The quarterback's order reminds her that pro football players aren't supposed to consume booze in public. Same goes for the Dallas Lonestars Cheerleaders.

As she leans forward and studies Royce closer, she sees telltale signs of exhaustion—like he hasn't slept for a week.

"The memorial service was rough, emotionally. Wouldn't you say?" she asks.

"Brutal. There aren't sufficient words for the loss of someone so young. Jentry Rae Randall had her whole life ahead of her. And the way she was found in all that blood—horrific. Her father must be up in arms. Have you seen him on the news? The man keeps emphasizing how much his daughter was humiliated." He pauses. "I'm just glad she had *some* clothes on when she died."

Nikki nods offhandedly.

The server delivers Royce's virgin beer and then sets her Pinot Grigio down. Once they're alone again, the quarterback sighs. "Christ Almighty, all this morbid talk . . . I wish I was drinking something with a kick."

"Then order it." Meeting his stare, Nikki presents a challenge.

Signaling the server, Royce asks for a scotch and soda. Luckily, he and Nikki are at a secluded table in the rear, so nobody notices them.

The discussion flows. Nikki learns that Royce grew up in Boston where he met his now-wife in high school. When he attended Seton Hall University, he was hailed as their football star. Three years ago, he was drafted by the Tennessee Renegades, but since he wasn't used much, his talent wasn't on display. Now that he's been traded to the Lonestars, he and his wife Piper have settled in the expensive Westover Hills area of Fort Worth. Their daughter, Rianne, is in preschool.

He falls silent. Before the entrées are delivered, Nikki watches him enjoy his cocktail. Meanwhile, she notices that he isn't wearing a wedding ring.

"Um," he speaks up, "I hear your documentary is coming along. Word is you're beyond qualified."

"I'm really happy with it." She flushes.

"If you were to do something bad, Nikki Keegan—and don't we all want to be bad?—would you ever take advantage of the situation and make a true-crime mockumentary? Or a docusoap? Aren't those all the rage?"

Her nerves ping. "My contract would stop me," she lies.

"But the murder of a Dallas Lonestars Cheerleader is a hell of a thing, isn't it?"

"It's completely shocking." She sets her handbag on the table close to the wall. "Did you know Jentry Rae personally?"

"Nope. Cheerleaders can't fraternize with the players."

"Right. Which reminds me of a joke. What can the Dallas Lonestars and their cheerleaders do apart but not together?"

"What?" he asks.

"Score."

Royce laughs—louder than he probably would without having slurped high-proof scotch. "Good one. But, you know, I'm all for the rule. If pro players hook up with pro cheerleaders left and right, it'd be like the Wild West. Or a bad telenovela."

"Except, all of you are adults. Aren't you? To me, it's like keeping children separate in kindergarten, so that the boys can't pull the girls' hair."

"The idea is to prevent performance distraction. But resisting temptation is hard sometimes." His tone turns somber.

Nikki spins the saltshaker, trying to access his expression. "Given that you're such a flirt, how did you court your wife?"

"We were lab partners in biology class. Then we became friends. Piper is a knockout, but mostly, she has a huge personality that screams confidence. I like that. We went to prom, one thing led to another, and she chose Seton Hall because of me. We dated all through college, and then I proposed to her in a field of poppies with a violin player in the background."

"I saw the photos on your wife's social media. Very romantic. But I also read some nasty comments about you as a couple during that time in your lives."

"What comments?"

Nikki thinks for a second. She wants to say, *"Critics hated that you gave Piper a 'Shut Up' engagement ring . . . a diamond a man gives their girlfriend to appease them. Some trolls say Piper was sick of you stringing her along, so she set forth an ultimatum after six years of dating: Marry me or get out."* Instead, Nikki says, "You were a confirmed bachelor for a long time. Am I right?"

"If you're suggesting that my wife pressured me into marrying her, you're mistaken. In all the years we've been together, I have been dedicated to her. We want the same things. God— that's why I hate social media."

"It's a ruthless kingdom."

141

"So-called fans think they know famous figures, but they have no clue." Fury slashes Royce's cheeks.

He's quick to anger, Nikki notices. But that won't stop her from egging him on. "Are you saying you one hundred percent wanted to get married?"

He shrugs. "I *did* want to keep moving through the goalposts. I mean, I wanted to graduate college, start my FFL football career, and then get settled. Piper was ready for a family before I accomplished those things. I gave in to having our daughter, I guess."

"Piper seems like an amazing person," Nikki says. *If not bossy and self-absorbed.*

He chomps on his steak. "My friend Chase keeps me on the straight and narrow, too. Well, he used to. These days, we aren't that close. Chase is jealous of me. He encroaches, and his competitive streak is toxic. It's sad that he had a traumatic upbringing. I mean, one of his foster dads beat the shit out of him." Royce lowers his voice. "Can't abusees become abusers? I worry that Chase is capable of some bad shit."

"Wow. He sounds scary."

"That's why I've distanced myself. I'm just focused on the prize now."

"What prize?"

"The FFL Trophy. It's what my dad wants for me. He QB'd for the New England Heralders back in the day. The great Halftime Holt fans called him." As Royce waves his scotch passionately, displeasure tinges his expression. "I'm always in my dad's shadow."

"That must be difficult."

"Fuck, yeah. But as you can tell"—he slurs his words—"I like to talk. I've said too much, though."

Turns out if you don't drink often, it doesn't take much to get drunk, Nikki thinks.

"It's just . . . you're a good listener, Keegan. You're calm and focused. Thanks."

She is about to ask the quarterback why he was loitering at Jentry Rae's apartment complex when he asks *her* a question. Does she want another pour of Pinot? She answers affirmatively, but when he reaches out to pick up her half-full wine glass, he knocks it over.

Crying out, she snatches up her handbag. Her cell phone falls out, showing that it's set to "Record."

"You're *recording* me?" Royce roars. "What the hell? This was supposed to be an off-the-record meeting!"

"I—" Nikki falters.

He lunges for the device but stops himself. "Please give me your phone."

"No, it got wet. It's ruined." She hangs on to it.

"Motherfucker! Stay away from me, Nikki Keegan." Throwing cash on the table, he storms off.

She composes herself, which isn't easy. Royce's temper just went from zero to sixty—faster than he can throw a football. And if he always does that when provoked, did he become angry enough to kill Jentry Rae?

Uncomfortable, she uses napkins to sop up the wine. Then she asks a busboy for a cup of uncooked rice. While her wet phone stays in the rice to absorb the moisture, she orders Vince a to-go burger to make up for the lousy baked potato she microwaved.

"Royce's me-first attitude can go to hell," she mutters as she leaves Bogart's. Hurrying to the van, she checks to ensure the recording is okay. It is. And on it, Royce validated that the only reason he agreed to meet with her tonight was to throw suspicion on Chase Campbell.

Some best friend Royce is.

He was also Jentry Rae's boyfriend, so Nikki wonders what, if anything, is out-of-bounds for the ego-inflated quarterback. Will he stop at nothing before reaching the top of his game?

INSTAGRAM POST

@PIPER_DUPREE28

PINNED REEL: Dressed in all-beige, the Holt family is sitting on an ecru sectional inside their all-white living room. The house is ultra-modern, clean, minimalistic. Caption: Family time.

1.2 million followers / 279,990 likes

#trending #WAG #neutralpalette #homelife #FFL

"Are you ready for our next baby to be born, beautiful Mama?" Royce asks Piper. Their pudgy toddler fidgets between them.

"If you help out more with this one, I'm ready!" She laughs.

"What do you mean? I changed a thousand diapers and did Rianne's midnight feedings."

"Those are small things compared to pushing a baby out of your v-jay!" Piper quips. Royce gives an uncomfortable laugh. The gurgling toddler seems upset, too.

Piper says, "Tell everyone how determined I am to LOSE my pregnancy weight after I deliver, *Monsieur* Dupree."

"You have been working out like a champ, babe; it's true. And you'll stay hot after Baby Two. We wouldn't want you any other way."

CHAPTER TWENTY-THREE

THE DALLAS LONESTARS CHEERLEADER

~ OCTOBER 22 ~

Shaunette is getting gussied up for her first appearance on *Boots and Babble*—the official DLC video podcast. The popular installments have a loyal, international subscription base.

While a makeup artist transforms Shaunette from girl next door to over-the-top glamorous, her anxiety ratchets. Has Sergeant Emerson already shown Vana and Tammie the phone recording of her fight with Jentry Rae? She can't deny saying *"I'll kill you."* The threat is right there on tape.

Will she be kicked off the squad?

Face criminal charges?

Be publicly ousted and chided by her mother?

Shaunette tries not to tremble as the makeup artist lines her lips.

Tempted to nip at a minibar-sized whiskey bottle inside her rolling bag, she looks down at it longingly. Too bad the makeup lady is standing so close. At any rate, Shaunette can't drink; she's driving. She is supposed to meet up with Sonny and Nikki after her podcast appearance. And since Nikki seemed angry with her during their last phone call, Shaunette is dreading getting together with the filmmaker.

Yards away, Vana and Tammie are in their typical sound-studio seats at The Depot. Together, they host the weekly podcast episodes, which feature one-on-one, upbeat interviews with the cheerleaders. However, instead of acting lighthearted and jokey, the hosts seem downtrodden today. Neither of them is speaking. And both seem lost in thought.

Dang it, Shaunette thinks. Being lighthearted and jokey is her goal this morning. If she can prove that she's a natural on camera and on air, she might be considered for more things within the DLC.

While she gets a final coat of lipstick, she watches Tammie in her peripheral vision. The choreographer starts to cry.

Vana reaches over and pats Tammie's arm. "Are you okay?"

"I'm a wreck," the choreographer replies. "Don't you get it? One of our girls has been murdered, so we've become the Deadly Lonestars Cheerleaders."

"Just try and relax."

"I can't."

"You're on in two minutes, ladies," a studio technician calls out.

Vana asks Tammie if she wants to delay the broadcast. When Tammie replies yes, the squad director gets up and has an exchange with the technician. He removes his headset, saying something to the effect that he'd be on edge, too. A cold-blooded murderer has infiltrated the DLC ranks.

"Thanks for that, Bruce. Super comforting," Vana replies derisively before rejoining Tammie.

The ladies seem to have forgotten that Shaunette is nearby.

"We need to be resilient for our dancers," Vana urges. "If we show them we can handle whatever comes our way, they will, too."

"That's an eloquent speech, but a killer is out there," Tammie replies. "He wants to topple the Dallas Lonestars Cheerleaders. I live for this organization! Maybe this lunatic is part Manson, part Ted Bundy. I mean, will he strike again?"

Thank God they are finally focused on safety, Shaunette thinks. Social media naysayers are blaming the DLC directors for how much their girls are exposed. If sexy dancers strutting their stuff does invite danger, Jentry Rae's death might not be an isolated incident. So, Vana and Tammie should definitely cease all performances.

Tammie presses a tissue to her bloodshot eyes. "At least one person is looking hard for the murderer—that snoopy film director, Nikki Keegan. She has been asking our dancers outrageous questions. She isn't being paid to pry, Vana. She's crossing the line."

"I'll look into it. But you need to pull yourself together, Tammie. Think straight. There won't be a DLC squad if we don't wear our business caps."

"It's not all about the money!" The choreographer stands and rips off her headphones. As she flees, Vana follows her into a hallway.

Shaunette trails behind both of them, trying to be discreet. She hopes to hear more about their vision for the future. Does it include showcasing her?

"Jentry Rae has become the poster child for the cheerleaders," Tammie says in a low voice. "But she was far from innocent. She broke some league rules when she was alive. I followed her one night. To see what she was up to. I won't tarnish another cheerleader's name, but somebody *else* is acting up, too. My advice? Watch our girls closer, Vana."

The idea lassoes Shaunette like barbed-wire rope. Do they mean watch *her*?

By now, everybody must know about the argument she had with Jentry Rae in the locker room. And if Tammie is overly tuned in to the cheerleader's private lives, the choreographer must also know that Shaunette doesn't feel like she deserves to be a Dallas Lonestars Cheerleader.

Shaunette thinks her appearance on the podcast went well. At least her amped-up nerves didn't take center stage.

Now that she's alone in her car, she removes her makeup with a wipe and studies her colorless face in the mirror. Vana and Tammie still haven't mentioned the recording of her argument with Jentry Rae. Are they playing it cool? Making her sweat?

Then again, they might not know about it yet. They certainly maintained pleasant faces during her on-air interview.

The notion of meeting Nikki at Sonny's hotel in a half hour is leveling Shaunette like a wrecking ball. Is the filmmaker ready for a battle?

Shaunette hopes not. She wants to be friends because Lord knows she needs an ally right now. Especially after her weird conversation with Chase Campbell. The emotional way he talked—he seemed to be utterly fixated on Jentry Rae. Were the two closer than anyone guessed? And if Jentry Rae was Chase's drug, could it be that he was addicted to her?

Worse, if Chase is consumed with measuring up to Royce . . . *sakes alive*. Maybe the sports therapist hurt Jentry Rae to punish and frame his childhood rival.

JENTRY RAE'S DIARY ENTRY

OCTOBER 10

Mother of pearl . . . I'm pregnant. Notice that I am NOT writing the news with happy exclamation points.

Mostly, I'm ashamed because I'm not certain which of my men got me pregnant. It's my biggest blunder yet. I need to figure out who the baby daddy is right quick.

I DID skip some birth control pills—half hoping I'd conceive. Only now, everything is too real and too scary. What will people think of me? What does my future look like? And what will the baby's father do?

If this child belongs to who I want it to belong to, I wonder how he will react. He has a temper, but only because he's a passionate person. I would never deny him his role as a father—but if news of this baby becomes public knowledge, it'll go viral. Then our worlds will explode into a million pieces, like confetti at the Supreme Bowl.

As I waited for the pregnancy test results last night, I kept looking at my DLC uniform hanging on the bathroom door. I don't have the heart to get rid of my baby. Only, I won't be able to hide my bump for long. Should I go to Vana with the announcement? The Dallas Lonestars Cheerleaders' policy on getting knocked up isn't good. I signed a contract. Now, I'm roped into the stated terms. So, goodbye short-shorts . . . that I won't fit into anyway!

What will my daddy say? I love him but he's old-fashioned. He won't approve of his grandbaby being born out of wedlock.

I would marry the love of my life in a second—I'm crazy about him. But why does he keep saying that love is a zero-sum game? Maybe, if I act excited for this child, he will be, too. It'll convince him to be with me. And if he stays close, I won't ever tell him that I skipped a pill on purpose.

I'm so tired. Tonight, I'll lie in bed and talk to the baby. I aim to protect him or her, so I bought a gun. (Coincidentally, I ran into Ryder outside the firearms store. It's a small world, isn't it? I've been bumping into him a lot.) What I want to record here is that my negligence affects lots of people. And one person in particular might do something rash. Violent, even.

I've written this before, but my other man will hate being the runner-up. Second is the first to lose; Shaunette learned that doing beauty pageants.

CHAPTER TWENTY-FOUR

THE FILMMAKER

~ *OCTOBER 22* ~

Nikki marches into Sonny's hotel lobby and seeks out Shaunette. As they stand face-to-face, everything about them is a contradiction. Nikki is exuding determination while the cheerleader is showing humbleness. Nikki's worn, ripped jeans contrast Shaunette's pink peplum dress, and their fragrances—earthy versus floral—clash greatly, too.

Nikki locks her hands on her hips. "What do you have to say for yourself, Shaunette?"

"First of all, what were you doing recording me without my permission? It's illegal."

"Not in Texas."

"Wrong. It's only okay to record someone in a *public* place. And if the recorder is part of the conversation. You caught me unaware on Lonestars' private property."

Busted. "Sue me." Nikki grits her teeth. How does the cheerleader know so much about recording shit, anyway?

Shaunette exhales. "Look . . . I one hundred percent knew Jentry Rae was seeing Royce Holt, all right? I alluded to it instead of revealing it outright so I could protect her memory."

"That may be true, but do you see why I'm confused? You're on a first-name basis with somebody you and your friend shouldn't have been in contact with in the first place. I mean, you even chatted with Royce on the phone—so, what the hell? It seems beyond friendly."

"You think *I* was sleeping with Royce behind Jentry Rae's back?" Shaunette's voice could shatter glass.

"I think you have a thing for him."

"You're mistaken. Royce and I are friends. That's all. I don't have to explain anything to you, anyway. You're not my mother."

"True again. It's just—I thought we were allies in this." Nikki's voice hints at disappointment.

Shaunette takes a breath. "I'm sorry if I didn't confide everything to you, but I swear there is nothing between me and Royce. I begged Jentry Rae not to get involved with him. He's married. Married to a viper, by the way. His wife could've decimated Jentry Rae on social media."

The cheerleader looks pale without makeup, and her usually manicured fingernails are chewed to the nub. What's more, her desperate facial expression seems to be screaming, *"You have to believe me."*

Nikki has a lightbulb moment. Maybe the rookie dancer *is* being sincere. Does Shaunette really want to protect her friend's memory? "Wait. You sent me that text, didn't you?"

"What text?"

"The one that read 'Someone on the Lonestars' roster is breaking rules.'"

Shaunette hems and haws. Sitting on a sofa, her shoulders cave in—as if she knows she isn't getting out of this one. "I did send it, okay? I wanted to implicate Royce in a roundabout way. An app on my phone lets me use dummy numbers."

"Cut the horseshit. You hated Jentry Rae. You probably wanted her dead. But now that she is, you're trying to preserve her reputation because it's the least you can do. Correct?"

The cheerleader's mouth droops. Her dark, under-eye bags make her appear even more defeated. "You're good at reading people."

"Filmmakers observe. It's our art. Tell me everything in a nutshell," Nikki urges in a kinder voice as she sits on the sofa, too.

"It's just . . . being competitive has been drilled into my head. It started when my mama put me in kiddie pageants. She only gave me sweets and high praise if I won. I was jealous of Jentry Rae. Of how she got everything she wanted with little effort. I coveted how she had the kindest father, too. But I didn't kill her."

Nikki can't criticize. She has done things she isn't proud of, as well. Obstacles have always been in her way, and Shaunette seems to know what that's like. Evidently, neither of them is above finagling, lying, sandbagging, and stacking the cards to reach a goal. Maybe they're more alike than opposites.

Nikki wants to do better and be better . . . eventually. After this ordeal is over.

"Talk to me straight next time, Shaunette," she says.

"I will. If you stop recording me without permission."

They exchange smiles. It warms the ice between them.

"We should see Sonny now," Shaunette says, standing.

They start for the elevator.

"Tell me something," Nikki coaxes as they walk. "The entire universe knows that Royce Holt is married. It's all over his social media: his perfect wife and perfect life. Oh, and can you believe the Holts' all-beige house? Hardly kid-proof. But Royce looks miserable in every photo. What am I missing about the couple's popularity?"

"Celebrity-hating can be fun. Piper Dupree's followers see that she's Team 'Me.' I mean, she'll say that everything is dandy to keep up appearances. People are on to her, and they can't look away." Shaunette presses the Up button.

"Jentry Rae must have been scared to death to break up that marriage. The world was watching. I'm saying that being pregnant must've rocked Jentry Rae's world."

Shaunette nods. "Her downfall was . . . she acted first then thought later. Unfortunately, I never got to talk to her about being pregnant. I told you—I learned about it at the autopsy."

"But you knew Jentry Rae was dating Royce and another guy at the same time. Right?"

Shaunette flushes. "Yes. And I'm starting to think the second guy is Chase Campbell."

Shock races through Nikki. Her mouth falls open. "Chase? Really?"

"I wasn't going to talk about it, but clearly you can tell when I'm holding something back. I had the strangest conversation with him. He says he was infatuated with Jentry Rae. And he told me he wants to vindicate her death. But I'm wondering if he hurt her to punish Royce."

"That's insane!"

"I know. What's also scary is . . . Chase thinks I was terrible to Jentry Rae. She called me a backstabber, among other things. It sliced our friendship apart. We weren't really talking at the end, and Chase seems mad about how I treated her."

"He should give you a break. You lost a close friend."

"Yes. And pathetically, I have trouble with friendships, in general. My mama raised me to be a lone wolf. I always push people away."

As they step into the elevator, Nikki crosses her arms. She isn't a lone wolf on purpose; she has always been the low-class outcast . . . the hand-me-down clothes, dirty girl at school because her mother was sick, her dad was at work, and her brother was never home. "I'll tell you my own secret. I overthink and have a fear of failure. Oh, and I could never wear short-shorts and show my midriff."

Shaunette cracks another smile. "I'll top that. I'm the screw-up Dallas Lonestars Cheerleader."

"No kidding! You'll have to tell me about that one day." Nikki pauses. "But right now, I want to solve Jentry Rae's murder for Sonny, don't you? My own dad isn't doing well. He's depressed. He lost his job. Money is tight. I'm not the best with money, either, so I'm getting credit card advances to help him out. Only, I don't get paid in full by the Lonestars until the documentary is complete."

"I'm sorry. Um, my mom is sick—stage-four breast cancer."

Nikki reaches out and rubs Shaunette's arm. "How are you holding up?"

"Not great."

It further explains the cheerleader's dejected vibe.

"Both of us are worried about our parents, huh?" Nikki realizes even more that they're not so different. As they reach Sonny's door, she adds, "Well, you need a distraction. Do you want to help me out with something? I swear you won't get in trouble."

"Says the woman with Watergate tendencies."

Her face heats. *Guilty.* "I'm creating a true-crime series about Jentry Rae's death. The Lonestars have given me permission," she fibs. "So, after this, I'm paying a visit to Dante Marconi. You know, the stadium guard on duty the day Jentry Rae was killed?"

"You are?"

"Yeah. He might open the door if he sees your familiar face. How about it?"

"If it means avenging Jentry Rae's death," Shaunette replies, "count me in."

CHAPTER TWENTY-FIVE

THE DALLAS LONESTARS CHEERLEADER

~ OCTOBER 22 ~

Stooped and slack-jawed, Sonny slowly opens the door for Shaunette and Nikki. He is wearing the same shirt as yesterday, and according to his bloodshot eyes, grief has him in an even tighter vise-grip.

When Shaunette enters the suite, she glances at the elderly man's sparse belongings: a tatty suitcase, medication bottles, and a comb on the sink. Sorrow stabs at her. The simple, seventy-seven-year-old man is not only out of his element in Dallas, but he's also a breath away from dying.

"Come in and get comfortable, ladies." He gestures them toward the main sitting area.

Shaunette sits on a sofa. Nikki sits, too, adjusting the strap of her handbag. Meanwhile, Shaunette hopes the filmmaker isn't secretly recording this get-together. Surely, Sonny is an off-limits interviewee.

The old man settles in an armchair facing them. "Ladies, I'm not feeling like myself this afternoon. My apologies." Sighing, he steeples his shaky fingers. "Years ago, I was a pillar of strength. Now, I'm a puddle of emotions."

Nikki says something about her own father who is struggling. After Sonny makes a compassionate comment in return, he gets to the point. "I asked you gals here because I ain't closer to finding Jentry Rae's murderer. Which is destroying me." On the verge of crying, he blows kisses to framed photographs on the nightstand. One is of his lovely, late wife. The other of his daughter. He adds, "I'm overwhelmed at the thought of my unborn grandbaby. Boy or girl, it wouldn't have mattered. No doubt the tike would've had Jentry Rae's looks and ringin' laughter. My daughter was the spittin' image of Nellie. Both of 'em were deep-hearted romantics."

Shaunette chokes up. *Their good genes should have kept going.*

"Why didn't Jentry Rae tell me she was pregnant?" Sonny asks a rhetorical question. "I wasn't aware she even had a boyfriend."

Melting at his pain, Shaunette thinks of her ill mother. She really ought to leave the DLC and be by Mama's side, but nothing would push Kaylene Simmons closer to the end of life.

Sonny gulps. "It's too bad Jentry Rae's pregnancy will be publicly announced soon."

"That information won't look good for the Lonestars," Nikki insists. "For that reason, the franchise might delay the release of the news."

Shaunette hopes so. Sonny might want to blame the powerhouse football league for the tragedy at hand, but the Dallas

Lonestars Cheerleaders put Jentry Rae on the map. She loved being on the cheer squad more than anything else.

"See what they're showing now?" Nikki looks down at her phone. She blows up an image . . . the official DLC group photo for the 2024–2025 season.

Everybody leans in.

The thirty-six dolled-up dancers are carefully arranged in six rows while a gigantic American flag hangs in the background. Some of the cheerleaders are on the floor, legs to the side, leaning on their hips, while others are on their knees or standing. Jentry Rae is located smack in the middle of the cluster. Shaunette is to her left. As the women form a sea of voluminous hair and sparkly lipstick, their kilowatt smiles could light a power grid.

Shaunette expels a breath. Fortunately, she was able to mask the tension between herself and Jentry Rae that day.

"It's a darn near perfect photo," Sonny says. "I was proud of my girl. But the media needs to leave her alone." Hands shaking like a bull-riding arena at full quake, he reaches inside his pocket and extracts what looks like a diary.

Shaunette's heart leaps to her throat. *Wait.* It's the same journal she read. *Gracious!* Jentry Rae's innermost thoughts are about to be revealed.

"Don't judge me, ladies," Sonny says. "The other day, I used an extra key my daughter gave me to get into 'er apartment. Once I was in, I searched for her cheerleaders' pinkie ring but found this instead." He holds up the diary. "I haven't read it all . . . maybe I don't *wanna* learn everything about my girl. But since I'm running out 'a time, I'm gonna read one passage aloud that startled me."

He opens the book.

"Hold on," Shaunette speaks in a panic. "Burrowing into Jentry Rae's revelations is an invasion of her privacy, Sonny. She's gone. Reading her diary won't bring her back to life. And it might even drag you deeper into grief."

"I disagree. It might be the only way to know who fathered my grandchild and who killed my daughter."

Nikki flings Shaunette a "What the hell?" expression.

Clasping the diary tightly, Sonny reads: "Today is June 16, 2024. I made it! Veterans are required to reaudition for the DLC squad, and I was selected again for the third year. I can't believe it!

"Today's auditions felt different, though. While Vana and Tammie were as sweet as pie, I felt my squad mates' jealous eyes on me the entire time. Also, when Dante Marconi appeared, I got a weird vibe from him. He 'belonged' there, I reckon. He's the chief security guard at the Americana Memorial Stadium. But after I finished my solo, I noticed a spooky, dark look on his face.

"It freaked me out. Dante has always given me the willies.

"When I passed by him, I wasn't overly friendly. I didn't offer him a smile.

"One bright spot was meeting Duke McCade, the Dallas Lonestars' new owner. He gave a congratulatory speech to us girls who made it to training camp. Despite being an older guy, he isn't bad-looking. He keeps himself in shape, and his pep talk was darned funny. 'I'm healthy, ladies, but I might keel over from an overdose of beauty,' he joked.

"His people have reached out for my phone number. Should I give it to them?"

Scowling, Sonny shuts the journal. He looks like he might get sick. "What do you make of that?"

"Jentry Rae's bright beam captivated lots of people," Shaunette replies. *She could also be an LED light that zapped insects.*

"I hate how slimeballs like Dante Marconi and Duke McCade were in her orbit," the old man says. "Again, if McCade's initials are inked on my baby's body, that varmint better run for the hills." He takes a breath. "Okay, ladies. I have another announcement. Pages are missin' from this here diary. My baby might have discovered that somebody was sneaking peeks at it, I don't know."

Guilt over reading the diary heats Shaunette's face. She hugs a pillow to hide her trembling hands.

"I bet Jentry Rae named her mystery man in the lost entries," Sonny continues. "Can you help me find them?"

Nikki sits forward, acting intrigued by the idea.

In contrast, alarm races through Shaunette. If Jentry Rae tore pages out, she had a reason to. Can't they let her memory rest?

The second Nikki offers her help to Sonny, it forces Shaunette to do the same. However, Shaunette knows she'll encounter roadblocks. Duke McCade's initials are D.M.—the same letters scrolled on one of Jentry Rae's hips. If Nikki gets permission to question McCade, Shaunette cannot be there for that. She would risk her spot on the DLC squad.

"Did Jentry Rae know about your dealings with Duke?" Nikki asks the ailing farmer.

"Just before she died, yes. She asked me some questions about it. I told her because as much as I wanted to shield her from wickedness, she needed to know what she was up against."

Sonny hesitates. "If y'all really want to help, take my baby's diary and study it. I can't bring myself to read more."

Nikki readily accepts the journal.

"One more thing." He stands and extracts a pink pistol from a drawer. Then he sets the firearm on a tabletop.

Shaunette sucks in a sharp breath. "Hold on. This is getting too real for me."

Looking even more intrigued, Nikki steps closer to the gun.

"My daughter bought this pistol," Sonny informs them. "I know, we're in Texas . . . lots of people have loaded guns for no particular reason. But I knew my girl. She'd only buy a weapon if she was out-of-her-mind terrified. Who or what prompted that purchase is what I want y'all to find out."

"I can't be part of this, Sonny. I'm sorry. Gotta go." Shaunette stands. "Are you coming, Nikki?"

"I'll meet you in the lobby," the filmmaker replies.

Shaunette exits the suite wondering if Nikki, who accepted the diary, will accept the gun, too. And will Nikki divulge how friendly Shaunette is with Royce? The diary entries speak of just that.

Sonny might see it as a betrayal on Shaunette's part. He might even go straight to: Royce Holt's initials are *R.H.* The other initials tattooed on Jentry Rae's hip.

Ryder Hutchinson has identical letters, Shaunette thinks as she heads for the elevator. She recalls the afternoon the insufferable, seen-better-days QB flirted with Jentry Rae.

He even asked for her phone number.

Before her friend's death, Shaunette was jealous of that. Now she knows being a flame-attracting moth can be deadly.

CHAPTER TWENTY-SIX

THE FILMMAKER

~ OCTOBER 22 ~

Nikki hustles Shaunette out of the hotel lobby and they drive directly to Dante Marconi's residence. On the way, the cheerleader is unusually quiet.

Nikki wonders what she's thinking. That Jentry Rae having a diary was a surprise? That Nikki's offer to help Sonny makes her an opportunist? Somebody who'll do anything to discover the truth?

As they near their destination, Shaunette breaks her silence. "Did you take the .22 caliber?"

"No." Nikki shudders at the thought. "I don't feel comfortable with guns. Same as you."

"Good. But, um, did you tell Sonny anything else after I left?"

"No." Nikki isn't lying about that either. She'll keep everything she has gleaned on the down-low for now.

Thankful that a little online sleuthing produced Marconi's address, she pulls up to a rundown duplex located in gritty South Dallas.

Once she parks, she and Shaunette trot up a set of stone steps. Steel-gray skies are threatening rain again, so she quickly opens the screen door and knocks on the second, wooden door.

"Who is it?" a voice calls from inside the house.

Nikki gestures for Shaunette to speak.

"Dante, it's Shaunette Simmons from the DLC. Can we talk?"

The portly security guard opens up while a short-hair cat tries to escape the house. Dante grabs the animal and when he does, he reflexively opens the door a little wider. Nikki peeks inside. A massive, creepy shrine to the Dallas Lonestars Cheerleaders is plastered across a long wall. Color posters, calendars dating back to the nineties, and magazine clippings of the sexy dancers make up a disturbing collection that must've taken the guard years to assemble.

Startingly, a blown-up image of Jentry Rae's face centers the shrine.

It makes Nikki shrink back.

"Damned, temperamental feline," Dante complains as he swings the door closed a few inches. "Um, howdy, Miss Shaunette. This is an unexpected surprise."

"Hey, Dante. I want to introduce you to Nikki Keegan. You may know her. She's directing a documentary about the Lonestars."

"Yes, ma'am," he says gruffly. "But I'm kinda busy."

"My questions won't take much of your time. May we come inside?"

"It's the cleaning lady's day off, so no. What do you want to ask me?"

"How well did you know Jentry Rae Randall?"

His eyes jiggle rapidly at the mention of the cheerleader's name. As the cat hisses, he holds it closer like a shield. "Why are you asking?"

"Her murder is still unsolved."

"Right. Okay, *err*, Miss Jentry Rae was the number-one Dallas Lonestars Cheerleader for three years. *Everybody* knew and loved her. So, I knew and loved her how everyone did . . . ya know?"

Nikki nods. "I think I understand. Did she ever ask for extra security at the stadium?"

Lightning sparks in the overcast sky. At the same time, Dante's eyes flash with defiance. "Lady, are you insinuating that she wasn't safe inside my territory?"

"What do you think?" She shoots him a sarcastic look.

The guard grunts.

"Please relax, Dante," Shaunette pleads. "We just want to learn more about Jentry Rae's enemies."

"I apologize, but *you* were her best friend, Miss Shaunette. Don't you know about her enemies?"

"She stopped talking to me at the end."

The trio on the front stoop goes silent.

"Dante, do you remember how you told me you heard tinkling sounds in the locker room on the day of the murder? Like two objects fell? Jewelry, maybe?" Shaunette inclines her head. "Well, the police only found Jentry Rae's gold infinity bracelet. What do you think the other item was?"

Surprise rankles Nikki. This is new information.

Dante shrugs. "I have no idea. Now, if you'll excuse me, I got something on the stove."

Nikki shoves her foot inside the doorjamb. "Please wait. This conversation is entirely private. If you heard jewelry fall, why didn't you hear the murder happen? And I won't name names, but is it possible that Jentry Rae spent time with a Lonestars' bigwig?"

"Don't know jack shit about that." Dante glowers. "Remove your foot, ma'am. Then back away. You, too Miss Shaunette. I saw you re-enter the dressing room on the day Miss Jentry Rae died."

Stunned, Nikki walks off with Shaunette. Unease roils her stomach. Is it true? Forget mulling it over, she thinks. She needs to ask Shaunette outright. "Is Dante right?"

Shaunette goes pale. "Ah, I did step back inside the dressing room for my pom-poms. But for three seconds! We're supposed to take them home with us. I swear I went straight out the door without going inside the locker room when I left. Jentry Rae was in the shower, so she was alive when I walked out!"

Nikki nods, although she isn't entirely convinced. Shaunette has a super-strong motive to have killed Jentry Rae. *Jealousy.* Yet, going off instinct, Nikki doesn't believe the cheerleader has it in her to commit murder. Shaunette seems more like a wounded child who's buckling under her mother's expectations than a killer.

Nikki's mind flits to the other information Dante supplied. The idea of items falling reignites her initial suspicion about Jentry Rae reaching for an object on the locker room floor before she died. If somebody picked it up and took it, what was it? Could the item implicate them?

Getting in the van, she doesn't start the engine. Instead, she rolls down the window and continues thinking. Shaunette falls into silence, too.

Just then, an older woman pulls up to the duplex in a beat-up car. As she hurries out of the vehicle, she points an angry finger at Dante who's out fetching his mail. "A little birdie told me you showed up to the neighborhood poker game with a wad of cash, you rot! What about the rent you owe me?"

"It's coming, Mrs. Knudsen. I'm sitting pretty. I just got paid under the table for helping my boss."

Huffing, the landlady wraps her housecoat around her tightly.

Nikki and Shaunette look at each other. Assuming Dante just referenced the owner of the Dallas Lonestars, Nikki whispers to Shaunette, "Do you think Jentry Rae was *coerced* into getting one of those tattoos on her hip?"

"I don't know." The cheerleader knits her brows.

"You saw the freaky shrine of the DLC squad in Dante's living room. It proves he has an obsession with you dancers. So, maybe he's capable of deviant things."

RADIO TRANSCRIPT

OCTOBER 26

A radio announcer at Minneapolis's Metro-First Stadium calls a game between the Minnesota Vipers and the Dallas Lonestars.

"Welcome back, folks," the broadcaster says after a commercial break. "If you're just tuning in, the Vipers are being smoked at the halfway mark—34 to 12. Seems the tables are turning for Dallas. In other words, the Texan team might have a savior in Royce Holt. Could the Lonestars be resurrected this season?"

"Royce Holt just needs to stay focused on football and not get caught up in fame. Because have you heard, loyal listeners? He has signed a multimillion-dollar contract with Brookson Brothers Jewelers. The TV commercials are really something. They feature Holt and his wife in various costumes throughout the ages, doing their best acting jobs. The ad slogan is 'The only thing that stays the same is true love.'"

"Call in if you've seen the ads," the announcer encourages. "What say you? Inspiring or nauseating?"

CHAPTER TWENTY-SEVEN

THE FILMMAKER

~ *OCTOBER 26* ~

Nikki grabs a bottle of beer at her apartment and settles on the sofa with it. She's in the middle of watching the Dallas Lonestars go head-to-head with the Minnesota Vipers. Conveniently, one of Vince's friends in Minneapolis is filming for him. Good thing. The Twin Cities are blanketed in snow.

The game is at the halfway mark, and Bob Phillips, the head coach for the Lonestars, is being interviewed. He's wearing a team visor and is clutching a laminated play card with white knuckles. Looking anxious, he glances at the Jumbotron over his head. Team owner Duke McCade is visible in a stadium sky box wearing a "Your job is on the line" expression.

As a female commentator jabs her microphone closer to Coach Phillips's face, she points out that Ryder Hutchinson is in street clothes. When the camera pans to the sidelined QB, he seems pissed about not playing.

Meanwhile, Royce paces and holds his helmet. Nikki sets her beer down and sits up straighter the moment she sees him.

About to jog onto the field, Royce tries fist-bumping with Hutchinson. The unshaven, older player crushes a cupful of Gatorade instead of reciprocating.

Nikki turns the volume up. While she listens to the broadcast, she takes her beer over to the audio/film equipment. There, she presses "Rewind" on a digital tape and then "Play." As she rewatches the video footage Vince captured at The Depot, it shocks her a second time. "Get out of my face with that thing! Don't film me hobbling around—the murder of Jentry Rae Randall is the real tragedy!" Ryder yelled like a rabid dog.

When the declining quarterback breaks down in tears, caution jangles through Nikki all over again.

R.H.

She still wants to know what those tattooed letters on the cheerleader's hip represent. According to Nikki's brush with Ryder, he seems more devoted to Jentry Rae than Royce.

There is a knock on the door. When she opens it for Vince, he holds up a six-pack of lager like a trophy. "Wanna share a brewski or twoski?"

She shows him her bottle . . . the same brand.

"Great minds think alike, eh?" He smiles.

They settle on the sofa and clink bottles.

"Don't tell anybody, but the Vipers are my team," Vince says in a mock whisper.

Nikki shakes her head. "We should've gone to Minneapolis to film the game. Using your camera guy is cheating."

"My buddy is the best in the state. He'll capture stellar footage, Nik. Don't worry."

Personally, she's glad to remain in Dallas. The mystery is heating up . . .

"What's the score?" Vince asks.

"Vipers 12. Lonestars 34. Royce Holt is crushing it."

On screen, Royce buckles his chin strap and gathers the players in a huddle. They clap then break. The football is snapped at the line of scrimmage, after which Royce expertly grabs it. While he hangs back in the pocket, he decides to sling the ball to Marcus Armando. The wide receiver gains some yardage . . . a few up to the twenty-three. It's a slow and steady process. No gigantic plays for Royce, but he is being consistent. Smiling, he glances at the Jumbotron where his wife Piper is displayed. When he gives her a hand heart, she jumps up and down in the skybox, hugging another Lonestars' WAG.

Nikki frowns. Royce isn't wearing his wedding ring. Does he take it off for every game?

Then again, he wasn't wearing it during the Lonestars' practice session. Or at their dinner at Bogart's.

Several pump-fakes from Royce lead to sacks. The Lonestars go off the rails, and he is pounded to the ground by the opposing team. Shaking off the sacks, he manages to get back on track. Final result: the Lonestars whoop the Vipers' asses.

Vince grimaces. "I'm still a Minnesotan at heart."

Nikki figures that since her cohort has downed his third beer and is a little tipsy, it's a good time to come clean. She switches the TV off. Folding her hands together, she says, "Um, okay. Please don't freak out. I have a confession."

"Confession? Fine, my child. You may proceed."

"Very funny, Father Vince." She swallows hard. "Look. I told Sonny Randall that I'm definitely creating a crime docuseries featuring Jentry Rae's murder. But I lied to him and to Shaunette when I said the Lonestars gave me the green light for it."

Vince chokes on his beer. "Without consulting me?"

"I'm glad I did. There's a lot at stake. Take a gander." She shows him the anonymous text she received about someone on the Lonestars' roster breaking rules. She also tells him that Shaunette Simmons has a stalker. "I mean, *Shaunette* texted me this message, but some psycho tried to run *her* off the road. To harm her."

"Slow down, Nik."

"In addition, I believe Duke McCade gave Dante Marconi, the chief stadium guard, a stack of cash."

"What are you saying? That someone *inside* the Lonestars organization killed Jentry Rae?"

"Possibly."

Vince hesitates. "Why?"

"Jentry Rae knew things. And she was sleeping with Royce Holt. Everything came easily to her, but I think he was the one thing she couldn't have." Nikki scoots to the edge of the couch. "Jentry Rae was dating another guy, too. Shaunette thinks it was Chase Campbell. Our girl Jentry was pregnant, Vince. Her dad found her diary, but pages are missing so we don't know who the baby's father was. Sonny Randall is okay with me delving into the crime series for that reason. And here's more. The medical examiner discovered two tattoos on Jentry Rae's hips: R.H. and D.M. Worse yet, she bought a gun before she died."

"What the fuck? This is"—Vince's face changes—"crazy interesting! All right, tell me more."

"You already know that Shaunette made a clandestine call to Royce, but she swears they never dated. However, she has been getting hang-up calls from an unknown lurker. Naturally, she's scared of that person." Nikki finishes her beer in quick gulps. "What I'm saying is . . . Jentry Rae lived a big life that turned dangerous. So, not only did Shaunette fail to protect her friend from danger, but she also fanned the hazardous flames."

Vince bites his nails. "Do you think Shaunette knows more than she's saying?"

"I don't think she hurt her friend, but who knows? I'm going to find out."

"What did Duke McCade pay Dante Marconi to do?"

"I'll find that out, too."

"Okay, Nik," he says. "I'll dig up dirt on Marconi for leverage. But we're amateur detectives, so we need to be careful. This is serious shit. A killer is out there. If we drop the ball too many times, we'll find ourselves in the Red Zone."

CHAPTER TWENTY-EIGHT

THE DALLAS LONESTARS CHEERLEADER

~ *OCTOBER 28* ~

Tonight, the cheerleaders are rehearsing at the Lonestars' stadium in Grapevine.

Shaunette dislikes on-field practice sessions. Not because she is required to wear her boots the entire time. Or because she hates October's cold weather. Rather, it's the *distance* the dancers are expected to cover on the football field during stadium rehearsals.

A hundred yards of turf at a fast jog.

With a slight incline up to the field.

Up and down. Side to side. Back and forth.

Having left skittish Beau Dog at home, Shaunette pushes through her disgruntlement and enters the DLC dressing room, pre-practice. A strained vibe assaults her. It's the first time the dancers have gathered at the stadium since Jentry Rae's murder.

Tension is strangling the atmosphere—punctuated by sizzling, unspoken accusations.

Shaunette feels those accusations all too deeply as her team-mates turn around and stare.

My stars. If everyone is aware that she and Jentry Rae argued in the locker room, are the cheerleaders wondering if her jealousy turned into a Venus flytrap that swallowed her ex-best friend whole?

Holding her chin up, she walks to her locker. She refuses to look at the area where Jentry Rae's body landed. The blood has been cleaned off the floor, yet subliminal residue of the tragedy remains. She steadies herself with the idea that Nikki is plowing full steam ahead to find the killer.

When Shaunette opens her locker, a dead rat falls out of it. *What the hell?* She screams at the top of her lungs.

Three dancers rush over. One gasps. One dry-heaves. And one snaps a pic of the rodent on her cell phone.

"Who did this?" Shaunette cries.

"What's all the fuss, ladies?" Vana hustles in. Spotting the eyes-open, claws-curled rat on the tile floor, she takes a step back. "Okay. Ah—nothing to see here."

"Nothing to see?" redheaded Ashleigh shouts. "That thing fell out of Shaunette's locker! You need to assure us we're safe in our own dressing room, ma'am."

"Rats can't kill you," Vana retorts. "Dead ones, anyway."

"You should watch the security footage out in the hallway. It'll tell you who entered here," Ashleigh suggests.

"That camera is broken. I keep asking Dante to fix it, but thanks, Ashleigh." Vana instructs everybody to get out. Next, she re-enters the locker room with Tammie, and the ladies begin a hushed conversation.

In the meantime, Priya tries to comfort Shaunette. "Girl, I have a half a Xanax in my cubby. Nibble the tiniest of pieces, and it'll take the edge off."

Juddered, Shaunette nods. She would kill for a glass of Bulleit Kentucky Bourbon, too.

Priya opens a drawer of her cubby. "What the—?"

Ashleigh bounds over. Hers happens to be the next stall over. "Priya Chandra! You have liquor and a joint in your cubby?"

"They aren't mine!" Priya argues.

Shaunette frowns. The liquor brand is her drink of choice. But who knows that? Then again, this infraction isn't being pinned on her. *Thank goodness.*

Vana hurries over, breathless. "My word! What do you have to say for yourself, Priya?"

"Those things don't belong to me, ma'am. I swear! Everyone knows that alcohol and recreational drugs are forbidden in the DLC, so think about it. You name me the Point and suddenly I'm breaking the rules? Seems I'm being framed."

"Maybe *you* did it, Shaunette," Ashleigh seethes. Her birdlike face turns pink as she spritzes her ginger mane with hairspray. "The fight you had with Jentry Rae isn't doing you any favors. Plus, you used to do pageants, right? Pageant girls are ruthless . . . famous for sabotage."

"That's enough, ladies," Vana interrupts. "I'll do some investigating, but for now, you need to leave, Priya. No game for you on Sunday."

"But ma'am!"

"No fussin'. Please do as I say."

Tammie picks up the weed and the whiskey and carries them to the trash bin.

"Who knows Priya's part in the dance routine?" Vana asks.

A beautiful rookie named Kamara raises her hand. Kamara is a stunner, with her flawless dark skin and long braids, but she has a knee injury.

Shaunette is slow to raise her hand next. Is she willing to attract more attention, positive or negative? Well, being featured is what she's here for.

"So, Shaunette and Kamara . . . rookies only?" Vana breathes hard. "Okay. Save that knee, Kamara. Shaunette, you're up."

Hating the strange circumstances, Shaunette grabs her pom-poms and smiles perfunctorily. She needs to get her head on straight and push down the idea that someone is harassing her, too. In other words, she mustn't perform like an acrobat falling off the highwire. She needs to do right by her mama.

Heart racing, she trails a few steps behind the dancers inside the tunnel. When she passes Dante, he gestures her closer. "Sorry there was a dead rat in your locker, Miss Shaunette. I don't know how it happened." Nervous perspiration shines on his upper lip. "I'm also sorry I wasn't friendlier when you came to my place. You caught me off-guard. It was wrong of me to blurt out that I saw you enter the dressing room."

"It isn't all right, Dante. But what's important is that we find out what happened to Jentry Rae. You understand, don't you? Can you tell me why Duke McCade gave you money?"

Concern darkens in his eyes. "Where did you hear that?"

"Your landlady. I overheard."

Turning red, he keeps his uneven voice to a whisper. "Mr. McCade didn't give me a bunch of cash. I told my landlady that to act like a big shot. Someone *else* paid me a few bucks, though."

"Tell me, Dante. Hurry! I'm about to go on." The first bars of the performance song boom on the sound system. In front of Shaunette, the cheerleaders whirl their pom-poms in anticipation of strutting on the field.

"I can't tell you who paid me." Dante shakes his head. "But I can give you the stadium's VIP visitors list from the day Miss Jentry Rae was murdered—to make up for what I said at my duplex. Is that helpful?"

"Yes, please."

"I'll email it to you."

"*Erm*—" She hesitates. She doesn't want this man having her email address. Besides, it's against the rules for her to give out personal information. But screw it. With the goal of clearing her name in the investigation, she rattles off her address and sashays onto the field.

The squad's rehearsal is a disaster. The cheerleaders dance offbeat despite the throbbing music, and a half-dozen run into each other. They haven't functioned the same since Jentry Rae died.

Shaunette is honored to be the Point and thank the Lord her dancing is decent. But in the larger scheme of things, all she can think about is the dead rat, her former murdered friend, and the possible death of the DL Cheerleaders' reputation.

PHOTO: Jentry Rae is sitting in a hairstylist chair, her head stacked with color foils.

401k followers / 32,004 likes

#TakeCareOfYourself #PamperingTime

Self-care is so important, girlies. I'm @beautycorral today, making the effort to do it all: hair, nails, skin care, and hydration. But foremost, it's our internal health that counts, right? Mental well-being is paramount to thriving. Can I get a heck yeah?

Announcement time. I have made the difficult decision to leave the DLC after this year. Thank you, fans; you're the best! I'll miss you fiercely!!

If you're a little stressed like me, close your eyes and count to zen. Remember: after a storm comes a rainbow. And rising suns bring new hope. Hope for mending friendships, possibly. Hope for creating new destinies, absolutely.

Put goodness out in the world 🎬 💝

Cheers & Godspeed xx

CHAPTER TWENTY-NINE

THE FILMMAKER

~ OCTOBER 28 ~

Nikki is in the middle of cooking eggs when her cell phone buzzes. Removing the skillet from the heat, she reads a text message.

Back off this investigation. You're risking your life.

What on earth? Oh my God!

The hair on her arms stands up while her sense of safety shrivels.

Fraught with alarm, she remains fixed in one spot as her empty apartment goes unnervingly still.

Who is doing this? Could Shaunette have sent the mysterious text? The cheerleader has a phone app that allows her to use dummy numbers, but she and Nikki trust each other at this point, don't they?

Nikki's phone rings, and she jumps. Seeing that it's Shaunette, she does her best to act unsuspicious as she pushes the "Answer" button. Inside, she's panicking over being next on the killer's list.

"Hey," Shaunette greets eagerly. "Do you have a minute?"

"Sure. You, ah, sound frenzied. Either that or you're out of breath from dancing."

"I have some good news I just told my mama about. I was named the Point. You know, the Dallas Lonestars Cheerleader who centers every triangle on the field? I'm the temporary Point, but it's still amazing, right?"

"Wow. Congratulations! But you seem more worried than excited. And why temporary?"

"A joint and some bourbon were discovered in the cubby of the originally selected dancer."

Nikki shifts the phone to the other ear. "Seriously?"

"Yeah. It's bizarre because Priya seems squeaky clean. The other dancers believe *I* planted the banned substances. Why, I don't know."

Because competitiveness is your kryptonite, Nikki thinks.

The cheerleader's voice grows raspier. "Here's something else. I found a disgusting dead rat in my locker. If I'm the one planting things, why would *I* have put that there? To scare myself?"

Shaunette sounds genuinely freaked out, so Nikki decides to give the cheerleader the benefit of the doubt. "No way you'd do that. But I'm surprised Vana gave the title of 'Point' to a rookie."

"She's all business. A consummate professional. She explained it to the squad as, I'm the strongest dancer who knows the routine the best."

"Right. Yeah . . . no. You deserve it. Congrats, again," says Nikki.

"Thank you. Wait, you sound a little nervous."

"A minute ago, I got a cryptic text—"

"What? I'm having trouble hearing you," Shaunette replies. "I'm headed home. Maybe we can talk later because—oh my God! Vana is calling me. She *never* calls me. Gotta go!"

"Drive carefully," Nikki says as she hangs up. She's still standing in the kitchen, frozen, thinking that none of this feels right.

No wonder Shaunette is jittery, Nikki laments as she stares at her uncooked eggs. A lot is going on in the cheerleader's life. Which is why Shaunette absolutely deserves the good news she received tonight.

Even so, Nikki works something out in her head. Why did Vana Lockwood break etiquette and make a rookie dancer the Point? And why are the squad members blatantly turning on each other by performing pranks and sabotage?

The Dallas Lonestars Cheerleaders are imploding from within while somebody is pulling the punishing puppet strings.

But who?

Fueled by worry, she calls Shaunette back and gets no answer.

TV TRANSCRIPT

Television anchorwoman Candice Chang is on camera at Dallas's Channel 5 news desk. Cued, she puts a hand to her earpiece. "This just in. Dallas Lonestars Cheerleader Shaunette Simmons has been rushed to a local hospital in critical condition. Her car swerved off an embankment near the Americana Memorial Stadium in Grapevine—a road marred by heavy road construction.

"Eyewitnesses attest that Miss Simmons was unable to stop her vehicle from tearing straight into a cement pylon. Presumably, her seat belt and deployed air bag saved her life.

"Mason Boon is on the scene. Mason, what can you tell us?"

"It's a terrifying set-up, Candice. You have a lonely stretch of road. No moonlight. And mishandled road construction. As you can see behind me, first responders arrived and pried Miss Simmons out of her car using the jaws of life. She's in an ICU ward at a nearby hospital, but as of yet, there is no word on her prognosis."

Mason takes a breath. "However, an additional, startling element of this story has come to light. Police officers allegedly found an open bottle of bourbon inside Miss Simmons' car."

PART III

Win, lose, or tie.
I'll be a Lonestars fan 'til I die.

CHAPTER THIRTY

THE DALLAS LONESTARS CHEERLEADER

~ *OCTOBER 28* ~

Frail, battered, and barely conscious, Shaunette is wheeled into a hospital emergency room on a gurney. Nurses and physicians gather around her as she's lifted and slid onto a table.

Her vital signs are taken.

A doctor shines a small flashlight in her eyes.

Someone puts an oxygen mask over her mouth.

Delirious and numb from the trauma, Shaunette swears she leaves her body, ascends, and hovers over herself. Down below, she hears the words, "The victim has a broken arm and a punctured lung. Her deep forehead laceration needs stitches. Plus, she's showing signs of a concussion."

Her beauty—has it been destroyed? Shaunette jolts back into her body.

"You should've seen the car, Doc," an EMT interjects. "That girl is lucky to be alive."

Bright halogen lights keep Shaunette from passing out. Accelerating her heart rate, too, is the glance she gets from a police officer by the door. He's making a "Drinking" gesture by extending his thumb and pinkie at his mouth. When he points at Shaunette, the lead doctor nods.

But she WASN'T driving drunk!

A toxicology screen will show it.

Somebody forced her into a pylon and tried to kill her!

Struggling to breathe—even with oxygen—her eyes droop. She is frantic to give an explanation, but instead she slips into the murky abyss of unconsciousness.

In the morning, Shaunette locks eyes with a nurse who enters her hospital room. Her throat is drier than the Sahara, and she has a splitting headache.

Hopefully, the nurse has come to hang a new bag of painkillers.

Shaunette wants to ask questions about her condition, but delirium still has her woozy. As she tries shifting positions in bed, the movement punches pain through her bruised torso. Her forehead injury stings, too. To be in so much pain is debilitating, but it's probably a smidgeon of what Jentry Rae felt in her final moments. When the superstar cheerleader fell from the height of what turned out to be a cardboard castle, the agony she experienced must have been indescribable.

Why did Shaunette leave Jentry Rae with such nasty words in her final moments?

Trying to eradicate her guilt, she silently counts to ten. Soon, she notices a rep from the DLC sitting in the corner. Julie? Jess? Jill? It's someone from administration, anyway.

The woman gives her a nod and remains stoic.

Meanwhile, Shaunette wonders where her phone is. She wants to call Mama and Nikki because, have they heard what happened to her? Has anyone tried to visit? The car crash must be all over the news.

Julie or Jill stands and moves toward her. Offering a smile, the rep buttons her blazer, pats Shaunette's hand, then asks how she is doing.

"I've had better days," Shaunette replies.

The woman informs her that the entire Lonestars organization is sending well-wishes. Nothing like this has ever happened before, and everybody is stunned.

When Shaunette asks how Vana feels about her accident, the rep clams up.

As the unhelpful woman exits the room in search of coffee, Shaunette sighs with relief. She needs to avoid panicking. Hopefully then, she can go home. This is *not* her ideal morning routine. Ordinarily, she'll wake up, check her social media feeds, get out of bed, and go in search of her own coffee. Beau Dog has been keeping her company, too—on her patio while she enjoys a hot latte. What's that saying? You don't know what you have until it's gone.

Cute little Beau Dog.

He has become near and dear to her.

Shaunette wishes she could cuddle with him for reassurance right now. *Good gravy!* Her thoughts are all over the place while her fear keeps mounting.

Piercing through her scattered thoughts, however, is a standout notion. She is lucky to be alive. That being said, the automobile accident doesn't look good for her. She can't imagine what people think. That she tried to commit suicide? Or that she was inebriated behind the wheel and lost control like a blitzed idiot?

Either scenario is scandalous.

At least a blood panel will prove Shaunette had no alcohol in her system. For heaven's sake, the results better be available soon. She was just made the Point, if only temporarily. She wouldn't kill herself *now*.

Shaunette hears the phone ring in her hospital room. The nurse answers the call by saying, "Room 1456." Nodding, she hands the phone over. "It's your mother."

"Mama?" Shaunette says in a croak.

"Great balls of fire, Shaunette Lynn! What in heaven's name were you doing? Riding a blind horse toward a steep cliff? I saw your accident on Channel 5 News. Tell me you weren't self-harmin' when you hit that pylon. I'll kill you myself."

Her mother's lack of empathy is a gut-punch. "I wasn't trying to hurt myself, Mama. It was dark. And somebody ran me off the road on purpose."

Silence.

"Um, I'm really tired and upset, so I'm going to hang up—" Shaunette starts to cry. Wailing makes her head hurt more.

Her mother does something unusual then. She breaks down, sobbing, too. "I'm telling you, baby, you scared the bejeezus out of me. I'm at my wits' end. If I ever lost you—"

Shaunette swallows in disbelief. Did her mother actually speak those words? Caring phrases are what she has been waiting to hear her entire life. Jentry Rae might've stolen millions of hearts, but hopefully Shaunette has finally captured her mother's.

"Do you mean that, Mama?" she asks eagerly.

"Of course I do, baby. You're my daughter. A piece of me."

The sentiment wraps Shaunette in a hug.

The nurse signals for her to end the phone call. It's making her pulse rate soar. She acquiesces, but not for her own health . . . because she doesn't want to worry her mother further. Mama has enough on her plate.

Still crying, Shaunette ekes out, "I'm being told to hang up, but I love you."

"Ditto." Although her mother's cold tone returns, the conversation is progress.

"Your accident is making national headlines," the nurse says as she ends the call and switches the TV on. "See?"

Shaunette dares to look at the screen. Her eight-year-old smoking Honda is crunched to bits, and beside it, two idling police cruisers chirp their sirens urgently. She gasps. How fortunate she was to walk away from the crash is startling.

A news reporter dashes her good feelings when he says, "An open bottle of alcohol was found inside Miss Simmons' smashed vehicle."

What? He didn't just say that!

A clammy chill spreads up her spine. *This is bad*. She did NOT drink and drive. But what are the police thinking?

"Please shut the television off," she instructs the nurse in a weak voice. "Um, do you know if anyone is caring for my dog?"

"I'm not sure, dear."

Shaunette will ask the DLC rep when the woman returns.

Once she's alone in the hospital room, Shaunette's thoughts turn to Vana. Vana was calling just before the accident. To retract the position of the Point, maybe? Shaunette only remembers snippets of their conversation before the black SUV forced her into that intimidating wall of road construction. Her cell phone flew out of her hands at that moment. Then it landed somewhere unknown. What she does remember is Vana bringing up a disturbing new subject.

Shaunette's breath catches as more thoughts jumble inside her sedated head. Where is the SUV driver now? And if Sergeant Emerson has her phone, how long before he comes across the calls between her and Royce?

Hot drumbeats of worry thud in her ears.

Will she be the next body on a morgue slab?

She *has* to stay alive. It's her only goal. As is Sonny's goal. But unlike Sonny, Shaunette wants to find Jentry Rae's killer in order to eliminate herself as a murder suspect.

She might be laid up in the hospital, but Nikki isn't. She desperately needs her new friend's help.

CHAPTER THIRTY-ONE

THE FILMMAKER

~ *OCTOBER 30* ~

Nikki has made several attempts to visit Shaunette at the hospital but was turned away. This morning, she hopes she will be allowed to see the injured cheerleader.

Like everybody else, she learned about the car crash on the news. She watched in horror as an ambulance carted mangled Shaunette to a local Dallas ER. Wanting to do something, she sent Vince to photograph the crash site. She also called the police numerous times but learned nothing specific about the accident.

Nikki knows Shaunette is alive—but that's about it.

When she called Sonny to share the shocking news with him, he was despondent. "What in tarnation is this world comin' to? Young women don't seem to have a chance these days."

Her optimism exceeds his. At least Shaunette survived the bad collision. But who caused it? She doubts the cheerleader was trying to end her life. Not after being named the Point. The accolade means too much to her.

In Nikki's opinion, so much media attention is focused on crimes that never get solved . . . crimes involving innocent women. And she isn't going to let Jentry Rae's murder and Shaunette's car wreck be included in that statistic.

Details. She needs to learn details.

Grabbing her handbag, she leaves her apartment and walks to the equipment van parked on the street. Startled, she halts on the curb. *What the fuck?* All four tires are slashed!

"Goddamn it," she cries. *Who has it in for her?*

Feeling her legs grow wobbly, she reads an anonymous text that pops up on her phone: **Stop while you're ahead!**

Obviously, the punctured tires are putting the exclamation point at the end of that sentence.

Shaky and full of fear, Nikki glances over her shoulder at her apartment building. The front doors are outward facing, so a Ring camera might've caught the culprit. She doesn't have time to ask each neighbor now, so she'll have the police find out. Except, they must have their hands full with what's going on within the DLC.

Deciding she's on her own, Nikki tries to stuff away the intimidation pounding through her. She calls Vince and asks him to take care of buying new tires. Then she Venmos him her last four hundred dollars. Now, she's legitimately in the poorhouse. How will she tell her father?

Nikki compartmentalizes her fright and Ubers to the hospital. Whoever is sabotaging her and Shaunette will pay. Is it Dante Marconi? Vince has been conducting some research on the seamy security guard, and fingers crossed her sidekick will uncover the reason behind Dante's recent windfall of money. As luck would have it, Vince isn't just a videographer. He's in contact with some interesting people—namely an underground web expert named The Dark Lord. They play World of Warcraft together.

"His real name is Owen," Vince revealed to Nikki the other day. In his best *Scarface* voice, he added, "But don't tell nobody nothing."

Nikki enters the hospital lobby. She won't take no for an answer when it comes to seeing Shaunette. She is about to speak to the front desk receptionist when a large floral arrangement arrives.

"These are for Shaunette Simmons," the delivery guy says.

After the receptionist accepts the gardenias, she asks an orderly to take the bouquet to Room 1456. Nikki follows the flowers into the elevator where their cloyingly sweet scent chokes the space. When she emerges on the fourth floor, she hangs back and watches the arrangement make its way to a room at the end of the hall.

The instant a nurse leaves her desk post, Nikki slips into Shaunette's room. She gulps. The cheerleader's tiny frame looks even smaller than usual, dwarfed by a sea of pillows and tubes. Shockingly, her bloated face is blown up like a puffer fish, and a massive forehead bandage indicates where she smashed her head.

Shaunette tries to sit up as soon as she sees Nikki.

"Stay still," Nikki protests. She pulls over a chair and sits in it. "Vince sends his well-wishes. He's busy researching Dante Marconi."

"Duke McCade didn't give Dante money," Shaunette slurs her words. Likely from painkillers.

"We'll talk about that later."

The cheerleader points to her forehead. Tears rim her eyes.

"I'm sorry you're hurt, but you're still gorgeous," Nikki jokes with a smile. "More importantly, you're alive."

"I might not be alive for long. I knew I'd be next."

More worry floods Nikki as she tries to stay above water herself. "Don't say that."

"Do you think I'm being dramatic?"

"No, because someone is after me, too. I got a threatening text message *not* from you. And my tires were slashed."

"Oh my God," Shaunette moans.

"You should have security outside your door, Shaunette. Have the police come yet?"

"No. I can't tell them much, anyway. I—I didn't see my assailant."

The mingled smells of ammonia, microwaved food, and pungent flowers make Nikki wrinkle her nose.

"I just want Beau Dog—"

"Please don't get upset," Nikki urges. "Do you want me to get the pooch from your place and keep him for the time being?"

"Yes, thanks." Shaunette indicates a drawer that contains her keys. "N-Nikki, do you think we'll survive this?"

"Of course we will. But tell me. Did you see the license plate of the other car?"

"No. I was . . . distracted. The rat in my locker. And Vana called just then—"

"Why was Vana calling you?"

"Help me. My mouth. So dry . . ."

Nikki helps Shaunette drink from a water cup. Then she resumes her seat. The atmosphere in the room feels repressive. Nerve-racking, even.

"Vana came here an hour ago," Shaunette explains. "At first, she acted concerned. But then she was furious with me. The police gave her a phone video that shows me arguing with Jentry Rae."

Nikki bites her lip. "Don't think about that right now. When you get out of here, you can stay with me. I'm scared, too. We'll get through this together."

"Thanks. But you don't understand. I said some heinous things on the video. Things that will probably take me off the squad." *Bleep. Bleep.* The EKG machine monitoring Shaunette's heart rate goes nuclear.

Nikki implores the cheerleader to calm down, but her pulse is thrumming, too. Now isn't the time to ask, but she wants to know the whole truth about that recording. It must be profoundly incriminating.

"I didn't kill my friend!" Red-faced Shaunette nearly breaks out of her prison of tubes.

"Take it easy. I'm sure you're telling the truth." At least, Nikki *wants* to believe her new friend. She has always been a good judge of character, and something tells her that the cheerleader's display of desperation is genuine. Which makes her own fright escalate. What is this dangerous situation they're in? Will each of them be tormented to death?

A nurse enters the hospital room and checks Shaunette's vital signs. Nikki goes rigid in her seat as her concern for herself and Shaunette grows.

"Maybe I deserve to die." Shaunette clenches her jaw after the nurse leaves. "I might not have killed Jentry Rae, but I *wanted* her dead."

It's impossible for Nikki to summon comforting words like, *"Don't carry heavy baggage while trying to climb a mountain of healing."*

A quarter of an hour passes, each of them lost in their own thoughts.

"The pain!" Shaunette exclaims.

"Is it time for morphine or something?"

"Almost, b-but I need to tell you a secret I've been keeping. Somebody filmed me drunk-dancing on a bar top. At a place called Swindler's. They . . . ah . . . sent the recording to Vana. It's another reason she called me before the accident. And it's why she paid me a visit here."

Swindler's Bar? By my rental apartment? Strange. Nikki frowns. "Who's doing this to you, Shaunette?"

"I wish I knew. Oow! C-call for the nurse, please." After a pause, she says, "Can you do me some favors, too? Find out who ran me off the road and clear my name. Erase the audio you captured of me speaking with Royce and talk to Chase Campbell."

As a nurse injects a painkiller into Shaunette's IV, Nikki's suspicions take a turn. It seems fishy that the injured cheerleader wants the audio destroyed. Does she have a good reason?

While Nikki can't agree to all the demands, she considers that if Chase is behind all this, she'll start there. And if she finds out that the cocky sports therapist holds the key to this shit show, she is more than willing to bury him with a few extra shovelfuls of righteousness.

CHAPTER THIRTY-TWO

THE DALLAS LONESTARS CHEERLEADER

~ OCTOBER 30 ~

Shaunette's terror evaporates during her nap. But the moment she awakens without Nikki by her bedside, a tsunami of anxiety splashes over her. As she looks around the clockless, windowless room, she feels disoriented. The only thing she knows for sure is how violently her world has keeled over.

Peeking at the door, Shaunette realizes Nikki was right. A security guard should be stationed in the outer hospital hallway. What if the hostile SUV driver comes back for her?

Worry causes her to stiffen at every noise.

As she inhales unsteadily because of the tube in her lung, she eyes a cup of water on the side table. Her mouth quirks. Unfortunately, the cup is adjacent to her arm cast, and her lung is burning like a forest on fire. *Screw being thirsty.*

It sucks being by herself.

Footsteps echo in the hall, and a new influx of fright flushes through her. The door opens, and Sergeant Emerson and his partner come through it. Judging from their expressions, they mean business.

Shaunette wishes she could feign sleep. But the cops have already seen that her eyes are open. She gives them a terse nod while more fright tap-dances on her brain. Are they here to charge her with a Driving While Intoxicated? Where is that damned toxicology result?

Emerson stares her down and begins with: "You're a brave young lady. I won't ask what it felt like to slam into a cement pylon."

If that's his idea of a joke, she's in no mood to be teased. Maybe the investigators will clear out if she exaggerates the level of her pain. "*Ooo . . .* my chest—"

"This is my partner, Nico La Rosa," Emerson interrupts. "So, we're here with good news. Your tox screen is back. No alcohol was found in your system. Dallas's police chief will make the public announcement on Friday, along with the news that Jentry Rae Randall was pregnant."

"Pregnant?" Dabbing her eyes, Shaunette acts surprised. Secretly, she's relieved that being cleared of lawbreaking increases her chances of remaining a Dallas Lonestars Cheerleader. She breathes easier until the sergeant adds, "However, Texas has an open container law."

Her emotions plummet again.

"Lucky for you, your car is a hatchback, Shaunette. It was legal for you to have had an open bottle of liquor tucked into the space behind the rear upright seats."

She nods. "This proves I wasn't impaired behind the wheel. But I've already proclaimed that."

La Rosa, a younger version of his partner with a lot more hair, pulls a chair across the floor. It squeals loudly. As he sits, he says, "You weren't driving under the influence, ma'am, but we're here for another reason."

Emerson puts his hand up to stop his partner from speaking. "Shaunette, you and I didn't have the best conversation when you came to the station. I'm sorry if I was a prick. Now I realize you need help."

"Excuse me?"

"I don't normally do this, but I want to suggest some self-help centers."

"Self-help? You th-think I tried to commit suicide?" she stammers.

He wags his chin solemnly. "Guilt is a terrible thing to carry around. It makes people do impulsive things."

"I was wearing my seat belt!"

"You could've strapped in at the last minute. Also, where are the skid marks you would've left behind if you tried stopping on a dirt, off-road path?"

"Have you considered that maybe the assailant wiped them away?"

Emerson paces the room. "What assailant? Come on. You want us to believe somebody got out of their car and erased skid marks? They'd risk being seen."

"It's entirely possible. A cold-hearted monster is after me." She holds her arm cast.

La Rosa spreads his hands sincerely. "Ma'am, my Italian grandmother taught me to look at every side of a situation. It's something Sergeant Emerson has taught me, too. And here's the problem. Nobody except you had a motive to kill Jentry Rae Randall."

The statement whirls Shaunette into a mental tailspin. The police are laser-focused on her. *Is this for real?* Even if she were to vehemently proclaim her innocence, what good would it do? The detectives think she is a jealousy-powered runaway train careening out of control.

As the men stare her down some more, her mama's pervasive voice reverberates in the hospital room. *"Sometimes pageant judges get tunnel vision, darlin'. When they do, they pick winners out ahead of time."*

CHAPTER THIRTY-THREE

THE FILMMAKER

~ *OCTOBER 30* ~

Nikki returns to her apartment carrying a slobbery Beau Dog. The Uber driver scowled at her the entire way home because the dog peed in his car. She apologized profusely, but at least the dog is good for a while.

After the pooch releases a sigh, it curls up on a blanket and falls asleep.

Nikki settles in a chair by the window and begins reflecting on her conversation with Shaunette. The cheerleader asked her to call Chase Campbell, so she plans to set up a meeting with the sports therapist. Then again, surprising him at home might be best. He'll be caught off-guard with no time to prepare what to say.

She is about to text Vince and put in a request for Chase's home address (compliments of net-savvy Owen) when there's a knock at the door. She is surprised. Halloween isn't until tomorrow; it's too early for trick-or-treaters.

Moving to the peephole, she sees a large, bald man shove a police badge against it.

"Who's there?" Her pulse quickens as she acts clueless that it's Sergeant Wes Emerson.

"Police detectives, Miss Keegan. May we have a word?"

She unlocks the door.

"You might remember me from the coroner's office. I'm the officer in charge of Jentry Rae Randall's murder. This my partner, Detective La Rosa."

A stocky man behind him nods.

"Yes, of course." She allows the investigators in. "Can I get you gentlemen something to drink?"

They decline. Instead, they stand rigidly in her living room and look around.

"I'll get straight to the point," Emerson says. "We just left Dallas Health-Central Hospital. Shaunette Simmons is in bad shape."

"I know. It's terrible."

"We saw you leave her ward."

Nikki shrugs. "Say what you came to say then."

"We'd like to take you to the station for a recorded interview, ma'am." La Rosa clasps his hands in front of him.

She sinks back on her heels. "Can't we just talk here? I have the dog."

"Jentry Rae's dog, correct?"

"Yes. What of it?"

"Ah, filmmaking duties don't usually extend to pet-sittin'," Sergeant Emerson intervenes. "I'd wager that you're embroiled deeply in this story, Miss Keegan."

"Is that a crime?"

He huffs. "Never mind. I reckon that if you consent to being recorded, we can do the interview here."

"Fine."

The detectives sit on the sofa while Nikki returns to the chair by the window.

After Emerson pushes "Record" on his cell phone, he sets the device on the coffee table and talks into it. "This is an interview with Nikki Keegan on the thirtieth of October at two-twenty p.m. Session is being conducted at her apartment by investigators Emerson and La Rosa. Okay, ma'am. A police complaint was filed by Royce Holt, the starting quarterback for the Dallas Lonestars. Why have you been harassing him?"

"Harassing?" Blood rushes to her face. Then her mind scrambles like an angry swarm of bees. "All I did was ask Royce a few questions for my documentary."

"Like I said, this film 'a yours is taking you in thorny directions."

"Is there a question in there somewhere, Sergeant?"

"Mr. Holt claims you singled him out and confronted him at the Lonestars' practice arena. Afterward, you recorded him during a meeting you two had at a restaurant without his permission."

Her throat constricts. She manages to say, "Gathering information is what I do. For my job. Anyway, Texas is a 'one-party' consent state, correct? I was part of the conversation, and I recorded Royce in a public place. All legal."

"It's still damned underhanded, is what it is." Emerson's mouth turns downward. "We're advising you to stop playing amateur detective in your spare time."

Nikki tries to act nonchalant, but the tops of her ears are burning with outrage. She wonders if she should divulge that Royce Holt was pursuing Jentry Rae. Perhaps got her pregnant, even. The revelation would blow his reputation sky high. And just as his career is taking off.

It's tempting.

"Do you admit to armchair sleuthing?" La Rosa asks.

"I wouldn't call it that. I heard a rumor about Royce Holt and the murder victim, Jentry Rae Randall. Word is they were friendly."

"As in, they knew each other intimately? Who told you that?"

"I didn't say intimate. I said friendly," she corrects. "All I know is dull docudramas need a little embellishment. Which isn't against the law either. Right?"

"You're pushing the envelope, and it's annoying." Emerson folds his arms. "I'd be careful if I were you. Football is a religion in Texas."

"I'm aware, Sergeant. But I hope slashing people's tires and sending sinister text messages aren't what Texans teach in Sunday school."

His cheeks turn red. He puffs out his chest. "If those things happened to you, file a report."

"Like it'd do any good."

He pauses. "Hear me clearly, ma'am. Let Royce Holt do his job. LEAVE-HIM-ALONE."

"Are you seriously throwing some misogynist vitriol in my face?"

"You don't understand, Miss Keegan," La Rosa speaks up. "Royce Holt conducted some research on you. He claims you aren't who you say you are. Allegedly, you didn't go to film school—a prestigious one or otherwise—and you never interned with Hollywood mentors."

Time stops. The curtain has been pulled back on the Wizard of Oz. As the ground drops out from beneath Nikki, she clings to the chair for support.

"Have you been lying about your credentials?" La Rosa asks.

She thinks *Yes. I also lied to my producer about having football knowledge. So . . . son of a bitch!* The exposure isn't a lethal Tomahawk missile zooming her way, but it's embarrassing. She prefers that nobody has inflammatory information they can use against her; she has worked too hard. "Does it even matter?" she replies curtly. "My work speaks for itself."

"Nevertheless, you don't want to find yourself in a pile of crap without the proper shoes for it," Emerson growls.

As if on cue, Beau Dog waddles over and pees on his loafers.

"Control your pet, damn it!" The bald detective leaps to his feet.

Nikki smiles. "He isn't my pet, remember?"

Seething, the sergeant wipes his shoes with Kleenex from the table. Next, he gestures to her crossly. "I saw the worry on your face just now, Miss Keegan. But I'm willing to keep your lies in my back pocket if you cooperate."

She scoops up Beau Dog, surging to her feet, too. "You mean, *if* I back off with my inquiries? Get the hell out of here. Both of you. And don't come back unless you have an arrest warrant."

NEW PINNED REEL: Piper films herself coming out of an obstetrician appointment.

1.5 million followers / 310,007 likes

#trending #FFL #sportswife #WAG #mother

"The countdown is on!" she gloats. "Baby Number Two will arrive in two weeks by a scheduled C-Section. I'm stoked to return to pumping, diaper underwear, and round-the-clock feedings. But for a sec, can we talk about my incredible husband? *Monsieur* Dupree, AKA Royce, is on fire. When he QB'd against the Minnesota Vipers last week, he was there ON LONESTARS' BUSINESS. Whoo-hoo!

"I'm so proud of him for fulfilling his dreams. He and I have been a team since high school."

She rubs her belly. "And since Royce and I make great partners, we aim to protect myself and this little one 'cause . . . have you heard? Another Dallas Lonestars Cheerleader has come into harm's way. Shout-out to Shaunette Simmons. I have never met her, but I hope she's okay. It's getting kinda scary out there, Dallasites."

CHAPTER THIRTY-FOUR

THE DALLAS LONESTARS CHEERLEADER

~ OCTOBER 31 ~

Pneumothorax is the medical term for a collapsed lung. As a hospital patient, Shaunette has learned more about the condition these past few days than she cares to.

She is healing well, though.

That's what the staff at Dallas Health-Central tell her, at least.

But if she really is on the mend, why won't her "I've-been-run-over-by-a-forklift" level of pain subside?

An Asian man in a white lab coat enters her room. Shaunette recognizes him as her attending doctor. Adjusting his eyeglasses, he pokes at a touch tablet and asks, "How are we feeling today, Miss Simmons?"

"Like I've been sucker-punched by a semi-truck."

"Good, good."

Is he even listening?

"According to your chart, the most severe injury you sustained is a collapsed lung. The nurses may have explained this to you, but a small catheter has been inserted to remove the air from the pleural cavity. That catheter helps the lung re-expand. It will be removed before you go home."

"When *can* I go home?"

"I don't see why you can't be released tomorrow afternoon. But you'll be closely observed for four to six hours before you're given exit instructions—to see if your lung rebels. You'll be sent home with painkillers, too."

"No painkillers, please." *Not a good idea with my addictive personality.*

"Heed my words, Miss Simmons. Take it easy. No waving those shiny pom-poms for a while. Doctor's orders."

She probably couldn't perform if she wanted to.

"Are you feeling well enough to have a visitor?" he asks. "Mrs. LeAnn McCade, Duke McCade's wife, is here."

Her heart skips a beat. *Really? The first lady of the Dallas Lonestars is paying me a visit?* Nodding, she self-consciously fixes her bedraggled hair and rubs at her chapped lips.

A beautiful woman in her forties appears. As if illuminated by a spotlight, LeAnn McCade floats forward wearing a fluffy crème-colored coat atop her shoulders. It complements her electric blue sweater and gold dress pants: a loyal array of Lonestars' colors.

As she reaches Shaunette's bed, her bouncy blonde hair shines brighter than her dazzling veneers.

"Hello," Shaunette says. She knows a pageant girl when she sees one.

All the woman needs is a sparkling crown.

A timid man with owl eyes and an underbite is on LeAnn's heels. He's holding a cell phone at arm's length, filming. Shaunette gathers that he is her media assistant.

"Shaunette Simmons, you poor thing!" LeAnn says as she hands a huge bouquet of Halloween-themed flowers to the nurse. "If you're feeling up to it, I hope you won't mind if Fletcher records this important moment."

Shaunette is too flabbergasted to oppose.

"I was so sorry to hear about your accident," the regal woman says. "I do charity appearances at this hospital . . . for my many community causes. Today, I wanted to pop in and offer well-wishes." She takes a breath. "Are you healing fast, darlin'?"

"Miss Simmons is a stellar patient, Mrs. McCade," the doctor answers with a starstruck expression.

"Fantastic." LeAnn claps her manicured hands together.

The assistant yanks a chair over for her. As soon as LeAnn sits beside the bed, she strikes another commanding pose. "You and I have something in common, my dear."

"What's that?" Shaunette asks in a scratchy voice.

The woman's red lips curve into a proud smile. "I was Miss Teenage Texas. And you were Miss Nacogdoches County. Oh, and Little Miss Sippy Cup, as I understand it. We know that world well, don't we?"

"Beauty pageants are in my past."

"No, no. Competin' for crowns stays with us. Chin up, chest out, am I right?" LeAnn laughs delicately. A moment later, she asks the doctor, the nurse, and her media assistant for a moment alone.

The assemblage scurries out of the room.

LeAnn leans in. "Bless your heart for crashing your ole car, darlin', but I hear you're fightin' spirits."

"Spirits?"

"Booze," she clarifies. "The devil's drink. And your unfortunate incident happened just when our football team was getting back on track—thanks to hunky Royce Holt. We really don't need negative jibber-jabber. In other words, we cannot have you embarrassing this franchise." LeAnn's expression is frosty, and her voice is stern.

Shaunette tears up. "I would never drive intoxicated, ma'am. Somebody ran me off the road." More incrimination—let alone from the queen of the kingdom—is something she can't handle.

"That's your story? *Hmm*. Well, listen to me carefully, Shaunette Simmons. Your fellow cheerleader Jentry Rae was doing something she shouldn't have, just like you. Y'all need to straighten up on that damned DLC squad!"

Cornered and speechless, Shaunette feels battered by mistrust. Soon, anger replaces her astonishment. "And if we don't straighten up, Mrs. McCade?"

"All I'm saying is: stay in your lane."

CHAPTER THIRTY-FIVE

THE FILMMAKER

~ OCTOBER 31 ~

Nikki is still reeling from yesterday's visit by police detectives. She is guilty of coloring the facts—that much is true—but it isn't career suicide. What's really bothering her is the ridiculous way Royce ran off to the authorities about how she padded her résumé.

Obviously, he wants payback for recording their conversation at Bogart's. She could throttle him.

But Royce isn't the only one who can dig up dirt. Nikki plans to go to Chase Campbell's house right now and drill the sports therapist about problematic Royce. The men have been friends since childhood, but supposedly they've grown apart recently.

Climbing into the equipment van with Vince, Nikki is glad that the vehicle has four new tires. Only, it was money she could've sent her dad. Sadly, he hasn't gotten out of bed in five days. How much longer can he put off paying his utilities?

Once Vince enters Chase's home address into Google Maps, she steers northeast. They arrive within the hour at a mid-century-modern home on a tree-lined street. She parks two houses down. Then she and Vince sit immobile as the sun descends.

"Should we be confrontational assholes when Campbell opens the door?" Vince asks. "Or friendlier than Mr. Rogers?"

"Let's take our cue from him." She switches the engine off.

Just then, Chase backs out of his garage in a gleaming black SUV.

Christ, Nikki thinks. *Shaunette was trailed by the same type of vehicle.*

Except, how many black SUVs are there in Texas? As many as churches?

She and Vince scoot down in their seats until the sports therapist passes the van and zooms off.

When Vince pops up, he turns his baseball cap backward, ready for action. "Follow him, Nik. Quick as a bunny."

Complying, she tails the SUV two cars apart for a good half hour. The van's fuel gauge depletes in the meantime. She starts to worry—especially when Chase's car enters a seedy part of Dallas. "We might run out of gas in this sleazy neighborhood," she tells Vince.

"Fuck. Don't manifest it."

Chase arrives at a strip club called Les Girls, and he parks around back. Nikki edges in behind him, slipping into a rear parking slot, as well. As soon as Chase gets out of his car and leans against the vehicle, it gives Nikki and Vince a clear view of him.

They wait and observe. Crack the windows and listen.

Several exotic dancers with hardened faces exit the club from a back door. Next, a fresh-faced dancer with pretty features and smooth skin comes out. She lifts her chin and heads straight for Chase. As the girl tosses her tawny-red hair over her shoulder, Nikki ascertains that the dancer is in her early twenties.

Vince starts to film on his 35 mm camera.

Chase pushes off his car and faces the woman while a throbbing rap song ends.

"I have one thing to say to you, Chase," she says. "Your friend is a jackass. Even though I dance for a living, I have some dignity. Tell him that for me."

"Hear me out, Rosie. He cares about you."

"Really? He used me and then tossed me away like trash."

"I owe him a lot because he helped me when I was young. But believe me, I give him hell in private about the way he treats women," Chase replies.

The stripper gathers her jacket lapels together. "Your stupid bromance reminds me of little boys in a sandbox. I have no hankerin' for men who won't grow up."

"I met you first, Rosie. And it wasn't here. Or online. Things might have worked out between us, until you-know-who swooped in."

"Then why are you loyal to someone who steals girlfriends away?"

"I told you. I owe him a lot. It's complicated shit. And he's kind of a mess." Bitterness and empathy blend in Chase's voice.

The dancer says nothing but her anger flames hotter than a furnace.

Chase reaches inside his pocket. He withdraws a small box: some sort of gift. "It's from him," he says as he hands over the present.

Rosie opens it, smiling.

Damn it that Nikki can't make out the contents of the box. It could be a piece of jewelry, but she isn't sure. After Chase whispers inaudible words in the dancer's ear, they get into his SUV and drive away.

"Whoa," Vince says. "That was freaky."

"Very. But let's go. The show is over." Nikki starts the van, disappointed that she can't report anything back to Sonny about tonight. On that note, curiosity is burning a hole in her brain. Is Royce the jerk of a friend who discarded the dancer? Maybe conquering women makes him feel untouchable . . . like a real "man" in an emasculating marriage.

On the other hand, bachelor Chase Campbell might be a bad influence on Royce. Is he the one introducing Royce to these women?

Pulling onto the street, Nikki remembers how, according to Jentry Rae's diary, Shaunette called Jentry Rae a homewrecker.

And considering that Royce is married, did Jentry Rae only date married men?

As Nikki stops the van at a stoplight, she looks to her left. Chase pulls up in his SUV without Rosie. When he motions for the van to turn into a nearby fast-food lot, Nikki nods. "We're busted," she complains to Vince.

"Yikes." He gets his phone ready to film discreetly again.

Once she parks, she hesitantly lowers her window.

"You're a terrible detective," Chase calls out from his vehicle. "Plus, I'd spot your praying mantis of a videographer anywhere. Stop filming me."

Vince scowls at him.

"What do you want, Chase?" Nikki asks.

"I should call the cops and report you for unlawful surveillance."

"Unlawful surveillance? Are you smoking something? This isn't a sting operation. And before you say anything else, have you been calling Shaunette Simmons and hanging up?" She takes a guess.

"Yeah." Clutching the steering wheel, Chase looks straight ahead. "Every time I think I'm ready to talk about Jentry Rae, I get overwhelmed."

The statement would've thrown Nikki for a loop if Shaunette hadn't prepped her about Chase's adoration of the murdered cheerleader. Maybe his love for Jentry Rae did run deep.

"Royce is my buddy," Chase says. "He's Shaunette's, too. But I don't want things to go further, so I'm going to spill the truth. Royce is a habitual liar. Track down his ex-girlfriend, Emma Hollander. See how he treated *her*."

Nikki decides to take another stab in the dark. "Hold on, Chase. You gave Jentry Rae her bulldog, didn't you?"

His face changes. "What if I did? She was sad. I wanted to make her happy—as a friend. She named the little guy Beau Dog because she's from Beaumont, Texas."

That much is cleared up.

Nikki looks at Vince, whose eyes get large behind his glasses.

"Chase, did you buy Jentry Rae a gold infinity bracelet with a sapphire inlay, too?"

"Excuse me? On my salary? Hell no. Like I said, find Emma Hollander." He screeches away.

Adrenaline rushes through Nikki all the way to a gas station. As Vince fills up the tank, she sends Royce a text: **I know you hate me, but we need to talk.**

He replies almost immediately. **Not even if you and I were the only people left standing after the world burned.**

Fuck him. Pursing her lips, she types another message. **I know about you & Jentry Rae. I also know about Rosie and Emma Hollander. Call me.**

CHAPTER THIRTY-SIX

THE DALLAS LONESTARS CHEERLEADER

~ NOVEMBER 1 ~

Thank God no medical complications arose prior to Shaunette's discharge from the hospital. However, she never thought getting out of bed, pulling on clothes, and stepping into Nikki's van would feel so torturous.

Hobbling into Nikki's apartment, she tries to steady herself. "I really appreciate you picking me up and letting me stay here," she tells the filmmaker.

"Sure thing." Nikki smiles.

Shaunette has a piercing headache, and her broken arm won't heal for eleven more weeks, but she is facing bigger problems. What's her future as a DLC? Will she even be alive to worry about it?

As Nikki carries her bag to the apartment's only bedroom, Shaunette protests. "I won't take your bed. I'm happy on the couch."

"Forget that. You need your rest. I'm not the one who wrapped my car around a cement pole."

The idea that she almost became the victim of a maniac races a shiver up her spine. *Mercy.* Who wants her dead? It might be a violent whistleblower, but if their goal is to punish her for making the "I'll kill you" threat to Jentry Rae, why don't they just blow the whistle at high volume and get it over with?

"I'm glad to have you," Nikki says. "I'll try to be a decent hostess."

"Thanks. I'd be terrified at my place alone."

"Same." The filmmaker takes a breath. "Okay, *soo* . . . the kitchen's there. And the bathroom's in the corner. Feel free to shower and borrow my robe."

The last thing Shaunette wants to do is look in a bathroom mirror. She hasn't removed her forehead bandage yet, and she wonders what kind of scar she'll have after the laceration heals. Plastic surgery isn't within her financial realm. Then again, a scar is a small price to pay for her life.

Nikki pats the sofa. "Sit. I'll make us some hot tea."

As Shaunette settles on the cushions, she studies her surroundings. The rental apartment is tastefully decorated in shades of gray and white—sparsely furnished yet inviting. She likes the light wood floors, the built-in bookshelves, and the cozy throw rugs. And she especially likes the lived-in desk area overflowing with video and audio equipment.

The scale of what Nikki is doing hits her. Hopefully, the documentary will turn out to be a quality project. Not a cheap profile. On that note, it's hard to know who she can trust. The higher-ups at the Lonestars organization? Vana? Certainly not spiteful LeAnn McCade.

Nikki hands Shaunette a mug of steaming tea. The aroma soothes her. "*Mmm*. What's this flavor?"

"Hibiscus blossom. *C'est la tea*." Nikki taps her mug against Shaunette's. "Before I forget, how do you know Duke McCade isn't giving Dante Marconi money? It's what you said in the hospital. Or were you delirious on morphine?"

"Dante whispered that to me during a DLC stadium practice. Someone else is paying him under the table."

"Who? Did he say?"

"No."

Exasperation darkens Nikki's face.

"I'm not sure I believe Dante, though," Shaunette adds.

"Why?"

"Duke McCade's wife, LeAnn, visited me at the hospital. She's a piece of work. She is *so* intimidating. First, she barked at me for putting the Lonestars in a bad light with my car accident. Then she told me to stay in my lane."

Nikki sits up. "Stay in your lane? Isn't that the phrase somebody painted on your car?"

"Exactly. Scarier still, Dante sent me a list of stadium visitors from the day Jentry Rae died. LeAnn's name is on it."

"But naturally her name is on it, right?" Nikki stuffs her hair into a messy bun. "She's married to the team owner."

"Yes, except that list indicates visitors who came to the *DLC dressing room* area. And LeAnn has never visited that section before. If she's capable of threats, she and Dante could be involved."

Nikki raises an eyebrow. "This is getting out of control. Okay, um, I'll try and set up a meeting with Duke and his wife. They need to be in the same room for me to tell what's going on."

Shaunette's hands shake around her tea mug. She can't believe the mess she and Nikki are in. Finding the killer is their only way out of it, unless they simply skipped town. But they would be eternally looking over their shoulders if they ran. And what kind of life is that?

The conversation stalls as icy rain patters the windows of the apartment. Soon, ominous thunder joins in. Shuddering, Shaunette glances at the front door to see if it's locked for safety.

Nikki hugs her knees. "I followed Chase Campbell last night—to a strip club. What a scumbag, right? Anyway, here's the most upsetting part. He drives a brand-new black SUV."

"What?" More fright ripples through Shaunette. Again, she regrets not catching the license plate number of the one that reamed her.

"Vince captured Chase on tape talking to a dancer. Watch this. See if you know this girl." Nikki stretches out her phone.

Shaunette studies the clip. "I've never seen her."

"Her name is Rosie. And she might've hooked up with Royce Holt."

"I wouldn't be surprised. Clearly, he's a serial cheater. You know, my lung might ache, but not as much as my heart does for Jentry Rae. She believed everybody was inherently good, so she must've included Royce in that assumption. Maybe she thought he'd leave his wife for her. She was in love, and if he returned the sentiment, she would've expected him to do something honorable about it."

"That makes sense." Nikki rubs her chin. "And since I want to hear about Royce's serial cheating, I messaged him. He is refusing to talk to me."

"Knowing him, he's working out a damage control plan. He's all about his image. He has a temper, too. Jentry Rae told me how he threw a lamp at her apartment wall, and it almost hit her. She excused it away, though, saying he was stressed. She never thought Royce would hurt *her*."

"That's concerning." Nikki frowns.

"I agree. What's more, Royce shares a secret with Chase. I told you that much, remember? Jentry Rae told *me* about it, but she wasn't privy to the details."

"Whatever Royce has on Chase must be leverage. I want to know what it is."

Shaunette listens as rainfall thrashes the windowpanes in harder lashes. Cringing at the wet, whipping noises, she reaches for a throw blanket and cowers beneath it. All at once, a gust of wind blows a window open and whooshes Nikki's Dallas Lonestars' access badge off the desk.

The women look at each other, getting goose bumps.

"I'll tell you something else," Shaunette rushes on while Nikki shuts the window and picks up her badge. "Jentry Rae told me that Royce got involved with a Tennessee Renegades cheerleader last year."

"Really?" Nikki asks. "When he lived in Nashville and was part of that team?"

"Yeah."

"What's the cheerleader's name?"

"I don't know."

"Could it be Emma Hollander?" Nikki gets on her phone and googles 'Emma Hollander' along with 'Tennessee Renegade Cheerleaders.' "Bingo. Look."

Shaunette sees a lithe, pro cheerleader in a bright red uniform. The blonde is grinning from ear to ear while shaking a pair of silver pom-poms. "How do you know the name 'Emma', Nikki?"

"Chase mentioned it last night."

"It's pitiful how Jentry Rae held out hope for Royce. But I'll tell you—when she heard about his fling with this Renegades' cheerleader, she was furious! She assumed she was Royce's only mistress. She tried contacting Emma—I didn't know her name then—to no avail. I told Jentry Rae to drop it. It's one of the things we argued about the day she died."

"Oh my God." Nikki goes still. "Do you think Jentry Rae got pregnant on purpose?"

"M-maybe. *If* it was with Royce's child." Shaunette's heart beats in quick patters. As the storm howls to the same rhythm, it heightens the anxiousness plaguing her. She uses the moment to say a prayer for Jentry Rae's unborn baby.

"Tell me more about Chase," Nikki urges.

"He's blameful of everyone else. He hated that Royce would call me sometimes. To talk about Jentry Rae, but that's all." She slides Nikki a look. Does Nikki believe her? Her association with Royce isn't a positive. It's why she feels caught in a sticky spider web. What Nikki shows her next ensnares her even more. Comments on the DLC's social media page read *Y'all need to protect your own. The cheerleaders' strict rules are making them turn to drink. And guilt drives people into concrete poles.*

"Lord!" Shaunette grimaces. "Now that Lonestars fans want answers, I'm low-hanging fruit. Vana must be beside herself over this bad press. She's probably flipping out over my dancing on a bar top, too. I wish I never made a spectacle of myself that night."

Nikki's phone rings. Worry coats her face as she explains that her brother is calling. She excuses herself.

Even though she moves into the hallway, Shaunette can hear fragments of the phone conversation. "Pop is taking more meds, Nikki." And "I loaned him money to keep the water on, but the energy company has sent two shut-off notices." And "Come home, sis. I have my own family to take care of."

"Give me a few more weeks, Dave. Please," Nikki entreats. As soon as she hangs up, she returns to Shaunette. "Sorry about that."

"No need to apologize. Your situation must be stressful."

"Extremely. It's hard watching a parent suffer. Um, how's your mom?"

"Fading fast."

"I'm so sorry."

"Thanks." Shaunette's emotions tug at her. Then she yawns. "I think I'll lie down now. I'm exhausted."

As Nikki's phone rings again, her eyes go wide when she looks at the caller ID. Tensing up, she hesitates to answer the call.

Shaunette shuts the bedroom door with a firm *click*, wishing desperately that she could shut out the entire world, too.

CHAPTER THIRTY-SEVEN

THE FILMMAKER

~ *NOVEMBER 1* ~

The air crackles like an electrical current while Nikki's phone rings with Royce's call. In her mind, the about-to-happen conversation feels like a pressure valve being tightened. The quarterback went to the police about her, for Christ's sake. How defensive will he be right now?

Taking a breath, she turns on a recording device before tapping the call to speaker mode. "Hey, Royce."

"Why did you encourage me to drink cocktails at Bogart's, Keegan?" he snarls.

"I—"

"A waitress from there posted about how I guzzled scotch and sodas at a table with a mystery lady. The Lonestars hit me with a ginormous fine. Piper is pissed at me, too. Are you going to include *this* in your sports documentary?"

"Ordering booze was your own choice. And I can't control what people post. But forget the documentary for a moment. Here's what you don't get. If you're worried about image control, I'm willing to feature you on a limited crime series I'm creating. Don't worry. I have permission to film it," Nikki lies.

"You're making a crime show? But you're a phony. Your work will be discredited."

"The Lonestars believe in me so far. And my portfolio proves my talent."

He hesitates. "Go on."

"Each episode will feature a new character in the murder of Jentry Rae Randall. *If* you come clean about your affair with her, I'll dedicate an entire episode to you. But if you don't agree, remember what I wrote in my text. About your revolving door of women."

Royce makes a fuming noise. "You hippy-dippy Hollywood flunkie! Of all the backhanded, shitty things—"

"Slow down and have some class, Holt. Or isn't that part of your five-million-dollar league contract?" She starts to pace. The guy pushes her buttons like few people do. He also makes her stoop low, which she despises. "I know you tattletaled to the investigators about me, Royce, but we'll discuss that in a minute. For now, let's say we're even. Here's the thing: a woman is dead, and another Dallas Lonestars Cheerleader is in danger. Both mean something to you. Am I right?"

"Yes," he grunts.

She smiles. This is better than him admitting to the affairs.

"But how can I trust you, Keegan? You might be recording me now."

She shakes her head as she holds her phone. "Do you think I want the cops knocking on my door again? Give me *something*, Royce. I want to ensure that no victim is ever forgotten, so my motives are pure. Plus, you owe me for siccing those detectives on me."

He mumbles profanities under his breath. "I'm sorry about that, but you did jeopardize my career."

"Let's start fresh. Tell me why you're such a womanizer. I mean, Jentry Rae? Rosie? Emma Hollander?"

"Maybe I'll explain if you tell me why you embellished your résumé."

She pauses. "I come from nothing, okay? And since women today have to be twice as good as men to get a job and keep that job, I made stuff up early on. Simple as that."

"Understandable, I guess."

"Enough about me," she says. "Tell me why you can't be faithful."

"Short answer? My dad. His cheating sprees were my role model."

"That's too bad. But if I'm being honest, I'm even more curious about the secret you share with Chase Campbell. I know because I did some digging."

Royce's rapid breathing slows. Maybe he is contemplating being cooperative. "Ah, I'm not sure I should say."

"Everybody has a story to tell and secret to share. Don't you want to be the one controlling the narrative?"

"All right, yes . . . fuck it. I need to get this off my chest, so here it is once and for all. Chase accidentally clipped a kid while he and I were riding an ATV in the woods behind my family's house in Massachusetts. The eleven-year-old boy came out of nowhere. He was walking his bike along a remote trail, and it's Chase's fault he died."

"What happened exactly?"

"We were stupid enough to get stoned and romp on a four-wheeler. I was riding on the ATV with Chase . . . on the seat behind. We sped along the path like clueless idiots." Royce pauses. "If I could do it over, I'd never take that joyride. Chase regrets it, too."

"Did he ever own up to it?"

"No. But he thinks about that poor kid every day. So do I. Except, there was nothing we could've done for him, so I covered things up."

Revulsion gurgles Nikki's stomach. "What? You fled the scene?"

"Chase was sixteen and I was fourteen. We were kids, ourselves. We didn't have a choice."

"Yes, you did. You could've stayed in the woods and admitted to the accident. Or gone to the police with a confession."

"And ruined both of our lives?" Royce asks defensively. "Besides, Chase is like my brother. He didn't want to confess, so I supported him."

"Your father had the money to hire the best attorney," she points out.

"I couldn't tell my dad I'd fucked up. Anyway, it's too late for speculation. I won't spill my guts about the accident on camera, Keegan, but I will say this. Chase was jealous of the way Jentry Rae pined after me. He had a thing for her. Ryder Hutchinson was in love with her, too."

Nikki's mouth quirks. *After my encounter with Ryder in the parking lot, I tend to agree.*

"You need to check out those guys." Royce hangs up abruptly.

She isn't sure she believed anything the nervy quarterback said. As the conversation weighs her down, she wonders who else in this drama is lying.

She grabs her vape pen and a beer to calm herself. Then she scrolls mindlessly through her phone. A social media reel shows pregnant Piper coming out of an ob-gyn appointment, bragging about her husband. The famous sports wife sends well-wishes to Shaunette next.

Nikki draws Shaunette's attention to the reel as soon as the cheerleader rouses from her nap. Anger blooms on Shaunette's face.

"Piper claims she has never met me. But she has." Shaunette clasps her hands together tightly.

"When and where?"

"The day Jentry Rae and I were at a hair salon called The Beauty Corral. We went there early in the Lonestars' season— for DLC makeovers. We bumped into Piper who showed up with my squad mate, Ashleigh. I guess they're friends, but still, I doubt the encounter was a coincidence. I'm not sure who set the run-in up, but Ashleigh introduced Piper to me and Jentry Rae. And the livid, kill-shot look Piper gave Jentry Rae is something I'll never forget."

CHAPTER THIRTY-EIGHT

THE DALLAS LONESTARS CHEERLEADER

~ *NOVEMBER 4* ~

Today, Shaunette has been summoned to Vana Lockwood's office. Since the squad director has the power to either retract or maintain her Dallas Lonestars Cheerleaders' status, the thought has her on a razor-sharp edge.

Shaunette is preparing for the meeting at Nikki's apartment. No doubt she'll need to explain to Vana about the bottle of booze found in her car, the rat left in her locker, and the threat painted on her Honda.

Will Vana believe that every act was done out of sabotage?

To either frame Shaunette or scare her?

Everything was. *Mostly.*

She is being unfairly singled out as the black sheep of the DLC, and she can't believe it. She would never damage the organization on purpose. Which confirms that people don't know crap about anything. The good thing is Nikki will be accompanying her to The Depot this morning. Having her as a wing woman will be helpful. Yet, as Shaunette drinks a different flavor of herbal tea, her spirits fray even more.

"Thanks again for offering to come with me," she tells Nikki as they gather their bags.

"Your car was crunched, so I *have* to take you," the filmmaker quips. She stops to fill Beau Dog's food bowl. Then she pats the animal on the head.

"I was up all night thinking. When you told me about your phone call with Royce, it made me believe he has some remorse about stringing Jentry Rae along."

"Really? I didn't get that at all." Nikki shakes her head. "But I've been thinking about that phone call, too. Royce mentioned how Ryder Hutchinson had a thing for Jentry Rae. We have to remember that Ryder's initials are the same as Royce's: R.H. What do you know about him?"

"Nothing." Shaunette shrugs. The motion roils pain through her. "Jentry Rae was like the sun, and people orbited around her. She was sweet too, so lots of guys were infatuated with her."

"Royce didn't say Ryder was *infatuated* with Jentry Rae. He said Ryder was *in love* with her. Let me see something." Sitting down at the computer, Nikki screen-surfs for an archived video. "Here it is."

Shaunette pulls up a chair and peers at the screen, too. Jentry Rae is shown on a clip with three other Lonestars Cheerleaders. The women are at a publicity event for the Dallas Museum of Art, and on a cloudy day Ryder Hutchinson gets out of a limo then struts up the museum steps like a rock star. Fans shout, vie for a closer look, and snap pictures of him. Meanwhile, Jentry Rae, who's in her DLC uniform, drops a pom-pom. As Ryder picks it up and hands it to her, he whispers something in her ear. She giggles like there's no tomorrow.

Before the aging quarterback enters the museum, he turns around and gives her an enamored look.

Nikki points at the screen. "Did you see that? Maybe I can link Ryder to Jentry Rae by his phone records."

Shaunette nods at the possibility.

Nikki google-speaks a question on her phone. "How-long-has-Ryder-Hutchinson-been-married? Okay. He's been with his wife for fifteen years. She is a statuesque brunette who writes children's books. They have three kids with names that begin with K. What's with that trend? Anyway, the guy has a lot to give up."

Antsy, Shaunette stands. "We should go." *What can't Nikki dig up? Even if the info isn't on Google?*

As they exit the apartment building, Shaunette hears Nikki's phone chime. When Nikki looks at the screen, her face loses color. "What the ever-loving fuck! I don't believe it. Oh my God! Shaunette, look at this video somebody filmed of me."

Shaunette stops cold. The eerie recording shows Nikki asleep on the sofa while ambient light from an intruder's phone floods her apartment and creates odd shadows. The intruder gets near enough to film her close-up. Nothing can be heard but her soft, rhythmic breathing. The scene resembles something out of a *Paranormal Activity* movie.

Shaunette gasps. She must have been unaware and snuggled in bed at the time. "That's the most terrifying I've ever seen! Someone broke into your place? How'd they get in? Or get hold of your phone number?"

"I have no clue." Nikki clicks her phone screen to dark with a trembling finger. The second she does, she gets a text. She looks at it, wide-eyed. "Jesus, the same lunatic who just sent me that video and all the other anonymous texts wrote, 'Mind your own business. Or I won't leave you alone next time.'"

"What the hell is happening to us?" Shaunette asks, completely freaked. "You have to go to the police."

Nikki doesn't respond because she begins to sob. Crying seems to be a big deal for her, which makes Shaunette swim with more fright. The stakes keep getting higher and higher, and their lives are more and more at risk. It feels like too much. This twisty cat-and-mouse game they're ensnared in is hurtling them through a mind-bending labyrinth, so is there light at the end of the tunnel? Or will they disappear into the darkness for good?

While they hurry to the van parked outside, Shaunette barely notices that the weather is clearer today. It's a glorious fall morning—splendid by Dallas standards—but too bad she and Nikki are about to face a whirling storm at Vana's office.

Nikki starts the van. "I can take care of myself, don't worry," she says in a quavering, unconvincing voice.

"You don't have to put on a brave face for me."

As Nikki cries like a floodgate released, Shaunette consoles her again. What they're going through is unbelievable. And only they can commiserate about it.

"Okay, shit. I'm getting it together." Nikki wipes her eyes. "Let's talk about what you'll say to Vana. Do you still want to be a DLC?"

"Yes."

"Keep it simple then. Tell her you screwed up. You're human. The police haven't publicly cleared you of drunk driving yet, so if you deny having a bottle of booze in your car, she might not believe you. Instead, reference how upset you are about Jentry Rae's death. Say that the Lonestars are on Comeback Road, as are you. Fortunately, your arm will be healed for the play-offs in January—if Vana is nice enough to keep you on the squad until then."

"You think that'll work?"

"Absolutely. You'll be deemed the modern face of the Dallas Lonestars Cheerleaders. Fallible. Relatable. Forgivable. It's what the squad needs."

Shaunette nods. "I should hire you as my PR agent."

Once they enter Vana's office at The Depot, they see Vana seated behind an enormous desk wearing a glittery DLC warm-up jacket. A mass of cheerleading paraphernalia surrounds her—posters, photos, and calendars—and the array lends her extra authority.

As Vana peers at Shaunette over a pair of blue bifocals, her disappointment is as subtle as a chainsaw. "You're late," Vana says.

Shaunette apologizes. She sits in a chair close to the desk while Nikki remains standing at the back of the office.

Chin up, Vana leans back in her swivel chair. More tension fills the air. The DLC director seems to be analyzing and contrasting the two different versions of Shaunette: the polished, perfect Dallas Lonestars Cheerleader versus how she appears today. In Shaunette's defense, wielding a curling iron and applying makeup are things best done with two hands.

Her most obvious change?

The hideous, stitched scar across her forehead. A doctor has instructed her to let the wound air out, uncovered.

Vana begins to rant. "I swear to the Great Almighty, Shaunette! You have disgraced this squad something terrible. What were you thinking? A half-empty container of bourbon was found in your car? I presume you were driving plastered. Or did you intend to self-harm? I think you keep the cork in too tight. Explain."

"I'm so sorry, ma'am." She cradles her broken arm. "Someone was tailing me. I tried to get away from them. And I regret having the bottle—"

"Regret? No. Regret is when you cut your bangs too short. Or when you order a magical face cream off Amazon that makes your skin break out. You have stomped on DLC rules left and right. Like I told you at the hospital, I received a video of you dancing drunk at a bar. You refrained from doing an official routine, but all of this is beyond outrageous. Little girls everywhere want to be perfect, like you, and this is the garbage you give them?"

"With all due respect, Ms. Lockwood"—Nikki steps forward—"nobody's perfect. And you're missing the point. The police will release Shaunette's clean tox screen tomorrow. She wasn't driving under the influence, but sure, people are going to think what they want about her having that bottle of booze.

The smart thing for you to do is play up her humanistic side. It'll show that the Dallas Lonestars Cheerleaders aren't fixated on flawlessness. Don't you see? Social media sets unrealistic expectations for girls at a young age. The DLC organization is part of that. But you can change the dynamic by keeping Shaunette on the squad."

Go, Nikki, Shaunette thinks. At least somebody is standing up for her. She just wishes her mama shared the same philosophy. Will Vana agree?

"I'm doing damage control, Miss Keegan." Vana snorts. "Jentry Rae Randall was pregnant. The world's gonna know about it soon. We have strict rules at this franchise for a reason." She pauses. "But what really miffs me is that you have been sniffing around the murder investigation like a bloodhound. For what reason?"

Nikki pushes the sleeves of her army jacket up assertively. "It's part of the sports documentary I'm directing. Remember, the Lonestars are restoring their image. And Jentry Rae's death is a new obstacle on that journey, so it needs to be included."

"Speaking of restoring images, I aim to redeem myself, too," Shaunette chimes in. "In addition, I have a stalker, Miss Vana. He ran me into that pylon. And have you seen the message painted on my car?"

"Yes, dear. But the Dallas Lonestars Cheerleaders have had stalkers in the past . . . loonies who just want a closer look. Go to the police and file a report."

"That's your advice?" Nikki frowns.

Vana waits a beat. "You're incorrigible, Miss Keegan. In fact, if we're talking a vengeful stalker, maybe you ticked someone off with an interview you did."

Nikki scowls deeper.

Shaunette shifts uncomfortably in her seat because danger is plaguing everybody who knew Jentry Rae. Can't Vana see it?

The riled-up DLC director gets up and walks back and forth behind her desk. She locks eyes with Shaunette. "Your mother, Kaylene Simmons—do you know the whole story about her time as a DL Cheerleader?"

"I know she loved being one, ma'am. I understand she was a top dancer, too." *Mama was selected as the Point and Show Troupe Leader . . . amazing accomplishments. So, don't you dare speak ill of her!*

"Your mother was a magnificent performer. But she broke the rules and lost everything by dating a Lonestars' tight end."

Shock barrels through Shaunette. *That can't be*. Mega-tons of disbelief whack her on the head as her world flips upside down. "Excuse me? That's not what my mama said. She told me somebody other than her got kicked off the squad for fraternizing with a player."

"She lied to you, dear. She was dismissed and disgraced. For that reason, I reckon your mother is living under a cloud of regret. It wasn't her finest moment."

"My mama has terminal breast cancer, ma'am."

That stops Vana cold. Her bottom lip shakes. "I—I'm sorry. What a shame. She was such a DLC star back then. If I could change one thing about that year, it's how we went from friends to enemies."

Shaunette sits up straighter. *Like me and Jentry Rae.*

"I wasn't nice to your mother when the scandal happened." Vana tears up and reaches for a tissue. "I didn't stand by her side. Maybe I've always been too fixated on maintaining rules . . ."

Nikki sits down in an empty chair. "All of this is fascinating, Ms. Lockwood. Very touching. And if you give Shaunette a second chance, it'll make for fantastic viewing for the documentary. You'll be hailed as a sympathetic hero."

"I don't care about that, Miss Keegan. But Lord knows, I need to do *something* to calm the critics. All right, Shaunette. I'll allow you to reaudition next season. *If* your arm is healed by then. And *if* you lay off the sauce. Heck, maybe you could be the Point."

"Thank you, ma'am! I promise to clean up my act."

"Good. My advice is use pancake makeup on what will definitely be a scar. Keep in shape, too." The director pauses. "This is my way of apologizing to your mama. Please relay that to her."

"Will do. Thank you again," Shaunette replies. Her mother will be ecstatic. However, on her way out, she wonders why her mother lied about something so important. It's obvious that "mom" has been living vicariously through "daughter." Kaylene Simmons has been boldly using Shaunette to redeem her mistakes and restore her reputation amongst the cheerleaders.

That degree of selfishness is a slap to Shaunette's face. Forget building a sacred mother-daughter bond. *Mama doesn't really care about me or my dreams.*

Then a scary thought envelops her. Being the Point will put her front and center—a potentially high-risk position. For the first time ever, she isn't sure that taking Jentry Rae's place is a desirable move.

MISSING ENTRY OF JENTRY RAE'S DIARY

SEPTEMBER 1—SIX WEEKS BEFORE HER MURDER

After I met He Who Shall Not Be Named at a civic event, he pursued me like somebody chases cool shade in the summertime. We have been seeing each other for two weeks, and I'm so happy! But still. It isn't your typical "dating" scenario. He is a Lonestars' player, so we can't go out together in public. Also, he's married.

We slept together last night—and I'm not sorry! It's against Lonestars' rules, but our lovemaking felt right, not wrong. I describe it as tender and sweet and passionate. I actually came close to drowning in his satiny touch. God, I think I love him. He told me I'm different than his wife. Good-hearted. Not a nag. A better listener. So, if a girl can fall for a man faster than a shooting star rockets across the prairie, that's what I've done.

He spent the night at my place, and when I looked into his eyes, I saw my future. Huge obstacles stand in our way, though. I'm mainly scared of being kicked off the DLC squad.

I mentioned it to him, but he shrugged casually. Said players and cheerleaders date all the time without consequences. I'm not sure about that.

Guilt is eating away at me. If our against-the-rules relationship is found out, he will just get a rap on the knuckles while I'll be thrown off the squad . . . the ultimate double standard!

I'm going to talk to Shaunette about my dilemma, but I hope she won't snitch on me. Her mom dated a Lonestars' tight end during her time as a DLC. Shaunette never admitted as much, but our choreographer Tammie told me the story. (Tammie knows everything about the Dallas Lonestars Cheerleaders.) Shaunette's mom aimed to marry into glamour and money, and tragically, when that didn't work out, she married a small-town drunk who left her.

I am not a gold digger! I love my mystery guy! Things with him are happening quickly—and Daddy says that when you know, you know.

Well, shit heels. I don't KNOW what to do next. I'm starting to have a sinking feeling. Threats are being made . . .

CHAPTER THIRTY-NINE

THE FILMMAKER

~ *NOVEMBER 4* ~

Nikki drives Shaunette back to the apartment. On the way, she wonders how Vana's decision to stir up protocol will be received by the squad members. The Dallas Lonestars Cheerleaders have adhered to the same ancient rules for decades.

When Nikki stops the van in front of her building, she looks over at Shaunette. "Are you okay?"

"Uh, no. My mama doesn't prioritize me. And after learning why she's been pushing me to be a DLC star, I don't know if I want to be a cheerleader anymore. I was doing this all for her."

"I get that. But it's nice to have the option. Right?"

Shaunette shrugs gloomily and slouches.

"Go inside and take a nap," Nikki suggests. "That's enough excitement, post-car crash."

"Thanks again . . . for being so convincing in Vana's office. No one has ever advocated for me like that."

"You're welcome. But what I said was true. Nobody should be expected to be perfect."

"Maybe you can change my mother's mind about that."

"Me? No. Have a heart-to-heart with your mom and convince her yourself." Nikki pauses. "I mean it, Shaunette. Call her now, if you want. While you're feeling inspired."

"Should I?" Inhaling for courage, she borrows Nikki's phone and places a call on speaker mode. "Fair warning. You'll hear how hard-headed my mother is."

Kaylene Simmons answers with a sharp, "Who's this?"

"It's me. Shaunette. I'm borrowing a phone, Mama. How are you feeling?"

"I'm hanging in there, darlin'. Lost more hair this week, though. I look a fright. Faded looks are the worst. Beauty lies in the eyes of the be-have-er."

Shaunette exhales. "I met with Vana today, and guess what? I argued my case to stay on the squad. She's letting me reaudition next season. Isn't that great? But, um, Vana also told me something shocking. She said *you* broke rules when you were a DLC. *You* dated a Lonestars' player and were disgraced."

Kaylene Simmons clucks her tongue. "Hogwash! That woman is venomous! She was my worst enemy. I showed her up with my dancin' skills and took the spotlight away from her. Don't trust Vana. She might be asking you back so she can punish you some more on my behalf. How do you know she isn't behind running you off the road?"

"She wouldn't do that," Shaunette says stiffly. "All right, I'll check on you later. I have to go. Bye."

Nikki shakes her head as the call ends. "I didn't know about your mom's hatred for Vana."

"I didn't, either. But I think my mother is twisting things. I mean, why would Vana make me pay for being a screw-up DLC? It isn't in her best interest."

Nikki notices Shaunette's expression change just then. In fact, the cheerleader looks like she wants to share something, but the moment disappears. Maybe she'll open up later.

"Okay," Nikki says, "I'm off to meet Vince at a coffee shop. He invited me to his place, but I can't imagine what his apartment looks and smells like. I plan to ask him about getting in contact with Emma Hollander. And he's going to share some things he found out."

Shaunette starts to get out of the van when she asks to use Nikki's computer. She wants to check her emails. Who knows when the cops will return her phone.

Nikki gives permission before she drives off with a wave. Soon, she parks in front of a trendy café on Canton Street. As she enters the coffee shop, a mellow Alanis Morissette song drones while glassy-eyed hipsters drink thick-as-tank-fuel espressos.

"Hey," Vince greets. He looks jazzed on caffeine, too.

"Quirky café," she says as she sets her hot tea down and takes a seat.

"I walk here from my apartment all the time. Um, you look pale, Nik."

"Here's why." She shows him the creepy video somebody took of her sleeping.

"What the hell? You should contact the police."

"You mean, ask Mutt and Jeff for protection? Emerson and La Rosa will probably accuse me of fabricating the break-in. They don't trust me."

"Then get a gun," Vince suggests. "This is Texas. Everybody has one."

"I'll think about it." She can always ask Sonny for Jentry Rae's pink pistol.

Vince tugs on his worn Radiohead T-shirt. "Let's take your mind off being stalker-filmed. How did Shaunette's meeting go with Vana Lockwood?"

"Great. Technically, she can reaudition for the Dallas Lonestars Cheerleaders next season."

"Awesome."

She pauses. "Vince, remember how Chase Campbell suggested we look into Ryder Hutchinson? I watched an archived video of him flirting heavily with Jentry Rae at an art museum."

"Wow. Isn't he married?"

"Yeah, but that's not stopping anyone around here. Can you have your web expert delve into Ryder's phone records? For any matches to Jentry Rae's number? I want to see how much he was contacting her. Or following her."

"Sure thing." He clears his throat. "All right. Are you ready for this? Owen hacked into Jentry Rae's Venmo account. She received three payments of five thousand dollars from someone registered as MBQ99. Owen is working on that particular identity. Also, Owen dug into Dante Marconi's finances and learned that the security guard makes just over minimum wage. So, when a pair of payments for $25,000 showed up in his account, they were flagged."

"Who paid Dante those amounts?"

"Brace yourself." Vince leans forward. "The payments came from Piper Dupree."

Surprise steamrolls Nikki. "Royce Holt's wife?"

"Shocking, huh?"

"This is huge!"

"Totally."

"What did Piper pay Dante to do?" she asks.

"No idea, Nik. But I bet you can find out."

She'll have another talk with the stadium guard. "Did Owen track down Emma Hollander's phone number?"

"Yep—he did a reverse phone lookup. I'm texting it to you right now. She lives in Nashville proper."

"Thanks. Got it."

Vince crosses his arms. "You're calling her this second? I hate to be Johnny Raincloud, but nobody answers calls from people they don't know."

"I'll try."

The call rings and rings. Vince predicted correctly; Emma doesn't answer.

Not giving up, Nikki texts the Tennessee Renegades cheerleader the following message: **My name is Nikki Keegan. I'm a filmmaker, and I need to speak to you about Royce Holt. Our conversation will be confidential because I have your best interest in mind. You probably know already, but Dallas Lonestars Cheerleaders are getting hurt.**

She sends the text three times.

Fifteen minutes later, Emma Hollander calls. "Is this Nikki Keegan?"

"Yes. Thanks for getting in contact, Emma." Adrenaline rushing, Nikki pictures the woman from the photo she saw. She's the spitting image of Jentry Rae Randall: long blonde hair, twinkly blue eyes, pert nose, and an oval face. Probably the only thing missing at the moment is Jentry Rae's signature smile; Emma sounds petrified. "Is it okay if I ask you some questions?"

"We're speaking off the record, right?"

"A hundred percent."

"Good. I didn't want to get involved, but things are getting out of hand."

The idea piques Nikki's interest. "I appreciate your sticking your neck out. Ah, what can you tell me about Royce Holt when he was part of the Tennessee Renegades?"

"You don't understand. I'm trapped. I can't say anything about Royce. I signed an iron-clad NDA at the behest of his family."

"What? Why did the Holts arrange that?"

"Hence the definition of a non-disclosure agreement. I can't say a word."

"But somebody killed Jentry Rae, Emma. It's all over the news. And another Dallas Lonestars Cheerleader almost died. Do you think Royce Holt is involved?"

"He isn't a murderer. That's all I'll say."

Nikki plugs one ear to hear better inside the clattering coffee shop. "Before you go, what do you know about his wife Piper?"

The blonde beauty goes silent for several seconds. "Piper's a nutjob. She thinks she owns Royce. I mean, she simultaneously treats him as her property and her meal ticket. He hates that about her. I would watch out for her if I were you. Piper Dupree is a possessive, deranged bitch. Look into her past." *Click*.

CHAPTER FORTY

THE DALLAS LONESTARS CHEERLEADER

~ NOVEMBER 4 ~

Shaunette is sitting at Nikki's computer, resisting the urge to reach for a bottle of whiskey on a nearby shelf. Rolling her shoulders back, she navigates into her emails—a difficult action with one hand. Seconds later, stacks of bills and annoying junk mail pop up. To her disappointment, none of the emails shout "Open me!"

Jesus Christmas.

Where is the outpouring of concern for her? Her boss at the gym hasn't reached out. Nor have her fellow cheerleaders. The scenario is making her realize how much her competitive-ness rubs people the wrong way. Why did her mother teach her to view people as rivals? And how come Mama taught her to always claw her way to the top?

Beau Dog, who seems to sense Shaunette's dismay, comes over for a cuddle. She coos at him while scratching behind his ears. Bulldogs never return smiles the way other dogs do, but she swears she sees warmth in his droopy stare.

Exhaling, she clicks out of her emails and sits back. Nikki's screen saver stares at her—a black-and-white photo of what presumably is Nikki as a little girl. She's perched on a woman's lap, and the kind-looking lady with fine features and short brown hair is giving her a hug.

If the woman happens to be Nikki's mom, Nikki must miss her. Maybe her mother encouraged her in all areas instead of flogging her with "success" pressure.

Beau Dog waddles away as Shaunette sets her mouth in a thin line. She can't wait until Jentry Rae's killer is caught. When the truth comes out, it'll end her nightmare. Only then can she start on a fresh path. Her whole life needs to be rectified. If this experience has taught her anything, it's that.

Regarding harsh realities, something tells her to reread Dante Marconi's email. Does *he* always tell the truth? He seemed lambasted with nerves when he spoke to her inside the stadium tunnel. Obviously, he went out on a limb to send her the stadium visitor list from the day Jentry Rae was murdered. And on the list, Shaunette had discovered LeAnn McCade's name. However, she didn't scour the rest of the visitors that day.

Was somebody else inside the Dallas Lonestars Cheerleaders' dressing area on the afternoon of the homicide?

Holding her breath, Shaunette locates Dante's email link. As it blinks at her like a flashing arrow, her nerves go on edge. Fingers trembling, she opens the attachment and spots Piper Dupree's name buried low on the list.

Her pulse pings at breakneck speed. *What in the world?*

Why was Royce's wife allowed access to the DLC wing that day? And why didn't anybody notice her?

Alarmed, Shaunette is about to stand up and call Nikki when the landline rings. Her instincts tell her not to answer the call. Instead, she listens to an incoming message.

Vana Lockwood's clipped voice comes on the line. "We need to talk, Miss Keegan. I knew you were posing questions to Lonestars' employees about Jentry Rae Randall's murder, but now you're askin' my DL Cheerleaders about Jentry Rae's enemies? That's crossing the line. I would like to iron out stricter guidelines for you as you film your documentary. I was just notified that you have a history of lying—about your credentials, namely. I'm debating whether to tell Duke McCade about it. Call and schedule a sit-down with me very soon. Thank you."

Shaunette nearly falls out of her seat. Did Nikki lie to her? Aren't they friends? Close enough acquaintances to confide in each other, anyway?

Maybe not. It seems that Nikki is full of surprises. And secrets.

Who is Shaunette *really* working closely with?

CHAPTER FORTY-ONE

THE FILMMAKER

~ NOVEMBER 8 ~

It has taken a few days, but Nikki has finally been approved for an audience with Duke and LeAnn McCade. She's supposed to meet them at their penthouse tonight—under the pretense that she'll dedicate the sports documentary to them.

At eight p.m., she and Vince arrive at Quadrangle Fountains—a posh, gated condominium complex in downtown Dallas. Apparently, the place was designed and built by McCade Master Construction . . . one of the tycoon's many side businesses.

As Nikki steps in a glass elevator, she worries about the phone message she received from Vana. She doesn't plan to call the DLC director back, however. Not unless she finds herself in hot water with Duke McCade this evening.

The elevator shoots upward like something out of a Willy Wonka movie. Gripping the handrail, Nikki realizes that, of course, the prestigious, amenity-rich complex is fit for a king and queen. To that end, the McCades' penthouse has spectacular, three-hundred-sixty-degree views.

Fort Worth is to the west.

Plano is to the north.

And Waxahachie is to the south.

Impressive.

It's obvious that the McCades have invited Nikki and Vince to their place at night because the cityscape will provide a showstopping interview backdrop.

"I bet they're all about per-faux-mances," Vince says as he fumbles with his bulky camera equipment.

Nikki stays silent. The soaring view is giving her vertigo.

"Owen couldn't find anything that links Ryder Hutchinson to Jentry Rae. Sorry, Nik. But maybe Jentry Rae had a disposable phone. She could've made tons of calls from it to another throwaway phone. You think?"

She nods. "Did Owen say anything else?"

"You won't believe what he found out about Piper Dupree," Vince replies. "I'll tell you later. But cripes! I can't believe I'm lugging around this massive tripod."

"The idea is we're rolling out the red carpet for a 'rare' interview."

"Right. Anything for Big D royalty."

The elevator stops. Once they step out, Nikki rings the bell, and a housekeeper opens the door. Taking a breath, Nikki enters an opulent, Manhattan-style loft that smells like a fancy hotel. Flickering candles glow and shimmer against shiny finishes while a large white sectional anchors a spacious main room. What she likes best is the open sliding door that's welcoming in a cool breeze from the veranda. Dallas's nightlife twinkles and whirrs below.

Duke McCade appears. He's dressed in a pair of dark slacks, and his black shoes are polished to a high shine. With his flashy dress shirt unbuttoned a little too low, he looks ready for an evening out rather than an evening in.

LeAnn McCade materializes next in a cloud of perfume. Her crimson dress hugs her curves and the color of it accentuates her fire-engine-red lipstick. As she strides forward, her heels click-clack on the marble floor. "This is so exciting!" she preens.

The four of them shake hands.

"Miss Keegan," LeAnn crows, "I understand your first documentary might be nominated for an Oscar."

"Oh, no. That's not the buzz, ma'am. But you're kind to say it."

"You do know about flattering camera angles, correct?"

"Ah, that project was about an underprivileged woman who was stabbed in the heartlands."

The former beauty queen goes quiet.

"Where should I set up?" Vince asks.

LeAnn stiffly escorts him to the outdoor veranda.

Meanwhile, Duke moves to a fully stocked bar cart. "Care for a bourbon, Miss Keegan?"

"I'm a beer girl myself. And call me Nikki."

"Sorry. Fresh out of beer. Kentucky Bulleit? It's the top of the line."

She nods, and he hands her a glass. Then he clinks his drink with hers.

Glad that he hasn't thrown her out yet, Nikki notices a large animal cage in the corner. Supposedly, Duke rescued a rare lizard from the Galapagos Islands. She meanders over to check it out and sees that the custom-made pet enclosure does indeed contain a scaly, endangered iguana. "What have you named it?" she asks.

"He's Mr. Lizard for now. People say he's so ugly that he's endearin', but my wife says he is just hideous. Beauty lies in the eye of the beholder, don't you agree?"

"Sometimes."

"That's *my* go-to dictum, Nikki. I prefer rare, unattainable things—one-of-a-kind standouts. Few people have the best, and I'm lucky that way."

She sips from the crystal glass to hide her unease. Jentry Rae Randall was the best cheerleader the Dallas Lonestars ever had. She was pure in her beauty and talent . . . the epitome of a standout. Did Duke want to possess her?

"Hungry, fella?" the magnate asks the exotic pet.

After the lizard blinks, Duke drops a box of grasshoppers into the climate-controlled cage. The iguana thumps its tail and then sneezes. "He's expelling excess sodium. That part about iguanas isn't great."

Nikki bristles.

"Drink up, young lady. There is more high-end liquor where that came from. My chef set out sliders for you, too. Your cameraman looks like he could use a good burger." Duke glances at one of four TV screens in the background. The New England Heralders are playing the Miami Manta Rays. "Forgive me for glancing at the TV. I'm always scoping out the competition. It's vital when you run a multibillion-dollar sports franchise."

"That makes sense, sir." She pauses. "Royce Holt's dad played for the Heralders, right?"

"Correct. And on a more serious sports note, please tell me you are portraying my team in the best light." He tilts his head persuasively.

"Of course I am."

Maintaining his smile, Duke comes closer. "You scratch my back, I scratch yours. *Capisce?* I will recommend you to other teams in the FFL if I'm happy with your finished project, Nikki."

"Thank you," she says for a lack of a better response. But really, she's had enough of pro football.

"If I find out you're digging into restricted areas, I won't be happy about it. You know what you're paid to do." He drops his smile as he waves his cocktail glass.

"Message received."

"Right. Glad we cleared that up."

She is tempted to throw the bourbon in Duke's face but at least he didn't take her off the documentary. Also, making him mad tonight will cut short the possibility of obtaining any information about Jentry Rae.

"We're ready!" Vince calls out.

As Nikki exits the penthouse with Duke, she notices a framed photo hanging on a wall. Surprisingly, it shows LeAnn McCade hugging Jentry Rae. Both women are wearing broad grins and are sitting on the condo's sectional. *Hmm.* What was Jentry Rae doing here at the penthouse, hobnobbing with the football team's queen? Usually, the Dallas Lonestars Cheerleaders are kept away from everybody else inside the organization.

LeAnn is seated on the patio, perched in front of the sparkling landscape on a plexiglass chair. As she pats an empty chair for her husband, she gloats again. Getting attention has her in her element.

"Peachum, you look ravishing," Duke says as he sits.

"Thank you." They share a light kiss.

Steadying herself, Nikki starts the Q & A. She learns that, naturally, the couple met at a beauty pageant. The year Duke purchased the Miss Teenage Texas franchise, LeAnn happened to be an honorary judge. Since then, LeAnn has started and failed several businesses of her own, including a skincare line and a jewelry line. The McCades never had children because LeAnn can't conceive. She expresses genuine sadness about that.

During the interview, Nikki is blown away by how much the beauty queen is an older version of Jentry Rae. Same vivid blue eyes. Same gleaming blonde hair. And same Arctic-white teeth. Only, Jentry Rae's sense of innocence is missing.

Nikki clears her throat. "Mr. and Mrs. McCade, can you tell me what you liked about each other when you first met?"

Duke answers first. "Look at her. She's a knockout."

LeAnn blinks, seemingly unimpressed. "What else?"

"Uh, my wife has always been charitable, and she thinks of the bigger picture."

LeAnn seems satisfied with his answer. "And I like the way Duke takes charge and protects me."

"That's sweet," Nikki says. "All right. If I may, I would like to switch gears to something more serious. The murder of a

Dallas Lonestars Cheerleader on October 13 has sent shock-waves through the world. It must be spiraling the football franchise into a tailspin. How worried are you about it, Mrs. McCade?"

Clenching her hands together, the middle-aged woman goes a little green. She pulls on her husband's sleeve. "Do we have to talk about this, honey?"

"It's part of what's going on, Peachum. We can't hide under a rock."

Anger roils through Nikki. These people seem to be content living clueless in an ivory tower. Well, tonight they're going to get some major pushback. "If you prefer to talk about something else," she says, "your youthful glow is remarkable, Mrs. McCade. In fact, you and the late cheerleader Jentry Rae could be sisters. Can you give a girl some beauty tips?"

LeAnn's left eye twitches. As she spins her massive diamond ring around her finger in panicky circles, her heel raps the floor. Next, she starts to cry and gesture erratically—transforming from lighthearted and glamorous to odd and unbalanced. "Stop asking me questions!" she shouts. "I never liked being compared to Jentry Rae! She pried and meddled and stepped where she didn't belong!"

"Drop this subject now!" Duke jets out of his seat. As if to downplay his wife's kooky behavior, his tone turns more diplomatic. "The murdered cheerleader was LeAnn's friend. Whenever my wife hears her name, she gets very upset—as you can see. So, LeAnn doesn't know what she's talking about right now. I apologize."

Nikki looks at Vince. His expression is aghast, just like hers. "*I hope you got that on camera*," she mouths to him.

He nods.

"Let's take a break," she suggests to the McCades.

Vince whispers as the couple go inside their elegant penthouse, "What's up with Duke and Duchess Unhinged? If we speak out of turn again, McCade might send bone-crushing linebackers after us."

"I'll for sure dig into his past. Remember, his initials are D.M.—one of Jentry Rae's tattoos. Anyway, let's get the hell out of here," Nikki says.

"I'm right behind you." Vince starts to pack up. "In the van, I'll tell you what Owen discovered."

A glittering object on the ground catches Nikki's attention. Curious, she picks it up and realizes it's a gold infinity bracelet centered by a sapphire. What on earth? It must've fallen off LeAnn's wrist while she flailed her hands around in protest.

Remarkably, the bangle is identical to the ones belonging to Jenry Rae and Piper Dupree. Nikki's mind totters, but not from the high altitude. If LeAnn ever learns that she has one of many bracelets, the woman might come completely unglued.

MISSING ENTRY OF JENTRY RAE'S DIARY

SEPTEMBER 16—ONE MONTH BEFORE HER MURDER

I was at Duke and LeAnn McCade's penthouse last night. LeAnn has asked me to co-host a new podcast she's creating about beauty and wellness. Can you believe it? It's so exciting! She and I are planning to upload it after I leave the DLC. The title is *In Your Glory: From 20 to 40.*

LeAnn has already paid me for a few episodes we have taped. I assume Vana Lockwood is okay with the project. I mean, LeAnn is the team owner's wife; she must have the final say! However, when I asked LeAnn about PR and marketing, she got real quiet.

Something isn't sitting right with me. The woman is all about sucking up the spotlight and staying relevant, so why isn't she doing any promoting? Maybe she's fibbing about ever releasing the podcast. I want to know what she is up to.

Last night I ran into Duke at the penthouse. He made small talk and then asked if I was related to a man named Sonny

Randall. My insides dropped, and my mind raced. Figuring it'd be smart to lie, I answered, "Who is he?"

"Just an old coot from Beaumont—where you're from," Duke replied. "Years back, I tried doing business with him, and he screwed me."

The last thing I wanted to do was to fall into Duke's trap, so I said I was no relation to Sonny Randall. Duke looked at me in disbelief. (After all, my daddy is all over my social media.) As I left the penthouse shaking like a leaf, I decided that I'm not going back there. I'll also tell LeAnn to forget the podcast. If she wants her money back, so be it.

If I find out that the McCades are using me to get to my father, my anger will ignite like country wildfire.

CHAPTER FORTY-TWO

THE DALLAS LONESTARS CHEERLEADER

~ NOVEMBER 8 ~

Shaunette hasn't confronted Nikki about the way the film-maker misrepresented her qualifications yet. The timing hasn't been right. When it is, Shaunette is fully prepared to ask questions.

Stirring from a nap on the sofa, she hears Nikki enter the apartment. Stretching, she sits up.

"Sorry if I woke you," Nikki says.

"It's okay. I fell asleep watching television. What time is it?"

"Ten p.m."

"How was your meeting with the McCades?"

"Bonkers, to say the least." Nikki plops down on the coffee table with a perplexed expression. In a few sentences she relays what took place at the penthouse.

"What?" Shaunette blinks. "LeAnn lost her temper at the mention of Jentry Rae's name?"

"*Lost her shit* is more like it. You should have seen it."

"And you're saying LeAnn has the same bracelet as Jentry Rae?"

"Yeah. Strange, right?" Nikki crosses her arms. "I was tempted to take it but didn't. The good thing is only one local jewelry store custom-makes them. The shop has a partnership with the Lonestars. Maybe one anonymous buyer commissioned all three bracelets."

"All three?"

"Jentry Rae's, LeAnn's, and Piper Dupree's. Sorry. I didn't tell you, but I noticed that Piper was wearing a gold infinity bracelet at The Depot."

Shaunette runs a hand through her rumpled hair. "This is getting so twisted. But do you believe a single person purchased all three bracelets?"

"Maybe."

Somebody wants to scare them away from the answers. Is it LeAnn? The possibility seems especially valid to Shaunette when Nikki says, "I need to find out what's behind the McCades' overreaction. It could be that Duke wanted Jentry Rae out of the way to appease his insecure wife. And remember how Sonny mentioned that he and Duke McCade had a falling-out? Maybe Jentry Rae tried to chip away at that." She adds, "At the penthouse, I noticed a photo of Jentry Rae with LeAnn. Did Jentry Rae tell you they were friends?"

"No." Needing to clear the air, Shaunette swallows. "Um, speaking of secrets, I heard a phone message from Vana when I was alone here the other day. Why did you lie about your credentials, Nikki?"

A long silence ensues.

The filmmaker gets up. Striding back and forth across the carpet, she stuffs her hands in her jacket pockets. "That was a terrible time in my life. I probably needed therapy to deal with my mom's death but couldn't afford it. I was angry because the pain of her loss from my childhood into my twenties just kept growing. It left behind a big question mark, so I dove into my work. I knew I could make great films; I just needed somebody to give me the chance."

"So, you lied to get ahead?" Shaunette fills in the gaps.

"Yeah. But that's when my imposter syndrome started. I felt like a fraud. Not good enough. I don't believe people when they tell me I'm talented. I guess I got lucky when my first film was well received, but ever since, I've been on a hamster wheel of 'Can I repeat my success?'"

Shaunette nods. At the same time, unease vibrates inside her. She is guilty of telling lies and snooping, too. She and Nikki are similar. But still, she can't say she loves being deceived. She'll keep her armor on and her guard up.

Nikki sits on the coffee table again. "I hope you can understand. I've been dying to tell you. Anyway, Vince's darknet expert unearthed some surprising stuff."

"I'm all ears."

"For starters, Jentry Rae was taking payments from somebody registered on Venmo as MBQ99. I want to know what she was being paid for. Also, Dante Marconi *has* been receiving mysterious payments, so what he told you was true."

"Interesting." Shaunette pauses. "I discovered something crazy, as well. Along with LeAnn McCade, Piper Dupree was in the Dallas Lonestars Cheerleaders' wing of the stadium on the afternoon of Jentry Rae's murder. It's located on the opposite side of the arena from where wives watch the games in the premier skybox. To my knowledge, Piper has never visited our section before."

"No way. What do you think she wanted that day?"

"I wish I knew." Shaunette shrugs, and it sends an ache through her. Her arm and her lung are still tender.

"Do you think Piper found out about Royce's affair with Jentry Rae?" Nikki asks.

"Possibly. And believe me, I never want to be her punching bag. Rumor has it that she verbally laid someone out for not stocking a skybox with her favorite green juice."

"Shit, I believe it because, I have other news. Vince learned via his source that Piper attacked her college roommate. Threw a chair at her head. Piper and Royce were on a brief break at the time, and Piper went ballistic when the guy she and her roommate both liked went for the roommate. She's a head case . . . someone I wouldn't want to meet in a dark alley."

"LeAnn McCade seems just as nasty," Shaunette says.

"Yeah. As I witnessed tonight. Push her buttons and she goes AK-47."

Shaunette's phone rings. She answers it on speaker mode, saying, "Hey, Sonny."

"Hi, sugar. I've made an important decision. I'm bringing my baby home. So far, the police have turned up diddly-squat. I refuse to let them poke and prod my Jentry Rae anymore. She deserves a dignified burial."

Emotion stabs at Shaunette. "That's understandable."

"It ain't been easy, though. After I signed the Report of Death in Dallas, I had to wait for it to be filed with the Health

270

Department. Only now can I transport a dead body within the State 'a Texas."

Envisioning Jentry Rae in a casket sends Shaunette into a grief spiral.

Nikki looks ashen as she listens beside her.

"It's a pile of hooey." The old farmer snorts. "Jentry Rae was my little girl. No parent in mourning should have to jump through hoops to bring their child home." He sighs. "Will you and Nikki come to the burial tomorrow?"

"Vince can drive us in the van," Nikki says under her breath.

"Of course, Sonny," Shaunette answers. "We'll get a pet sitter for Beau Dog, and we'll be there."

The country air at Vale View Farm is rife with the smell of overseed, recent rainfall, and profound sorrow.

Shaunette notices that Sonny can hardly stay standing at the burial ceremony. Emaciated but dressed in his Sunday best, he studies his daughter's coffin as it hovers on pulleys over a dark hole. Minutes from now, his only child will rest four feet apart from his wife . . . forever.

There is even ample room for a third grave when Sonny's time comes. The idea makes Shaunette sob buckets. That'll be soon.

As the old man clasps his hands together, he whimpers. Obviously, he is fighting through physical agony as well as emotional anguish. Bowing his head signals a preacher to begin a touching eulogy for Jentry Rae. It speaks of lovely sunsets that disappear into oceans—which is what Jentry Rae was. A beautiful vision that vanished too soon.

Just then, a butterfly zigzags in the air. More tears form in Shaunette's eyes as she studies its yellow and purple outline. Jentry Rae loved butterflies, and her favorite colors were yellow and purple. Is this a sign that her friend's spirit is nearby, looking down on the whole assemblage?

When the preacher quotes a scripture about redemption and forgiveness, Shaunette doesn't like that part. The words seem hollow under the circumstances. Nothing can bring Jentry Rae back. And her violent death is unforgivable.

As her casket is lowered into the earth, Sonny leans over and places a rose atop it. Several neighbors and distant family members follow suit. While the descending coffin makes a horrible cranking sound, the old man whimpers louder. Soon, he falls apart altogether, and it's a heart-wrenching sight. "Godspeed, baby," he cries.

There isn't a dry eye among the guests. Everybody comforts the grieving farmer, or tries to. Meanwhile, the preacher directs the group into the house for refreshments.

Shaunette stays behind to compose herself. "My deepest condolences, Sonny," she says through her tears.

"Thank you, sugar. You and Nikki bein' here means a lot."

She takes a look around. "This place is lovely. I've always liked it. You tend to it with care; that much is obvious."

"Mighty nice you of to say." Sonny shuffles off the knoll to the swing set he built decades ago. Gray skies close in as he wedges his rear into a swing. "Jesus, Mary, and Joseph. I need a minute. This is a good spot for me. Swinging was Jentry Rae's favorite thing to do when she was four years old. She was always in motion, so it's strange to see her frozen in one place now." He weeps into a handkerchief.

Shaunette pulls more tissue out of her purse. "She was lucky to have you for a father. Um, I have a confession, Sonny. I'm overcome—not just today, though. I feel like this tragedy has changed me. I'm not as one-dimensional and unfeeling. Now I know that actions have consequences, and that big egos are unhealthy. I want to apologize to you for how I treated Jentry Rae at the end. There was room for *both* of us on the cheerleading squad."

The old man waits before he answers. "It takes a mature person to say that. And you're right, sugar. We should always keep empathy on hand."

Several minutes pass. As Shaunette shrinks beneath her thick black sweater, insects trill loudly. Then a hush descends over the farm.

Sonny gazes at his endless patches of strawberries with bloodshot eyes. "Life is simple here. If I had persuaded my baby girl to stay on the farm, she might be still alive."

"You can't change yesterday. But also, women have to discover who they are on their own terms. To do that, we need freedom." She needs to explain this to her mother. Her mama's outrageous expectations ruined her friendships with Jentry Rae and the other cheerleaders.

"Well said, Shaunette, honey. I just hope the police are close to finding my girl's killer."

She sits in an adjacent swing and slowly moves to and fro. "When will the DNA results come back from Jentry Rae's autopsy?"

"The first lab deemed the results inconclusive. They're re-testin'. I keep calling Brandon López, the assistant DA, for information. He tells me Dante Marconi has fled the jurisdiction."

"No kidding!"

The farmer's loose chin wags. "That coward must know something. And I keep thinkin' about how Jentry Rae dated two fellas. I tried ta speak with Chase Campbell, Royce Holt's best friend, but I was removed from the approved visitors' list at The Depot."

Shaunette revisits the fact that Chase could've been Jentry Rae's other mystery man. Although, she hopes not. Chase has always struck her as sketchy . . . much less refined than Royce. On the other hand, Royce is a sleek snake charmer with his own manipulative style.

Nikki comes out of the house. As she joins the private moment, she leans against the swing set pole. "It was a beautiful ceremony, Sonny."

"I thought so, too, sugar. But I barely got through it." As he balls his handkerchief into one hand, his expression turns dire. "Stay here a minute, ladies. I'll be right back."

Sonny lumbers into the house with pain-filled strides. Seconds later, he re-emerges carrying two objects. "Take these, Nikki." First, he hands her Jentry Rae's apartment key.

"No—" she protests.

"I won't be back there," he points out sadly. "And it will help your investigation. Now, listen carefully. You'll need this, too." He passes her Jentry Rae's pink .22 caliber gun. "You should have it since you're involved, and I won't take no for an answer. So, do three things for me when you get back to Dallas. Protect yourself and Shaunette. Find Jentry Rae's DLC pinkie ring and bring it to her gravesite. Then, find out who the father of her baby was. That person killed my girl. I guarantee it. Promise me, Nikki," he pleads in a wheezy voice.

"I promise."

Shaunette is reduced to tears all over again.

Nikki seems shattered, as well. "Sonny, we need to discuss the possibility that Duke McCade wanted to get back at you through Jentry Rae—"

The scene is interrupted by the clatter of a dark green Mini Cooper rolling up to the farmhouse. A slight man with a thin face beeps the horn. After he lowers his window, he waves enthusiastically and shouts hello.

"Who is that?" Sonny asks no one in particular.

All of them meet the man halfway down the driveway.

"Why in tarnation are you making noise, son? I just buried my child."

"My condolences, sir. You must be Sonny Randall. I'm Kevin Drummond, Brandon López's paralegal at the DA's office. I drove here all the way from Dallas. Whew! These country roads are killers. Oops, sorry. Bad choice of words."

"Maybe we should go inside," Shaunette suggests. "What do you think, Sonny?"

"In a minute, sugar. I reckon this gentleman has come for an important reason. Which is . . . ?"

"Prosecutor López sent me here with my computer so you can videochat with him, sir. He wants to share some new information about your daughter's murder."

"Summarize for me, man," Sonny urges. "My time's runnin' short."

The paralegal lowers his voice. "Basically, the State has received partial results of the DNA evidence. Mr. López will tell you who that evidence implicates."

A dank chill prickles the back of Shaunette's neck. Could they be one step closer to finding out who killed Jentry Rae?

CHAPTER FORTY-THREE

THE FILMMAKER

~ NOVEMBER 9 ~

Nikki leads Kevin Drummond into the farmhouse. As he sits at the kitchen table, Sonny says goodbye to the funeral guests, Shaunette starts to wrap snack trays with cling wrap, and Vince goes to the bathroom.

"I would love a glass of anything, please," the paralegal says to Nikki. "Driving on a tight schedule is dehydrating."

"Sure thing." She moves to the refrigerator and is about to pour some lemonade when her phone rings. Emma Hollander, the Tennessee Renegades cheerleader, is calling.

"I'll pour that," Kevin offers. "We have a few minutes before the video call starts."

"Thanks. Excuse me." Thoughts racing, Nikki steps outside with her phone in hand. "Hey, Emma."

"Hi, Nikki. Sorry if I was rude to you the other day." The woman's voice is even shakier than before. "It's just—Royce Holt is being hailed as a football hero more and more by the press. And his wife is having their second baby any minute. His perfect life is such a façade! Seeing his smug face everywhere is triggering."

"Understood. Can you expound on that a little?"

"Like I said, I really shouldn't be revealing anything. In addition to the NDA I signed, Royce was an up-and-coming league player when we slept together. He wasn't as well known then, but we shouldn't have dated in the first place. He told me he was getting divorced, and I believed him. Stupid me. Regret from that time still haunts me. I guess I just need to talk it out."

"Of course. What took place between you two, exactly?"

Emma doesn't answer. Instead, she cries softly.

How upset the woman is burrows under Nikki's skin. She has never liked Royce. The way he uses his charisma like enticing bait irks her. Does he realize how destructive infidelity can be?

Vince emerges from the bathroom and joins her on the porch. "You want me to record?" he whispers.

She nods.

Lifting his cell phone, he audio-captures the call.

"Listen, Emma," Nikki says. "Chase Campbell nudged me to contact you. This is your chance to tell your story full-out."

"You're in the dark about this whole thing! Chase is Royce's pit bull. He protects Royce with his life . . . because he *owes* Royce. The Holt family took Chase in when he was a kid. They raised him and put him through school."

"I know that. And Royce got Chase his job with the Dallas Lonestars, right?"

"Yes. But the thing is Chase accidentally killed a kid when he was younger. Royce covered up the incident. That's the real reason Chase owes him."

Nikki's blood chills. Hearing about the tragedy a second time feels like a double blow. She may not be throwing darts in the dark anymore, but hearing granular details is unsettling. "Chase's guilt must be enormous, but the way he and Royce covered up an accidental murder—that's not okay." She pauses. "Um, do you know more, Emma?"

"No. The guys never talked about it."

"Did Royce come on to you at first? Or was it the other way around?"

"He blatantly flirted with me when we met at a Nashville bar. Then he started to message me. He mentioned the accident when he was drunk one night, but he refused to divulge details."

The conversation stalls while Nikki thinks of what to say. Vince does a "keep it rolling" gesture. She clears her throat. "Emma, the NDA you signed at the request of the Holt family. You need to tell me the reason behind it."

The pro cheerleader seems to mentally drift away because a long silence follows. "Um, Royce can be amazing. He says all the right things. At least, he did when I first dated him. He knew how to seduce me, but then I realized I was second fiddle to his football career. He keeps his cool on the field, but he's able to act that way because he lets loose when he *isn't* playing."

Nikki's breath catches. "Are you saying he has a Dr. Jekyll and Mr. Hyde personality?"

"Kind of. His controlling wife drives him crazy. Piper is constantly demanding things of him, and he always wants to escape from the house. That's why he—" The cheerleader gets choked up. "God, I'm violating my NDA. I shouldn't be discussing anything!"

"Forget the non-disclosure agreement," Nikki pleads. "Any contract that conceals a crime is unenforceable. Please tell me what Royce did."

"It was more what *Chase* did."

"Pardon?"

Emma's voice cracks. "One night, I was upset about Royce being married and ignoring me, so Chase and I went for a drive. He was living in Nashville, too; he moves where Royce goes. We parked at a vantage spot on the edge of the Cumberlands overlooking the city. We were talking, but all of a sudden, Chase kissed me. He wanted to make out, but I was dating Royce, not him. When I pushed him off me, he . . . shoved me."

"Chase *shoved* you?" Nikki repeats.

"Yes. He took my shoulders and pushed me against the car window. I ended up with bruises. And a bump on my head. That night, he got madder than I'd ever seen him. 'Why don't you look at me the way you look at Royce, Emma?' he yelled."

Nikki's worry is a ringing bell in her head. Chase obviously competes with his friend on a warped, unhealthy level. So, how much violence is he capable of? "I'm sorry that happened to you. I believe you one hundred percent, but do you have any proof?"

"I took photos of my bruises. Then I marked them with dates and stored them in my mom's safe. It was my only retaliation. The Holt family pressured me heavily. They claimed they cared for Chase like a second son, and they said that if I had a heart, I'd forget how he lost his temper. I signed their NDA for one reason. Fear of what that powerful family could do to me."

"It's okay, Emma. At least you're speaking up now."

The cheerleader pauses. "Royce demands loyalty from Chase. And vice versa. I'm telling you. The entire thing is a clusterfuck."

"You still have the photos, right?"

"Yes."

"Okay. But please explain something," Nikki prods. "*Chase* told me to find you."

"It's probably one of his sick games. Maybe he thought I would never talk because I signed that stupid clause. Also, I had an affair with a married man." Emma takes a breath. "Sorry. I have to go."

"Unbelievable." Vince shakes his head once the call ends. The next moment, his phone pings with a Google alert. He stares at the screen. "Royce Holt's wife gave birth to their second baby. A boy. They named him Theo. Here's a picture of him with Piper in the delivery room."

Nikki looks at it. "The baby is adorable, but why is Piper in full makeup? She must have arranged for a photo shoot in the delivery room. Jeez. And Royce looks like he wants to kill himself." Her heart plummets.

As her Pop says, "*What is this world coming to?*" Morality in this digital age has gone off the deep end because falsehoods and vanity are like mind-altering drugs. What's real? What's not? Worse, why is it so hard for people to remain loyal in friendships or in love?

Sonny appears on the porch. "Ready, folks? We are about to talk to Brandon López on the computer."

Nikki and Vince follow the old man to the kitchen table. There, Kevin Drummond is waiting with his laptop open. Shaunette is seated next to him.

The paralegal taps his keyboard. A second later, López's face appears on the screen.

López waves. "Hi, everyone. I'll get straight to the point. Following Jentry Rae's autopsy, the DNA on the towel covering her body has been identified. It belongs to Dante Marconi, the lead security guard at the Americana Memorial Stadium."

Nikki looks at Shaunette. The pale-faced cheerleader wrings her hands.

"An arrest warrant has been issued for Mr. Marconi, a fugitive," López adds. "Unfortunately, I'm still waiting for the full lab results. Namely, I am waiting for a match to the DNA found on Jentry Rae's skin and under her fingernails."

Sonny glowers. "Don't stop until you catch that tomfool security guard. You need to see what he knows about my baby's death."

"You have my word, Mr. Randall. Furthermore, I believe Dante Marconi received payments from someone to, perhaps, follow you, Miss Simmons. Thus, making you crash your car. I am still trying to prove it."

Shaunette picks nervously at a hangnail. "Mr. López, Dante told me he heard *two* objects clatter to the ground inside the cheerleaders' locker room the day Jentry Rae died. The noises sounded like pieces of jewelry. One was Jentry Rae's infinity bracelet, but I wonder what the other object was. Speaking of noises, it's hard for me to believe Dante didn't overhear the murder happen. Obviously, he knows more than he's letting on. I'm glad you're after him, sir."

"Excuse me," Nikki interrupts. Everybody stares at her, bewildered—including the prosecutor on the video chat. "I just found out something about Chase Campbell, the Lonestars' sports therapist. He might have hurt Jentry Rae out of a weird competitive streak with his friend, Royce Holt. And if Chase thought Shaunette was also dating Royce in order to hurt her rival Jentry Rae, he might be trying to harm her, too."

INSTAGRAM POST

@PIPER_DUPREE28

Reel: Piper is standing in her home nursery in the middle of the night. The room is decorated in five different shades of blue, and it contains a full-sized bed for her. After doing a shushing motion, she points at the crib. Then she tells her viewers to check out a product list she has linked in her bio.

1.5 million followers / 576,009 likes

Link.bio/piper_dupree28

#trending #WAG #gavebirth #babybooties #FFL

"Midnight feedings are challenging, to say the least! To help, I've included everything I bought for Baby Bundle Number 2." She holds the camera on the lower half of her body as she whispers. "These are my FAVORITE item: Luxome Lounge Pants. They're on sale right now, so snatch some up! The funny thing is I wore these comfy sweatpants in the hospital even though people say I wear the pants at home. Ha!" She laughs loudly, waking her newborn up. Wailing fills the nursery. Piper starts to cry, too.

CHAPTER FORTY-FOUR

THE DALLAS LONESTARS CHEERLEADER

~ NOVEMBER 9 ~

Night falls, and Shaunette is lingering in Sonny's kitchen. As moonlight streams in from a nearby window, she leans against the counter while asking herself a question. Did Dante Marconi try to mislead her by giving her a list of stadium visitors? Maybe the security guard would do anything to throw people off his scent. And if Dante's DNA was found on the towel that covered Jentry Rae's body, what else did he do to the star cheerleader?

Chewing a handful of nuts, Shaunette thinks about Chase Campbell next. She makes a mental note to stay away from him. The guy isn't just a killjoy, but according to Nikki, he might have deadly intentions.

At least Shaunette feels safe here at the farmhouse.

She picks up Nikki's borrowed phone and clicks into her emails. Keeping in touch with what's going on within the DLC squad might distract her from the encroaching chaos. *Surprise!* A rookie cheerleader has finally reached out. Rehearsals have been catastrophes. And during tonight's practice, the dancers made extra-bad snafus and missteps galore. Plainly, they still need a capable leader after Jentry Rae's murder.

It's too bad Shaunette isn't coming back this season, the rookie writes.

Shaunette also reads that the new Point is Ashleigh. *What?* The announcement knocks her sideways. The redhead will grace the cover of this year's DLC Calendar, as well as lead the renowned Show Troupe.

No way!

It can't be!

Looking at a bottle of wine, Shaunette is tempted to chug the whole thing. She can't abide that Ashleigh has everything she wants. Everything her mama achieved, too, when she was a DLC.

Deciding to reach for a non-alcoholic beer instead of the wine, Shaunette does her best to tamp down her old obsession for crushing the competition. However, the flames of missed opportunity burn a hot hole in her gut.

Nikki appears. The filmmaker frowns as Shaunette hands her phone back. "You seem upset. I'll join you for a beer. Come on. Let's bring them out to the porch swing."

Once they sit and open their bottles, Shaunette hears a symphony of croaking frogs, singing cicadas, and hooting owls. Soon, a calm breeze blows in. She should be unwinding here, but it's impossible. Not after learning that Dante Marconi is on the loose.

Nikki takes a swig of the virgin beer and nearly spits it out.

Both of them swing in the chilly night for a stretch of time without talking. Finally, Shaunette relays the DLC updates, trying to keep bitterness out of her tone.

Nikki smacks her lips. "You're saying Motormouth Ashleigh is the new star of the Dallas Lonestars Cheerleaders? That's blasphemy. Didn't she *conveniently* find pot and booze inside another cheerleader's locker?"

"Yes, but her involvement was never proved. To her credit, Ashleigh is a three-year veteran and a good dancer. She has earned the accolades. I just hate her bad juju."

"No, shit. The girl seems conniving."

More nature sounds echo outside of Sonny's farmhouse. Inside the home, though, things are quiet. Kevin the paralegal has departed, Sonny is asleep in his bedroom, and Vince is fixing a midnight snack. Nikki and Shaunette should have departed long ago, but they wanted to ensure that Sonny was okay.

Shaunette looks up at the vast sky. A tapestry of stars flicker and twinkle, and the panoramic sight gives her a good sense of distance. She's glad to be among friends. If only trouble felt miles away, too.

When Nikki shares details of her call with Emma Hollander, it exacerbates Shaunette's worry. Chase's violent, jealous streak seems far-reaching. Only, what's the truth here?

"Everybody seems to be lying," she says to Nikki. "Piper Dupree, Dante Marconi, Royce Holt, and Duke McCade."

"It's a dumpster fire," Nikki agrees. "I wish I could tell somebody to call off their dogs, but I don't know who unleashed them in the first place."

They grip their beers in the moonlight.

"What made you want to be friends with Jentry Rae in the first place?" Nikki asks.

"I didn't know any of the cheerleaders early in the season. Jentry Rae happened to be my mentor, and I got lucky. She was the friendliest and the funniest out of all the girls. She used to joke that she was glad she had big boobs because she didn't always want to make eye contact with people."

"That *is* funny."

"I miss her. She gave me insider's advice, but more than that, she understood me. My fixation to be perfect—she didn't judge me for it. Instead, she used to say that perfection doesn't exist. Everybody has flaws, including her."

"Jentry Rae had flaws?"

"I know, looking at her, you wouldn't think it. But she admitted that sometimes she wanted too much."

Nikki nods. "There is danger in that."

Sensing that the filmmaker is studying her, Shaunette asks, "What?"

"You seem really tense. Maybe Vana's right. Maybe you keep the cork in too tight. And maybe you want a lot, too." Nikki pauses. "Please tell me what you started to say earlier. In my van. Obviously, you wanted to share something."

Shaunette wedges her beer bottle between her legs so that she can talk with her hands. "Okay. Stay with me on this. I have been doing some reflecting. When we get back to Dallas, I'll be stepping back from helping you investigate. I don't want to be part of your crime series."

Nikki's face flushes. "Is this because you learned that I faked my credentials?"

"No."

"Uh, not to sound rude, but you never helped much, Shaunette."

"What? I feel like I *did* help. But please understand. I have to keep my slate clean if I'm going to reaudition for the DLC."

"Come on. When are you going to stop pleasing your mom and live your own life?"

It sounds pathetic to hear. "You don't get it, Nikki. Being here and seeing Sonny's sorrow—I can't do it anymore. Jentry Rae feels like a fleeting dream that's disappeared forever. Even if we find her killer, she is never coming back."

Nikki shoves her feet to the ground to stop the swing. "You said it yourself: Jentry Rae wasn't perfect. None of us is. But she deserves justice. And don't you want to know who's putting you in danger? If you haven't noticed, a psycho wants to end your life! They're after me, too. So, what's with the about-face?"

"If the murderer doesn't want to be found, they probably won't be."

"That's a cop-out! I'm beginning to think you know who killed Jentry Rae but won't say. True or false?"

Shaunette's heart drops. The time has come for her to own up to what happened the day her ex-best friend died.

CHAPTER FORTY-FIVE

THE FILMMAKER

~ NOVEMBER 9 ~

Is Shaunette about to confess? Nikki's suspicion builds as the cheerleader blinks rapidly and doesn't speak.

Mentally scrambling, Nikki tries to assemble the puzzle pieces: the menacing text messages she received, the stalker who filmed her asleep, people being where they shouldn't have been on the day of the murder, and Shaunette's strange behavior surrounding Jentry Rae's death.

The elements might seem random, but are they interconnected? And once they're fitted together, what big picture will they paint?

Nikki is starting to believe that Shaunette's front-row seat to all the events aren't acts of chance.

"I have no idea who killed Jentry Rae," Shaunette finally replies.

"Really? You could've fooled me. Are you protecting someone? I want to know what you're playing at."

"Tread lightly," Shaunette grinds out.

"What's that supposed to mean?" Nikki's phone bleeps—an ill-timed intrusion. As she quickly lifts the device off her thigh, she studies the screen without Shaunette seeing it. Three messages from the person who filmed her asleep pop up in individual bubbles:

> **Don't believe anything Shaunette Simmons says.**
> **She told Jentry Rae that Royce slept with a**
> **Tennessee Renegades cheerleader.**
> **Not the other way around.**
> **Ask her if she was sober on the Lonestars vs.**
> **Condors game day.**

Shock thrums Nikki's pulse. The night air goes still, and the echo of her speeding heartbeat is all she can hear. Did Shaunette hurt Jentry Rae during a violent, drunken stupor?

Licking her dry lips, she slurps the beer. Not for taste. To stall. She knows two effective tricks for obtaining information. One: push the envelope. Two: just ask straightforwardly.

"You need to tell me what you know." Nikki turns her phone over again and taps it on her thigh. "My creepy intruder messaged me just now. They're trying to implicate *you*, Shaunette. And if I think about it, *you* were the only person in my apartment the night I was recorded while sleeping. There was no sign of a break-in."

"Huh? Are you serious?"

Nikki feels bad that she's at the end of her rope. She doesn't want to outright accuse Shaunette of sabotage—or of murder—but she needs to finish this and be with her father. Sonny's days are limited, too. God help her, she's lowering herself, but she will do better and be better as soon as this is over.

However, before she can goad Shaunette more, the cheerleader grabs her phone.

"Real mature," Nikki growls. "Give it back."

Shaunette shakes her head. Standing up, she silently reads the text messages. "This is complete bullshit!"

"If it *isn't* bullshit, you know you can come clean to me. I have your back."

"Don't use reverse psychology on me, Nikki. I've been honest with you. Jentry Rae told *me* about Emma Hollander."

"But let's revisit the dead rat in your locker. It seems one of your fellow DL Cheerleaders has it in for you. Why? Because you drink too much?"

Misery and anger coat Shaunette's expression. As she starts to pace, dejection joins in, too. "Um, okay. I'll tell you the truth but try not flip out. Here it is. One of my squad mates eavesdropped on my conversation with Jentry Rae in the locker room. It was Ashleigh—on the day of the murder. I'd been having problems with alcohol; it's the only thing that relaxes me and gives me courage to perform. So, I drank on a game day. *You* try dancing next to a live Barbie doll. My mama expects a lot, so I drank in my car before I entered the stadium. Which explains the bourbon bottle hidden in my back seat."

"What?" Nikki gasps. She surges to her feet, too. "You performed wasted? Isn't that the cardinal sin of the Dallas Lonestars Cheerleaders?"

"Yes! And I'm ashamed of it. It's the reason I floundered the routine that day. I tried to disguise my intoxication, but Jentry

Rae smelled bourbon on me. She filmed me so that she could show me later . . . as a type of intervention."

The revelation tears through Nikki like a tornado. She doesn't know what to say.

"Jentry Rae and I started screaming at each other," Shaunette goes on. "Our voices echoed in the locker room, and Ashleigh heard our fight. Days earlier, Jentry Rae told me that some-body had roughed up a Tennessee Renegades cheerleader in the past. Royce was a player on that team, so I got worried that he would hurt Jentry Rae. To wake my friend up, I threatened to tell Vana that Royce and Jentry Rae were sleeping together, but when Jentry Rae heard that, she swore she'd tell Vana *I* came to the game hammered." She pauses. "Here's the worst part. I thought Jentry Rae would always have my back, but she cap-tured me on her phone yelling that I would kill her."

Nikki nearly drops her beer bottle. "Oh my God!" The damn-ing information is seismic. Her mind clambers at high speed as she thinks about what to do. She can't record *this* encounter because Shaunette is holding her phone. Otherwise, she'd have proof that the jealous cheerleader could be Jentry Rae's murderer.

She doesn't want to believe it, though. In fact, she has not wanted to believe something less. She and Shaunette have been through so much, and she likes to think she has made a real friend in her. Was it too good to be true?

Then again, would Shaunette have plowed into a cement pylon, sliced open her forehead, deflated a lung, and possibly died to take suspicion off herself? Maybe it *was* Dante Marconi who forced her to crash.

"You were angry in the locker room. That's understandable," Nikki says. "But did you really say you would kill Jentry Rae?"

"Unfortunately, I did."

"Okay, wow. I mean, I can see why you lost your temper. If you got kicked off the DLC squad without the chance of return-ing, your mother would never have forgiven you. You couldn't take that. You live for your mom's applause. She's counting on you to redeem her involvement with the squad, and you're only fulfilled by her approval."

"So, I—what? Eliminated the one person standing in the way?"

All at once, Shaunette's face goes white. Wincing, she tilts off-balance and presses a hand to her forehead. Doubling over completely, she gets sick and then crumples to the porch floor, writhing in agony.

"Shaunette!" Nikki screams. She drops to her knees beside the incapacitated cheerleader.

Vince and Sonny rush outside.

"What's the matter?" Sonny asks breathlessly.

"Something's wrong with Shaunette! She's in pain. I need to take her to a hospital."

Rubbing sleep from his eyes, Sonny points east. "Beaumont Medical Center is up the road. Hurry!"

Nikki shouts at Vince to start the van. Once she helps Shaunette to her feet, they move to the vehicle as quickly as possible. Time is of the essence. Shaunette has survived incred-ible odds. Will she survive this, too?

CHAPTER FORTY-SIX

THE DALLAS LONESTARS CHEERLEADER

~ *NOVEMBER 9* ~

Shaunette passes out on the way to a local emergency room. When she comes to, she experiences a déjà vu scenario. Doctors and nurses are working on her diligently while a kaleidoscope of lights blaze in her eyes. An oxygen mask is placed over her mouth, and her pupils are checked. But this time, she doesn't hear the attending physician announce her injuries as a collapsed lung or a broken arm. Instead, a doctor diagnoses her with a subdural hematoma. A blood clot.

"A pool of blood is sitting between the patient's brain and its outermost covering," the attending doctor tells an intern. "She needs an MRI, STAT."

Teardrops stream down Shaunette's cheeks. Why do bad things keep happening to her?

As she's wheeled down a hallway for imaging, she sees Nikki.

Nikki waves. Then the filmmaker tells a nurse, "My friend's car accident was thirteen days ago. Is this related?"

"It could be," the nurse replies. "Subdural hematomas may not cause symptoms for days or weeks after a head injury."

Shaunette is put inside an MRI tube, feeling weaker and weaker. "Am I going to die?" she asks the technician.

"I can't say either way," he replies flatly. "But often a tube can be inserted to the brain to drain blood, pus, and fluids. The physician on your case will send you to surgery as a last resort."

Brain surgery?

Curling her hands in pain, Shaunette regrets trusting Nikki with her biggest secret. Nikki judged her—just like she has been judged her entire life.

She unfurls her fists like helium released from a balloon and loses consciousness.

When Shaunette wakes up in a hospital bed, she has no idea how much time has passed.

Nikki is in a chair beside her, reading Jentry Rae's diary. The instant the filmmaker looks up, worry coats her pallid face.

Meanwhile, Vince is propped against a wall eating a bag of Funyuns.

"You're going to be fine, Shaunette." Nikki reaches over and pats her hand. "Doctors drained the pressure on your brain. It was residual damage caused by the car accident."

Half lucid, Shaunette flutters her eyes and tries to clear her dry throat. The room goes in and out of focus like a camera lens.

"Loads of terms were thrown around," Vince informs her. "But to put it in plain, Webster dictionary language, you had a transient ischemic episode. A mini stroke. The cells in your body didn't have enough blood flow, so Nikki probably saved your life by bringing you here."

"Thanks, Doc." Nikki shoots him a look.

Overwhelmed again by her bad luck, Shaunette holds her bandaged head. This is too much. How much more can she take?

"Vince, I think Shaunette needs some quiet time," Nikki says. "Can you give us a minute?"

"No problem." As he exits, he whispers, "Be sure to show her what Owen discovered."

"I will."

Shaunette doubts she's on morphine while she sinks further into the pillow. It worked well at the other hospital, but whatever is streaming through her veins right now isn't making a dent in her pain. She locks eyes with Nikki. "I don't remember a lot before I passed out. Only that you practically accused me of murder."

Remorse is written all over Nikki's face. "About that. I was a total asshole. I'm sorry because I realize now that I was wrong."

"Huh?"

"Sonny says Jentry Rae was asking a lot of questions about Duke McCade at the end. She seemed scared of him. He's a possible suspect, and I'll see if ADA López thinks so, too. Also—" Nikki pulls something up on her phone. Standing, she turns the screen around so that Shaunette can see it. "Take a look at this."

"I can't really focus on anything. Just tell me."

"Okay. Vince's dark web expert found a reel filmed by a Lonestars fan. It shows you signing autographs in the parking lot of the Americana Memorial Stadium directly after the game against the Philadelphia Condors. On the day Jentry Rae died."

"Really?" Shaunette can barely breathe.

"The timestamp proves that you quickly grabbed your pom-poms from the dressing room then left *with* the squad while Jentry Rae stayed behind. She was heard taking a shower *after* you left the building. You couldn't have killed your friend."

What an incredible relief! Peace, once unattainable, shimmers and glimmers before Shaunette. She sobs until her chest burns. It's true that she came at Jentry Rae verbally that day. She even scratched her best friend's arm, but she didn't shove her into a metal locker. Finally, there's proof of that.

"Can you ever forgive me?" Nikki asks.

"I thought I lost you as a friend. I don't have many, you know."

"You're stuck with me, I'm afraid."

"Thanks for this. Can you show that video to the cops?"

"Of course." Nikki looks at her phone when it rings, and she swears under her breath. "It's someone from the Lonestars' organization." Opening the door, she gestures for Vince to come in. He does, still crunching his Funyuns.

"Hello," Nikki answers the call.

The conversation floods the room.

"Miss Keegan, this is Duke McCade's assistant, Bethany Platt. I'm calling to inform you that we're taking you off the documentary."

"Pardon me? The film is nearly done!"

"My instructions come from Mr. McCade himself. He wants all negative publicity surrounding Jentry Rae Randall's murder to die down."

"That could take a while."

"He wants all negative publicity surrounding *you* to subside, as well."

Nikki's jaw drops. "Me?"

"Don't pretend you didn't fake your credentials. We received an anonymous tip about it, after which our people verified your falsehoods. We are concerned that our fans will find out."

"That was in the past. And what does it matter? You're clutching at excuses—"

"You're right. It isn't just about that. You have been sticking your nose where it doesn't belong. What I'm really saying is you egregiously offended Mr. and Mrs. McCade with your line of questioning when you came to their home. On top of that, we know you're filming a crime series on the side."

The room goes still.

It's Shaunette's turn to feel badly for Nikki. Somebody slashed her tires, filmed her asleep, and now they are annihilating her career. Maybe bad luck is contagious. Then again, Nikki lied about having permission to make the crime series.

"I should've stuck to sports at the McCades' penthouse; I admit it," Nikki says into the phone. "But I can explain—"

"No need. We've already found a replacement director for the documentary. Somebody who isn't busy playing Sherlock Holmes."

"You can't!"

"Ah, we can. Turn in your access badge tomorrow. Same goes for your videographer."

Nikki shakes her head. "But you have our word that we are portraying the cheerleaders and the football players with utmost discretion. And we'll spin the entire film from a favorable angle during final edits. But keep in mind, the world wants an inside peek at an unsolved, tragic murder—"

"There you go again, Miss Keegan. We won't tolerate you spinning our franchise in any direction. Let alone a scandalous one." Bethany pauses. "The Dallas Lonestars Cheerleaders are going silent for a game . . . giving no performance. Which is unprecedented. Vana Lockwood has no choice because her dancers are scared out of their minds—thanks in large part to your dramatic interviews with them. And now Shaunette Simmons is being targeted, too? This is unacceptable. That's all. Good day."

"Goddamn it!" Nikki cries after she hangs up.

Vince winces. "There goes my Emmy. And my Ferrari, and my—"

"Not now." She grabs an elastic out of her bag and shoves her hair in a ponytail. "This is insane, Vince. The Dallas Lonestars aren't our bosses. Our producer is."

"Yeah, Nik. But our Producer Extraordinaire will be pissed off if we roll ahead with anything. We don't have *permission* to conduct any more interviews. And we don't have the *authority* to sniff around anymore. This is the end of the road."

"If you and I keep filming on the sly, we might capture the identity of the murderer. Then we can pitch our docuseries to streaming services."

"It might get us sued. No way." He shakes his head vigorously.

Ignoring Vince's protests, Nikki guides him to the door. "Put gas in the van. Then come back for me. We're headed to Dallas."

"I'll return to Dallas with you, Nik, but you and I need to part ways."

"What? You can't be serious."

An awkward silence hangs in the air.

Nikki turns to Shaunette once Vince leaves. "The doctors won't release you for another five days. In the meantime, rest up."

"I'm scared," Shaunette says in a blind panic. "I could be a sitting duck in this hospital bed. Don't leave me alone. Please!"

Nikki takes her hand. "I'm going to insist that Sergeant Emerson posts a local cop outside your door. I completely understand your fright. I'm scared, too, but luckily, you have an alibi, Shaunette. I still need to clear my name and be done with this. The cops think I'm a liar."

"You *are* a liar. You never had permission to make a crime series."

"Well, you lied to *me* when we first met. About being friendly with Royce Holt. Remember?"

Shaunette presses her eyelids shut for a second. "And look where dishonesty got us. Our lives are on the line." She locks eyes with Nikki again. "You may think I have an alibi, but there is no guarantee I'm in the clear. How long will you be gone?"

"As long as it takes, so be brave. When you get better, I'll need your help. Are you up for it?"

"Yes, except I don't have a car. You need to swear on the Holy Bible you'll come back to Beaumont and get me out of this hospital, Nikki. You owe me for thinking I was murderer."

"You have my word," the filmmaker replies. "But not because I owe you. Because you're my friend."

PART IV

A smart Texan can pinpoint
a whisper in a windstorm.

TV TRANSCRIPT

Another episode of the cable sports show *Field Talk*. Royce Holt strolls on stage, looking sharp in a brown three-piece suit. As he joins Barry Levin and Glen Paderowski at their enormous light-up desk, the hosts do a "bow down" motion.

Barry: There he is . . . Royce Holt, football legend-in-the-making! We'll get to the news of your second baby in a sec, but you're crushing it, man. (They fist-bump.) Major apologies for our previous teasing. You've proved yourself. How does it feel to have won the last three games for the Dallas Lonestars?

Royce: It feels awesome, but I can't take all the credit. My guys are the GOAT. Wins come from teamwork.

Glen: So true. Except, don't be humble, bruh. You have sports stardom in your genes, right? Your dad—Hall of Famer Halftime Holt—must've taught you some moves.

Royce: (Nods)

Barry: Speaking of your dad, we have a special "gotcha" treat. Halftime Holt is on the phone line right now. Nice surprise, huh, Royce?

Royce: (Appears shocked and displeased)

Warren Holt's voice: Hi, son. You haven't returned my calls, so I suppose this is the next best thing. (His sarcastic attempt at humor falls flat.) I want to say that I'm proud of you. You have finally achieved the level of success I knew you were capable of.

Barry: NOW you're proud of your boy. Eh, sir? (Laughs)

Royce: Thanks, Dad. (Satisfaction brightens his face like a school-boy who's been given a good report card.) I've been waiting a long time to hear you say that. Only, you have no idea what it's taken for me to get to this point.

CHAPTER FORTY-SEVEN

THE FILMMAKER

~ *NOVEMBER 10* ~

During the four-hour drive back to Dallas, endless flatlands provide boring scenery, and Nikki's lack of sleep is a killer.

She nearly nods off at the wheel, but she also feels like shit-crap for other reasons. The danger looming around her has multiplied, and being fired from the documentary is gnawing a hole in her dignity. What's more, her dad's financial straits are pushing her "Panic" button. She feels like she is locked inside a flaming building with her feet glued to the floor.

On the flip side, being kicked off the documentary means she's free to pursue the truth about Jentry Rae's death without the Lonestars getting in the way.

She can't forget that she made a pledge to a dying man.

Seeing a sign that reads *Dallas . . . 311 miles*, Nikki floors the gas pedal. Vince just finished angry-ranting at her because of how she overstepped and blew their opportunity. Now, he's asleep in the passenger seat, curled into a tight ball. Amid the silence, she slips into thinking mode. Glamorous Jentry Rae might have been a bold, iconic Dallas Lonestars Cheerleader, but she was also a hopeless romantic . . . someone who would've done anything for love. She desperately wanted to be with the father of her baby and settle down with him, but Nikki doesn't believe Jentry Rae was a maneater. The girl was just in over her head. Therein lay the rub. Intrinsically, Jentry Rae was positive and good, a rule-follower—until somebody pushed her to the breaking point. Her decision to trap her lover into having a child meant she crossed a line she wouldn't have crossed otherwise.

Self-hatred is why the charismatic star lashed out at her best friend, Shaunette.

It's also why she placed herself in a precarious situation and bought a gun.

Playing with the big dogs led her to fear ferocious bites.

And Jentry Rae was right to be scared. She brought infidelity into the equation, which put careers and marriages at stake. People's happiness hung in the balance, including hers. Sadly, she craved validation from men to make her whole. Hell, she even wrote that she was afraid she would cease to exist without her true love.

Driving faster, Nikki guzzles an energy drink. Soon, the caffeine revs her determination even more. She's well aware that female viewpoints about personal fulfillment vary. She seeks professional acceptance in a male-dominated industry while Shaunette derives her worth from her mother's approval. Lack of self-esteem is an age-old problem—as exclusive a club as the phone book. But why can't women accept their shortcomings? Strides in inclusion have been made, yet it's up to each person to do the work.

Women need to stop comparing themselves to other women and celebrate their strengths. After all, the only person you need to please is yourself. Because, if we can't love ourselves, who else will love us?

Social media needs to stay the hell out of everybody's way.

Vince stirs. Still looking perturbed, he sits up. "I know that look, Nik. What are you up to now?"

"I just realized how tricky it is to be a Dallas Lonestars Cheerleader. Critics might argue that when you display a certain thing—like dancing half-clad—you have to anticipate a certain reaction. But a beautiful woman on display never *asks* to be hurt. Or killed. Jentry Rae loved entertaining, it made her happy, and she built her self-confidence by using what she had. Good for her."

"Right on," he says without his customary smile. "But I'm telling you to stop. Let the police handle things from here."

"Not a chance. In fact, I'm going to pull out the heavy artillery. My name in the film industry will NOT be smeared. And the son of a bitch responsible for killing Jentry Rae and for terrorizing me and Shaunette will pay. I won't let him walk softly through life."

"What about *my* name being smeared?" Vince scoffs. "Also, what concrete theories do you have, exactly? I think you're trying to nail jelly. Meanwhile, you're putting your life in danger, and I don't want to see you get hurt." Sulking, he coils into a vexed ball against the door again.

Hoping he'll come around, she gets on her phone. She wants to find out if Medicare covers a hospice nurse for Sonny. The poor man is alone, and he could use help at the farmhouse.

Next, she reaches under the seat and touches Jentry Rae's pink gun and diary. A good director *feels* their characters' pain. But a great director *feeds* off their characters' agony.

It's the only way to make a powerful film. Fortunately, those requisites are Nikki's strong suit.

The first thing Nikki does when she returns to Dallas is drop Vince at his apartment. Then she heads across town with plans to confront Chase Campbell at his home. Munching a greasy meal from Skipper's Catfish drive-thru, she sits in the van near his house for an hour. She knocks on Chase's door twice but gets no answer. The inactivity starts to drive her crazy.

While she huddles inside the van, she wishes she could text Shaunette, but her friend is still without a cell phone. Nikki could ring Shaunette's hospital room, but that would risk waking her up.

Concluding that the sports therapist isn't home, she starts the van. As she steers it down the street, she sees a figure cycle toward her on a Tarmac bike. The man has his head down, so his identity is undiscernible. She sees that it's Chase once he looks up.

Her heart pounds.

Don't act nervous, she instructs herself.

Leftover daylight allows him to recognize her, too, so he indicates that she pull over.

"Hi," he says, walking his bike closer. "You aren't coincidentally in my neighborhood, right? What's up?" He breathes heavily from what Nikki presumes was an intense ride.

"I wanted to tell you I spoke with Emma Hollander."

Chase wipes his forehead. "What exactly did she say?"

"Her account was hard to hear. Essentially, she asserted that you shoved her when she wouldn't have sex with you."

"I'm not surprised." He shows no concern. "What I'm saying is it's a damned lie. Royce did it."

"What?"

Chase looks around to make sure they're alone on the street. "Emma probably said she only had bruises, but the truth is Royce put her in the fucking hospital. She didn't want to have sex one night, and she made that clear. She had reconstructive surgery on her face, and ever since, she's been afraid to blame Royce."

Surprise and confusion knot Nikki into a pretzel. "You're pulling my leg. The Holt family made her sign an NDA on *your* behalf."

"You have it all wrong. The NDA Emma signed was to protect *Royce*."

Nikki swears she's on an undulating funhouse floor . . . off-balance and disoriented. The problem is she didn't hear any of this from Emma, so should she believe Chase? Liars will do anything to insulate themselves.

She knows a little something about that.

When Chase goes to leave, she sticks her hand out the window to stop him. If more acting is required to get the truth, she'll do it. "Wait. This is so fucked up. And I can tell this is hard for you. Your loyalty to Royce—"

"I'm definitely torn. I owe him a lot, and I owe his family a lot. But his deceptions need to stop. I won't stay quiet anymore."

"Disclosing details is the right thing to do," she says. "Go to the police."

"I will. But there is something else you should know." His tone grows more serious.

"What?"

"Royce has battered other women."

As Chase cycles off, Nikki gets the chills. His story differs greatly from Emma's, but frankly, it was the ominous glint in his eyes that made him hard to believe.

CHAPTER FORTY-EIGHT

THE DALLAS LONESTARS CHEERLEADER

~ *NOVEMBER 11* ~

Shaunette uses the hospital phone to call home. As the line trills, she wonders how her mother is feeling. Is Mama hanging in there?

Her Aunt Noleen answers, "Howdy, love."

"What's the word on my mama's health?"

"Honey pie, we don't expect her to last the next forty-eight hours."

"What? No!" Desolation layers Shaunette's voice. Panic, sadness, and guilt fuse in her psyche, too. She should be there with her mother, but . . . does anyone know she is confined to a hospital bed after having a mini stroke?

"I'm so sorry to have to tell you," her aunt says.

"I can't believe it." Shaunette weeps. "I don't know what I'll do without her."

Aunt Noleen exhales. When she speaks again, her voice is melancholy. "Your mother loves you. She might have a strange way of showing it, but she does."

"I had a setback after my car accident. A blood clot in my brain. I'm okay, but I can't come home right now."

"Gracious! Let's do the next best thing, then. I'll put your mama on the phone right now."

There is a pause. Shaunette braces herself during the silence. A moment later, Kaylene Simmons gets on the line. "Hello?" Her crackly voice sounds thinner than melting ice. "Shaunette Lynn? Is that you?"

"Hi, Mama." She hopes it won't be the last time they ever speak. "Please don't let go yet."

"I'm at the end of the road, darlin'. Come home."

"I wish I could, but I'm at the Beaumont Hospital." She gives a brief explanation.

"You mean you can't move heaven and earth to see your mother on her death bed?"

Alone and in pain, Shaunette has never felt farther away from the woman who raised her. Crushed by emotion and at a loss for words, she breaks down.

While she cries, someone in the background gives her mama a sip of water. It allows Shaunette time to process the fact that her own health and safety don't count in her mother's eyes.

A disturbing question rings in her head. *Why have I lived to please Mama all these years? Maybe my problem isn't abandonment by my father. The harsh truth is the door to my mama's affection will never fully open.*

Shaunette realizes she will never cut the mustard. And as sad as this moment is she needs to stop seeking approval. Her sanity depends on it. She also needs to come up with a new dream as her aspiration. Hers and hers alone. Not her mother's.

Static crackles on the line.

"Hello?" Shaunette says. "Are you still there, Mama?"

"I'm h-here."

"It's important that I speak my peace, so I'm going to say a few things before we hang up. First off, there is more to life than being beautiful."

"You're wrong, darlin'. Beauty keeps the ugly out."

"Well, maybe I don't want to be a Dallas Lonestars Cheerleader anymore."

Her mother draws a sharp intake of breath. "If you loved me, you'd rethink that."

"It's time for me to focus on what I want, Mama. But I do love you. And I need to live my own life."

There is a taut, uneasy silence.

"You've cut me to the quick, Shaunette Lynn. Goodbye." Her mother hangs up.

Shaunette isn't sure what she feels. Except, she knows she must make a staunch self-vow. Never again will she allow anybody else's expectations to outnumber her own.

CHAPTER FORTY-NINE

THE FILMMAKER

~ *NOVEMBER 12* ~

Nikki is at her apartment when she gets a phone call from Shaunette. She quickly picks up. "Are you okay, Shaunette?"

"My mama passed away." The cheerleader sounds shot to pieces. "I heard the news from my aunt an hour ago."

"Oh, no! I'm so sorry!"

"Thank you. Her death was a waiting game, but it's still difficult."

"Of course it is." Heart aching for her friend, Nikki comforts Shaunette for a good half hour. They discuss the complicated feelings that come with losing your mother: confusion, denial, loneliness, and eventually, acceptance. "Let me know how I can help," she says sincerely.

"Thank you for letting me unload," Shaunette replies. "The last conversation I had with my mama offered no closure. We still didn't see eye to eye."

"Did you at least get some things off your chest?"

"I did."

"Then it *was* closure for you."

"Maybe you're right."

At the end of the call, Nikki changes subjects and mentions her disturbing encounter with Chase. "He claimed Royce demolished Emma Hollander's face. Then he called Royce a serial abuser."

Shaunette gasps. "Do you think Chase is being honest? He can be a jealous weasel, so he might be trying to cause Royce's downfall. You know, lying on purpose."

"I thought of that, and I don't know what to believe. But even if Royce didn't bash Emma's face in, he still covered up the ATV accident. That's unforgivable."

"I agree. Gracious!" says Shaunette. "That poor kid's parents. They probably don't know the truth, even to this day."

"You're right. Where have all the good men gone? To quote that song from 'Footloose'. Okay. Get some sleep. I'll check on you later." Hanging up, Nikki goes to the fridge for a real beer. As she reclines on the sofa with Beau Dog, they sit in a ray of sunlight pouring through the window. Overwhelmed, she descends into thinking mode. She needs to figure this the hell out. Who is the murderer?

Piper Dupree, maybe? If Piper found out her husband was having an affair with Jentry Rae, a public reveal of it would've destroyed her perfect family and her well-cultivated brand.

315

Dante Marconi? Judging from his shrine of the Dallas Lonestars Cheerleaders, he is obsessed with the sexy dancers. And who was sexier than Jentry Rae Randall? Maybe, if he couldn't have her, nobody else was going to, either.

Chase Campbell? He, too, had an all-consuming fascination for the dead cheerleader. Plus, childhood rivalry could have come into play. Did Chase take away the one thing he could from Royce—Jentry Rae?

Royce Holt? Is he 'He Who Shall Not Be Named'? If Jentry Rae was going to have his baby, his football career would have imploded. He is the focused type. Nothing will get in the way of his success.

And finally, who are R.H. and D.M.? Nikki rubs her chin. She's dying to know what the tattoos on Jentry Rae's hips represent. In her opinion, Duke McCade can't be D.M. Why would the cheerleader ink "enemy" initials on her body? Nevertheless, the McCades could have had Jentry Rae extinguished.

All at once, the apartment seems too quiet, and Nikki doesn't feel like being alone with her thoughts anymore. She decides she needs some fresh air, so she grabs her wallet and steps outside. A rousing blues melody wafts along the breeze, giving her an idea. Tonight is the night she'll join the locals at Swindler's Bar for a tequila shot.

Neon beer signs blink and rowdy customers chat shoulder to shoulder inside the hole-in-the-wall establishment. As Nikki maneuvers through the crowd, she spots an empty bar stool. Settling on it, she throws back two shots, and then she makes a phone call.

When a receptionist at the police station picks up, Nikki asks for Detective Nico La Rosa. He seems less hotheaded than Sergeant Emerson.

"La Rosa here." The investigator comes on the line. "Who am I speaking with?"

"It isn't important," she answers in a thick, liquored voice. "Now, listen. You need to talk to a woman named Emma Hollander. Either Royce Holt or Chase Campbell put her in the hospital three years ago."

"Excuse me? You don't know which guy did it, lady? Are you ripped?"

She doesn't respond.

"Do you have proof of what you're saying?"

"Emma Hollander does."

"Why hasn't this woman come forward?" La Rosa asks.

"*You* are the detective; ask her. She'll tell the truth to a cop."

Thank God he hasn't registered that Nikki is phoning. The investigator must remember their disastrous conversation at her apartment, though—when Beau Dog peed on Sergeant Emerson's shoe. However, Nikki is doing a weird British accent tonight. Plus, she's really feeling the Jose Cuervo.

"Ma'am, we believe our investigation is on the right track as far as the recent homicide."

"So, you don't need my help?"

"I—"

"Was Royce Holt seen on video leaving the Americana Memorial Stadium around the time of Jentry Rae Randall's murder?" she asks.

"I can't divulge that."

317

"Footage can be spliced, Detective." *I should know. I'm a filmmaker.*

There is a cool silence.

"Okay, ma'am. I'll double-check what you're saying," La Rosa finally acquiesces.

She hangs up and gives her phone the finger. In the next instant, she chides herself. She can't blame the detective for being untrusting; she called anonymously.

Her next tequila shot tastes extra fiery and bitter. As it slides down her throat, she thinks about Shaunette being drunk on a game day. Pro cheerleaders produce endorphins while booze is a depressant. The effect must've been paradoxical for Shaunette that afternoon. So, what made her so upset that she got inebriated in the stadium parking lot and performed that way?

Drama with her mama, is what Shaunette claimed.

Or was it the ripple effect of the green-eyed monster?

Holy crap. The shots hit Nikki like a two-by-four—although she isn't mad about it. She wants to feel uncaged tonight. Nothing has been going her way, but what's bothering her most is getting the cold shoulder from Vince.

How long will he stay mad at her?

While she hunches over the sticky bar, she wants to prove to him that she isn't clutching at straws. To that end, she tries to discern if Emma Hollander is fabricating the truth because, who is the Renegades' cheerleader really protecting?

It's apparent, too, that Shaunette defends Royce's innocence sometimes. Maybe they have a unique bond. He has a pressuring parent, just like her, so both are living the ill effects of that heavy dynamic. Only, Shaunette needs to stay away from Royce. If he is abusive, the world will be shocked to learn he pulverized a woman and forced her to get a new face. He deserves to be punished in a court of law.

Or did Chase do it?

As Nikki spins her shot glass in circles, she wonders whose DNA is under Jentry Rae's fingernails. LeAnn McCade and Piper Dupree were in the DLC dressing room area on the day of the murder. *Sketchy.*

Thank God Shaunette has an alibi. But the police lab needs to hurry up with the full DNA results. Sonny doesn't have much time left.

The tequila hits Nikki even harder. Good thing her apartment is within walking distance. She is about to leave when the bartender asks, "Another shot of Cuervo, sweetheart?"

"Nah . . ."

"Wait. I recognize you. Somebody came in here the other day and showed me a clip of a film you're making about the Dallas Lonestars."

"Um, *was* making. But really?"

"Yeah. Great job with the interviews, honey. And go 'Stars! They're my team!" He indicates a game schedule on a wall.

"Thank you." Swaying on her barstool, she gives a drunken fist pump. Then she summons the bearded bartender closer by crooking her finger. "Since you know that I ask questions for a living, are you willing to tell me who showed you that clip?"

"No can do."

"Come on, man." She discreetly slides him a twenty-dollar bill.

He lowers his voice. "Okay. You know her."

"Her?"

"Yeah. It was Tammie Turner, the choreographer of the Dallas Lonestars Cheerleaders. She comes in all the time."

Surprise hits Nikki like a hailstorm. It must've been Tammie who recorded Shaunette drunk-dancing on the bar top right here. Evidently, the woman doesn't mess around when it comes to the DLC. "Are you serious?" she asks. "I sent Tammie some dailies, but she shouldn't have shared them with anyone. The film isn't finished. It'll never be finished thanks to her and others."

"I'm not sure what you're saying, but it looked like real good work." The bartender shrugs.

Nikki's imposter syndrome takes a temporary back seat. She *is* good at her job. The sports documentary had style, substance, and inspirational elements. Why does she doubt herself?

She notices as she glances around the seedy bar that it's packed fuller than a tin of sardines. Pubs are great places to go unnoticed—and if Tammie is a barfly who does nefarious things after dark, the choreographer could be one person by day and another by night.

The lumberjack-esque bartender lowers his voice. "I'll tell you more if your wallet is fat."

Nikki slides him a ten-dollar bill.

"Tammie Turner refuses to see the franchise go down in flames. She tried out for the cheerleaders years ago but was never selected. Now, she's honored to be the DLC choreographer and plans to protect the institution 'til her dying day. She said that the only person who could've killed Jentry Rae Randall was someone inside the Lonestars' organization." He wipes down a glass. "But you didn't hear those things from me."

"Right. My lips are sealed."

He points at a DLC poster hanging next to the Lonestars' game schedule. "People give the cheerleaders a hard time, but really, they're hot distractions on the field. I mean, yeah, their uniforms are scanty, but they aren't naked or nothing."

Naked?

Nikki freezes.

A revelation hits her harder than a baseball bat to the head. Despite the world believing Jentry Rae was found nude by first responders, Royce mentioned at Bogart's that the star cheerleader had *some* clothing on. Not a towel. *Clothing*.

If it's true, that detail was never publicly revealed. In addition, images of Jentry Rae's corpse are continually blurred out for the media.

Could Royce be correct?

God help him if he is.

Nobody but the killer would know that detail.

Sonny phones just then. Nikki's pulse races faster. She'll ask him about how Jentry Rae was found.

Turning away from the bartender, she puts a finger in her ear and answers the call. "Hey, Sonny? Can you hear me?"

"Barely, sugar." He sounds weak. "Are you at a truck rally?"

"A bar."

"I see. Um, thanks for setting up the hospice nurse. She has no humor, but I reckon she's okay."

"Good. You're welcome."

"I have some news," the old man says. "That paralegal called me . . . Kevin Drummond. DNA results have come back. You know, for the tissue collected from underneath my baby's fingernails?" He takes a breath. "It belongs to Royce Holt."

The world stops. Nikki's skin crawls. The final puzzle piece is in place.

"This is huge!" she cries.

"We're darned near finished, sugar. But the assistant DA told me to contain my excitement. The DNA results prove that Jentry Rae fought with Royce. Not that he killed her."

"Understood. Okay. Well, on that subject, I have an important question, Sonny. Were you shown Jentry Rae's crime scene photos?"

"Yep."

"I'm sorry to be indelicate, but was your daughter naked when she died?"

"Jeepers. Why you askin'?"

"Please just answer."

The old farmer's voice hitches. "She was wearing a bra and panties. Apparently, she was about to put her jewelry on after taking a shower, too."

Oh my God. Nikki's heart thrums. "And in the photos, was Jentry Rae's Lonestars' cheerleading ring anywhere in sight?"

"I told you, no. And I gol-durned want it. That pinkie ring meant everything to her. She only took it off to bathe."

Nikki nods. What did Dante Marconi claim he heard? *The sound of two objects clattering to the floor. Probably jewelry.* The items must have been the infinity bracelet *and* Jentry Rae's ring. The ring that has disappeared. It's clear that Dante must have heard the murder happen. And that's why he's involved in some underhanded shit.

Unless, of course, what the guard heard was Royce dropping his wedding band that day. Is it the reason the QB hasn't been seen wearing it?

Nikki needs to force Royce to slip up. He needs to admit that he fought with Jentry Rae, hurt her, and then picked up whatever was on the floor. It must have been what the cheerleader was reaching for in death, according to the photos on the news.

Bastard. As Nikki finishes off a last drib of tequila, she realizes without a doubt that Royce was in the locker room that afternoon. His DNA says so, and science doesn't lie.

"Are you sure you didn't see your daughter's ring in those photos, Sonny? Or take it from her apartment?" She holds her phone tighter.

"I'm positive," he replies groggily.

"All right. Thanks. You take care. I'll check on you later. Goodnight."

It's obvious that Royce is a narcissistic sociopath who has caused cataclysmic tragedy. No more fanfare for him, Nikki pledges. He must be locked away.

Her phone bleeps. Ironically, Royce is texting her. Stiffening, she reads the message, and the next second, fear tremors her body with tsunami force.

"Something wrong?" the bartender asks when she swivels back around.

Dry-mouthed, she doesn't answer. Her nerves are shooting sky high because Royce wants to meet her at the Lonestars' practice facility in an hour. He'll tell her everything if she comes alone.

Is it safe? *No.*

Will she go? *Yes.*

PART V

You can go to hell, and
I will go to Texas.

—Davy Crockett

MISSING ENTRY OF JENTRY RAE'S DIARY

OCTOBER 12—ONE DAY BEFORE HER MURDER

Previously, I carefully avoided writing my baby daddy's identity in this journal. But considering the pickle I'm in, I'm going to write it now: Royce Holt.

I figured it out after doing the math. I slept with Royce before I slept with Chase—and I'm four weeks pregnant now. I tried to confront Royce yesterday about having the baby, but then I chickened out.

A few weeks ago, I was at his house. His wife and daughter were traveling, so I excused myself and pretended to use his bathroom. Really, I went to his home office where he keeps his computer. It was open to his wife's social media account. Piper refers to Royce as "Monsieur Dupree"—which is so demeaning. Does he like being under her thumb? Does he want to leave her?

I hunted around on the computer and discovered something alarming. Piper was charged with assault and battery when she was in college. She smashed her roommate's head with a chair and put the girl in a coma. But Piper comes from a wealthy family and had a good lawyer, so she didn't serve jailtime. The incident was kept out of the papers, too. Still, the woman isn't right in the head. Royce told me she's in therapy for anger management issues.

What will Piper do if she learns that I'm sleeping with her husband? I should run for the hills! She is the reason I bought a gun.

The Holts appear to be the perfect family, but they're not. Maybe I can convince Royce to be with ME and OUR baby. I love him so much. He deserves a support system, instead of an unbalanced wife. She's a spinning ball of rage, and her anger is a tipping point for his temper. But I know he'd never hurt me. What's important now is that he and I are together. Forever. What we have is special. I feel it when we make love.

I'm going to ask Royce to meet me in the DLC locker room after tomorrow's game. That's when I'll tell him about the baby. He can sneak over after the other cheerleaders have cleared out. The guard Dante will let him in.

I can't wait to talk to him! I've already given our baby a gender-neutral name: Drew Marlowe. I hope Royce likes it. If not, it doesn't matter. I already got D.M. initials tattooed on my hip—in honor of the new love of my life.

I'll do my best to persuade Royce to leave Piper and marry me. If he agrees to help me raise our child, we'll be happier than pigs in mudpuddles. My daddy will be proud of me, too.

CHAPTER FIFTY

THE FILMMAKER

~ NOVEMBER 12 ~

Flustered, Nikki gets behind the wheel of the equipment van and presses the gas. She replied to Royce's text at Swindler's Bar and agreed to meet him tonight at The Depot at one a.m.

After that, she went to her apartment and made a pot of coffee. That's when she called Vince for backup. She was going to ask him to borrow a car and wait for her in The Depot's parking lot in case she needed him. But her call went to his voicemail after two rings. He rejected it.

Jesus. How far will Vince take their fight?

He is the Robin to her Batman, and she feels off-kilter without him.

Nikki pulls the van onto the freeway, nerves firing at the idea of meeting a potential murderer. Showing up alone at The

Depot isn't wise, but unless she speaks with Royce one-on-one, he won't spill the beans. No way will she miss this opportunity. She'll prove to the world that she was right about him all along. Prove it to Vince, too.

Maybe then she can atone for getting them fired from the documentary.

The good thing is Nikki has Jentry Rae's gun inside her waistband. She has her cell phone tucked into her knee-high boot, too. She *could* leave her phone under the driver's seat in order to regain Royce's trust, but she needs a way to contact somebody. In case she gets in trouble inside the complex.

Gripping the steering wheel tightly, she goes over her game plan. She might be able to tap into Royce's deepest thoughts using her interview skills. However, that feat will require being her most clear-headed and calculating self. Right now, she's a jittery mess. She needs to sober the fuck up.

Her phone rings. Jumping at the noise, she answers it on speaker mode. "Sonny? Are you okay?"

"I'm better than all right, sugar." He sounds loopy thanks to the painkillers. "I've decided I like the nurse. And hours ago, Jentry Rae spoke to me."

Nikki gulps more coffee in a takeaway cup. "What did Jentry Rae say?"

"My angel," he murmurs.

"I bet that was wonderful, Sonny. Do you want to share what your daughter said?"

"She urged me to find the pages she tore out of her diary. She'd keep secrets from me that way as a girl, and it drove me batty. The pages are somewhere in her apartment."

"You can't go back to Dallas in your condition."

"You don't understand, sugar. I'm asking you once more to go to Jentry Rae's place and look around. You still have the key, right?"

"Yes, and I will go. But right now, I'm meeting Royce Holt at The Depot. Please tell Brandon López I dove into the investigation, after all. What's startling is Royce swears he'll reveal everything." She pauses. "I think he did it, Sonny. I think he used his charm to seduce your girl, and then he killed her to stop her from ruining his life."

"Catch that sumbitch for me, Nikki," the old man growls.

"I will."

"Tell me you have the gun with you, sugar."

"Yes."

"Good. *Bee caareffull.*" Sonny's voice trails off. Seconds later, he comes back on the line. "You and Shaunette are like second daughters to me. I don't wanna lose y'all, too."

Emotion blocks Nikki's throat. Sonny has a pure, golden heart, and he was a caring father. Jentry Rae deserved to be with a sweet man like her dad. Unfortunately, Royce thought love was a zero-sum game.

Nikki floors the van. Royce can fool other women, but he can't fool her. If he hurt Jentry Rae it was out of selfishness. Supposing he was the father of her baby, he could have just insisted that she raise it on her own. Or he could have offered to pay for the child's life and then stepped back. He didn't have to kill her when she wouldn't get rid of the baby.

Did Royce snap in the heat of the moment?

Is there anything more chilling?

"Sonny? Hello?" Nikki calls out.

When she hears the old man snoring, she hangs up.

331

It's past one a.m. by the time she gets to the practice compound. Usually, the place is abuzz with activity—coaches blowing whistles and players grinding out tactical drills—but tonight the compound is sleeping under a full moon.

She pulls the van through the guard gate without a problem. Either Royce re-added her to the approved guest list, or he swore the guard to secrecy. The guard happens to be the one who flirted with Nikki before. He is probably wondering what she's doing here at this hour. She felt like telling him she wasn't one of Royce's mistresses.

After she parks, she hurries to the central practice building where the football players hold court. A revolving door leads her into a shiny lobby, and as she steps across the team's lassoed "L" logo engraved on the tile floor, she shudders. She has been banned from this place. But as luck would have it, the foyer is empty; the only sign of life is coming from a mounted television playing the Lonestars' Network.

Trying her best not to be scared, Nikki moves deeper into the building. The phone in her boot feels heavy, as does the gun in her back waistband. Hopefully, the long dark sweater she is wearing hides the firearm well.

Reaching for her vape pen, she puffs on it, but the nicotine just accelerates her anxiety. She stuffs the pen away and begins to peek inside the physical therapy room, the weight-lifting room, and the locker room. There is no sign of Royce.

Instinct tells her to cut across the practice field to the Lonestars Club—where the cheerleaders rehearse. Her heart pounds faster as she traverses the dim indoor playing field. Just when she reaches the fifty-yard line, spotlights boom on.

"Jesus!" she cries. "Is anyone there?"

Nobody answers.

Presumably, the lights are hooked up to an automatic sensor. She hates to think somebody is toying with her.

Pulse roaring, she approaches the Lonestars Club but finds the door locked. After she pulls repeatedly on the handlebar, she looks around as her impatience and fright grow. "Royce, if you're in there, let me in!"

She waits and waits.

Hurry up, you psycho.

Moments later, he opens the door.

"How did you get in this building?" she asks, dry-mouthed.

He has a bizarre look on his face—as if he's a million miles away. He points to her pockets without speaking. She shows him that they're empty, and then she fibs about her cell phone being in the van.

Doubt layers Royce's expression. He asks Nikki to turn in a circle while he scans her body. Red-faced, he gestures to her right boot next. "What's that bulge?"

"You got me." Her heartbeat gallops. "It's my phone."

"Goddamn it, Keegan! You're recording me again? Hand it over."

Shit. There goes her chance to call anyone or get anything Royce says on tape. Should she flee now? At least she still has the concealed gun.

She fakes nonchalance when the quarterback shoves her phone into his pant pocket. Then he instructs her to follow him. Royce guides her down a corridor flanked by DLC images, staring straight ahead and not speaking.

"Hey." Nikki taps him on the shoulder. "Are you all right?"

He makes no reply.

Scared, she follows him into the rehearsal room. There, a pile of blue and gold pom-poms shimmer in a corner. Pupils dilated, Royce motions to them with eerie conviction. "Jentry Rae told me they keep extras on hand in case the girls lose one. She was an amazing cheerleader, wasn't she?"

Nikki nods. The gun is sliding further down inside her stretch pants. And while she's glad that the safety is on, she wonders if she can go through all the movements needed to take the safety off and shoot in time. She has only fired a pistol once.

"Let me show you something." The on-edge QB indicates a framed memento of Jentry Rae on a wall. It displays her uniform and a glossy photo of her.

Both of them step up to it.

Nikki cocks her head. She knows that the Lonestars Cheerleaders are required to turn in their uniforms at the end of the season, so this is a sad exception. In the color photograph, Jentry Rae's beautiful face glows with eternal youth.

"Faces are strange things, aren't they?" Royce asks. "They can mask a lot of pain."

"I suppose. But they can also relay joy and fulfillment. Look at Jentry Rae's expression there. Nothing made her happier than being a DLC."

He shrugs. "I agree. She had a bright light. But she also knew how to goddamned push. She sure pushed my marriage to the brink." An overhead light falls on the angled planes of his face, lending him a ghostly appearance.

"If I'm being honest, you don't seem to take your marriage seriously, Royce. You never wear a wedding ring."

"Never have." He continues looking straight ahead. "It's locked in a drawer at home." He pauses. "Let's talk about what's important. Everybody knows that football has end zones and goal posts. Plus, basketball has the hoop, and hockey has a goal cage, but no player scores any points when it's Judgment Day."

What the hell does that mean? Nikki wonders.

Acting like an unfeeling cyborg, Royce shoves his hands inside his pockets. When he extracts them to gesture, a gold DLC pinkie ring falls out and clatters to the floor.

Nikki's heart skips a beat. *Holy Christ!* It must be Jentry Rae's.

Flushing, Royce flings her a guilty look. Then he quickly snatches up the ring.

Concern pings sharply through her. She knows she isn't safe here, but she needs to hear the truth. "Tell me everything, Royce. I'm listening."

"No one can be ready for this, Keegan. But you're going to hear it anyway."

CHAPTER FIFTY-ONE

THE FILMMAKER

~ *NOVEMBER 12* ~

The anger on Royce's face deepens as Nikki's anxiety catapults.

She suspects a confession is coming, and she regrets all over again that the football player spotted her cell phone in her boot.

Tilting his head, Royce stares at the photo of Jentry Rae. "I met with her in secret after the game against the Philadelphia Condors."

"And?"

He clams up, shaking his head like a petulant child.

"It's okay. Nobody else is here. Tell me and I won't repeat what you say."

"It's hard. What I did to Jentry Rae was horrible." Royce sniffs back tears. "I'm a monster."

Nikki's blood is rushing at a furious rate, but she tries to keep her voice steady. "I promise you'll feel better once you get everything off your chest."

His faraway look returns. "I wasn't put in the game that day. Hutchinson was appointed QB1, and it pissed me off. My ass got numb from sitting on the bench while he screwed up. My father watched that game."

"Queuing up is tough for you, huh?"

"Hell, yeah."

"What did you do once the game ended?" she asks.

"Jentry Rae wanted to meet me in the cheerleader's locker room. We both had burner phones, and she messaged me before the game to come. I kept texting back 'no.' Finally, she sent me a message that 'someone has a bun in the oven'—with a winkie face emoji. Can you believe it? I panicked. I needed her to understand that I couldn't be with her, so a guard named Dante let me in that section of the stadium. He must have been sweet on Jentry Rae."

"You met with her when you were already riled up?"

"Yeah. Which was stupid. I was *too* worked up. My father— he demands perfection. A secret baby would've ruined my career and disgraced him. I needed the chance to make him proud." Going pale, Royce rakes his fingers through his hair.

"What happened next with Jentry Rae?" Nikki asks.

"I refused to raise her child, and she broke down in tears."

"*Her* child? It was yours, too, right? You should've given her a break."

"No fucking way! She tricked me!"

Royce is growing more unstable by the minute. *Maybe*, Nikki thinks, *I should reach for the gun when he isn't looking.*

337

Debating, she presses her shoulders down. "Jentry Rae was in a complicated situation. It could be that she feared losing her father's respect." She pauses. "You can relate to being a tight spot, can't you?"

"Stop. You aren't a psychiatrist, Keegan."

"Sorry. Okay. How did you leave things?" She forces a compassionate expression.

"Jentry Rae's voice became high-pitched. Frantic. Her pleading still rings in my ears. She asked me one last time if I would step up and be the baby's father. I told her to terminate the pregnancy. That's when she threatened me. She swore she'd report our affair. She said she would also tell the Lonestars' administrators that I wanted to get rid of the baby. Word would get out. This is Texas. Full of conservatives. She threatened to reveal that I killed that boy on my ATV, too."

Nikki gasps. "You told me *Chase* ran him over!"

"It wasn't the truth."

"God! You're a liar and a murderer?"

He shoots her a furious look. "Shut up and listen. Jentry Rae was going to use my lies against me. Like powerful ammunition. I believed her because you should've seen the look on her face. She changed then. She tried to be strong. For a split second, I respected her for standing up for herself."

Sympathy for Jentry Rae makes Nikki's head spin. She got herself into a drastic situation. Her mother died having her, and she probably wanted help through the birthing process and beyond. Feeling gridlocked, maybe she didn't see another way out. *God.* Why didn't Royce have a shred of empathy?

Royce continues to fume. "I attempted smooth-talking Jentry Rae next. She was wearing a sexy bra and panties, so I tried to be romantic. But when I touched her, she recoiled, and it enraged me."

Nikki looks at his large hands. *The strength he must've used . . .*

"Like I said, I'm screwed now. Even if I'm exonerated, my name is tainted and Duke McCade won't want me on his team. My life is spiraling down the fucking drain."

"You don't know that, Royce."

"I goddamned do! I shouldn't have dated Jentry Rae in the first place. She got in the way."

"Got in the way? She was a human being! Her life was more important than your career!"

"What do you know about hard work, Keegan? You climb over people to get ahead."

"That isn't fair. And don't change the subject. What happened next?"

"Jentry Rae picked up a towel, covered herself with it, and then she got in my face. She said I was missing out on an opportunity. She claimed her goal was to gather evidence about Duke McCade. He tried to slander her father and ruin his reputation in the farming world. She wanted *me* to use that little scandal to find out if McCade had other underhanded dealings."

"Blackmail?"

"Jentry Rae said McCade was in the wrong."

Nikki steps back. "But implicating Duke McCade would've cost her her spot on the DLC squad, right?"

"She was pregnant, remember? She wasn't going to be a cheerleader anymore." Royce circles the studio like a caged animal. "The girl was crazy enough to name me as the baby father in her diary. I know because I had a key to her place and read the pages right after she died. Once I hid them where they wouldn't be found in her apartment, I left the building. A mob had gathered outside, so I was forced to hide in the crowd like a nervous idiot."

Nikki's stomach does backflips. She is playing along to the best of her ability, but it's a struggle. "I'm sure you were angry with Jentry Rae when you confronted her in the locker room. Right?"

"I was. I couldn't watch her bring me or the Lonestars down, so I grabbed her wrist. She dug her long nails into my arm. That's when she said she'd run to Chase. He treated her better, she claimed. She slept with him after she slept with me! She bragged that Chase would protect her. Christ, she was trying to control me like my wife does. And the way she looked at me . . . exactly how other girls I hooked up with looked at me when I—"

"Hit them?" Nikki's heartbeat goes warp speed.

He balls his hands into fists. "I made myself let go of Jentry Rae, but she came at me, screeching that I was done in football. She thought she could call the shots. Hold shit over my head. Fuck, I get enough of that at home, so I saw red."

"Is that when you shoved her against a metal locker?"

"It was an accident, all right? I lost my temper! I jostled Jentry Rae around a little and her towel flew off. She started hitting me, so I pushed her away. I guess I pushed her so hard that she sailed backwards against the locker. The impact cracked the back of her head open." Tears spring to Royce's eyes.

Nikki is tempted to reach for the gun that's tucked in her waistband. Except, her inner voice is urging her to leave the facility before the quarterback hurts her, too. She knows too much.

"Like I said, I snapped. But I can't go to prison," he hollers.

"Maybe plead temporary insanity—"

"My fate is doomed, Keegan."

"Do the right thing. Confess."

His hands shake. Then his expression changes. "You were right. I do feel better now."

No, no, no. A chill skitters up Nikki's spine. What has she done? It dawns on her that Royce brought her here with no intention of letting her go. It's why he just released a shocking sluicegate of truth.

Terrified, she edges backward.

"Dante Marconi must've covered up Jentry Rae's body with a towel afterwards," Royce says as he stalks forward. "And Shaunette told me that Jentry Rae filmed a catfight they had. There was scratching involved. The police must know that by now, so Shaunette might be blamed because of DNA. I'm hoping I can still walk away from this."

You're wrong, Nikki thinks. *Shaunette has an alibi. Also, her DNA isn't under Jentry Rae's fingernails. Yours is.*

While hot blood roars in her ears, she glances at the door. Should she make a run for it? How far would she get?

"I went home and told my wife everything afterward." An eerie smile curls Royce's lips. "Piper almost left me, but then she came up with a brilliant plan. She paid Marconi to say he heard nothing that afternoon and that I was never inside the locker room that day."

"Your wife's name is on the stadium visitor's list . . . because?"

"She suspected before the game that I had a thing with Jentry Rae. My wife came to the DLC area for a confrontation, but then she changed her mind and left." He pauses. "She and I are counting on no witnesses."

Skin chilling, Nikki trips as she backs up. "Don't worry. I'm going to leave, but you have my word that I won't repeat anything you said."

"I can't let you go, Keegan. You have the ambition gene. You'll rat me out. Now, keep quiet and accept your fate." Closing in on her like a creeping spider, Royce lunges forward, grabs hold of her neck, and squeezes. Panicked, she tries to fight him off, but he's too strong. Too infuriated. Too determined.

Time stops. As Nikki's larynx shuts off any air, she swears she is trapped under a thick layer of ice on a winter's pond. Everything on the other side is blurry . . . morgue quiet.

Her pulse slows as her mind races for a survival plan. But God help her that she can't think straight in this life-or-death moment! She can't call out, either—and it horrifies her to conceive that she wouldn't be heard even if she could scream.

Royce uses his athletic power to wrestle her to the floor. When he straddles her and pins her arms beneath his knees, she almost loses bladder control. She's unable to reach the gun, and the tighter he squeezes her neck, the more pain encircles her throat like a sharp ring of thorns.

"Stay still! It'll be over in a minute," he thunders.

She kicks and flails, fighting his weight with all her might. Except, it's useless. Her brain is starved for oxygen, so she becomes a flimsy kite in a raging storm. All at once, her life flashes before her like landscapes glimpsed through a train window. Her pop is singing her to sleep at age five. Next, she's at her high school graduation, accepting a photojournalism award. Then she's at her worst job at a Dairy Queen where the air conditioning goes out and all the ice cream melts. Finally, she sees Shaunette's and Vince's faces. Why didn't she ever tell them they were great friends?

This can't be how her life ends!

Nikki snatches one last glance at Royce's contorted expression. He might be a deadly parent pleaser, but underneath, he has tremendous, burgeoning talent. For a split second, she feels sorry for him. She lets her eyelids drop, knowing she is about to become his next murder victim. Everything goes dark.

Just then, a noise rises above Nikki's non-responsive state. The studio door bursts open, causing Royce to loosen his grip. Shuffling noises and muffled voices echo around her. She flutters her eyes open. Vince is there. Grunting and growling like an animal, he dives at Royce, wearing an expression she has never seen before.

"Get the hell off Nikki!" Vince shouts. After he tugs and yanks at the football player's hands, he finally pulls the quarterback away from her.

She scrambles to a corner, holding her raw throat. There, she watches a riveting scene play out.

Vince and Royce start to clobber each other in an all-out brawl. With primal blows and lightning-fast punches, they battle in what becomes a bloodbath. Tall, skinny Vince is surprisingly strong—that or fury is increasing his adrenaline. As he sends Royce flying into the wall mirror, the glass shatters and pieces spill to the floor in sickening clinks. Royce isn't fazed, though. He gets up and hammers Vince across the jaw.

"Stop, Royce!" Nikki yells, but her voice is an inaudible croak.

Sliced by a mirror shard and bleeding, Royce wrangles Vince to the floor. Suddenly, the tables turn. Vince flips Royce over and wallops him against a long wall. Next, Vince pummels the quarterback to the floor. While he steps away, breathing hard, blood on his mouth, Royce gets to his feet in a surge of energy, and the opponents resume their fight like a pair of dueling cannons.

Petrified, Nikki reaches into her waistband and grabs the gun. She's unable to hold it in her shaky hands, so it falls out of her grasp and skitters a few yards away. Royce's eyes flit to her. It's enough time for Vince to beat the shit out of him.

Vince throws one last punch, which knocks Royce out.

The football player crashes to the hardwood floor like a slain giant. If he'd have been wearing a helmet, it would've flown off.

"Game over, you sacked motherfucker!" Vince throws his hands up. Catching his breath, he looks at his cut-up knuckles. Then he hustles to Nikki's side. "Are you all right?"

"I am now," she ekes out. "Thanks. I owe you my life."

"I listened to your voicemail, Nik. I've been in the parking lot this whole time. Until I realized how long you were taking. And then I got worried."

She nods. "I was afraid you wouldn't show up. Or that the guard wouldn't let you through the gate."

"I never turned in my access badge," Vince admits sheepishly. "Here's more good news. I filmed from behind the door—until it got too dangerous."

"You waited a little long! Christ!" she complains in a scratchy voice.

"I'm ready to put together a bang-up crime series. But right now, I'm calling the cops." Grinning, he moves away and gets on his phone.

Nikki picks Jentry Rae's pink gun off the floor. Damn it that she blew her chance to shoot Royce. That would've felt good. At least Vince was her hero today. Impulsively, she catches up to him and gives him a hug. He seems thrilled.

As he searches for something he can restrain Royce with, she tries to settle down. The aura inside the dance studio descends into quiet relief at the same time. The ordeal was traumatic, but at least she and Vince are alive to talk about it.

When Nikki glances at a group photo of the Dallas Lonestars Cheerleaders, she hopes Jentry Rae heard Royce's confession. The cheerleader deserves a satisfying sense of justice.

Royce stirs in the blink of an eye. He leaps to his feet and snatches up a jagged slice of mirror. Raging, he darts forward and lunges at Nikki with it. She hustles backward, stumbles, and falls flat on her back. The gun tumbles out of her hands again, sliding out of reach. She screams at the top of her lungs, Royce nearly on top of her. As her heartbeat erupts in explosive booms, it signals that the end is happening.

Shaunette rushes through the door. Picking up the pistol, she aims it at Royce and fires a fatal shot at his heart. He halts and jerks, looking like a villain in a horror film, and then he crumples in a heap.

"That's for Jentry Rae!" Shaunette screeches. Her face is a mixture of gratification and mortification as she lets go of the gun. Next, she goes still; she's likely in shock.

Vince leans down and checks for a pulse. "Royce is dead."

"You saved my life." Nikki sags against Shaunette. Thank God for her friends. They were her saviors today. She might have done her best in the face of death, but she wouldn't be alive without Vince and Shaunette.

It gives her an idea. "Fuck Royce," she whispers in Shaunette's ear. "Let's say you weren't here at all."

Trembling, Nikki feels a sense of closure roll through her. Vince captured Royce's startling confession on tape, and that provides an incredible finale to the true-crime series of the decade. Yet deep down, the new her doesn't care about that. She is more grateful that she kept her promise to dying Sonny.

CHAPTER FIFTY-TWO

THE FILMMAKER

~ *NOVEMBER 12* ~

Moments before the police arrive at the DLC dance studio, Nikki wipes Shaunette's fingerprints off Jentry Rae's pink gun. Then she presses her own prints on the trigger.

In the meantime, Shaunette hurries to the ladies' room to wash gunshot residue from her hands.

"How did you know to come here?" Nikki asks her when she emerges. "I mean, how did you get here from Beaumont?"

"Sonny called and told me what was happening. I escaped the hospital—Sergeant Emerson never posted a police guard. Then I Uber-ed to Sonny's farm and drove his truck here."

"You should leave now," Nikki urges her. "If I don't pretend I shot Royce, you might not be a Dallas Lonestars Cheerleader again."

"I don't care about that," Shaunette insists.

"Okay. We'll do this for your future, then."

The cheerleader protests more, but Nikki won't change her mind. Shaunette has been through enough: the murder of her best friend, the suspicions of her teammates, a near-fatal car crash, a brain blood clot, and her mother's death. Besides, Vince caught Nikki on tape being throttled by madman Royce. Claiming that she broke away from his clutches and shot him in self-defense is entirely plausible.

One more step is needed to fully cover for Shaunette, however. Nikki must conceal the cheerleader's presence at the dance studio altogether. The guard on duty might be bribe-able; he likes Nikki. She might give him her phone number. Or feature him in the crime series.

Investigators arrive after Shaunette sneaks out. First, they spread out and access the scene, asking a litany of questions. A CSI unit gets to work, as well. In the end, Nikki and Vince behave cooperatively, and the police detectives conclude that Nikki justifiably shot Royce Holt in self-defense.

Vince hands over his cell phone to the investigators prior to leaving. Of course, he emailed what he captured to himself before the authorities arrived. "Let's go," he whispers to Nikki with a proud smile. "Thank God for contract loopholes. You and I have a series pitch deck to assemble."

Shaunette cries the entire drive back to Beaumont. The old, dilapidated truck barely gets her there, but breaking down on the side of the road isn't her main concern. All she can think about is Sonny. Perhaps she killed Royce as much for the sweet, old farmer as she did for Jentry Rae. He was the father she never had, for a brief time.

Royce committed a grotesque, merciless act of violence—and the vindication trilling through Shaunette feels amazing. It's better than a sugary, syrupy, confectionary high that robs your senses blind.

Maybe Royce would've gone to prison for ending Jentry Rae's life.

Maybe not.

Now there is no need to place wagers.

Shaunette never was a betting kind of girl, anyhow.

Actually, she is crying for all sorts of reasons. Because it's a new day and the tangerine sun looks magnificent against a brilliant blue sky. And because somehow, she senses that Jentry Rae is in the truck with her, seeing the sunrise. Ending somebody's life is a moral dilemma Shaunette will grapple with later. But for now, she wipes her tears, sings a Taylor Swift song, and reaches for a Jack Link's beef stick.

Nikki shuts down inside her apartment for days after the heinous episode at The Depot. She explains to Vince that she needs time alone. Exhausted, she tries to process all that's happened. When she finally comes to the point when she can move on, she forces herself out of bed and puts the crime series together with Vince's help.

A few weeks later, she holds her breath and sends the footage to an entertainment agent with ties to streaming services.

What she reads online in the interim nearly equals the shock of Royce trying to squeeze the life out of her inside the DLC dance studio.

ARTICLE—THE DALLAS MORNING NEWS

DECEMBER 11, 2024

A former employee at the Dallas Lonestars' home stadium has come forward with bold claims. Security guard Dante Marconi asserts that he innocently covered murder victim Jentry Rae Randall with a towel after discovering her dead body. It explains his DNA being on the item. Moreover, Marconi has admitted that Piper Dupree, wife of late first-string Lonestars' quarterback Royce Holt, paid him a total of $50,000 dollars to commit aggravated stalker crimes in the wake of the cheerleader's demise. The offenses include breaking and entering, vandalism, recording filmmaker Nikki Keegan while asleep, sending her threatening text messages, and running DLC Shaunette Simmons into a cement pylon.

Most importantly, Marconi asserts that he was paid by Dupree to hide the fact that Dupree's husband entered the locker room of the Dallas Lonestars Cheerleaders on the day of the murder. Holt, prior to his death, confessed to killing Jentry Rae Randall on October 13 of this year.

Investigators have seized Piper Dupree's computer. Allegedly, Dupree had been using an IP number voiceover to make a false identity. Now, she is facing four criminal charges herself: two counts of bribery in the private sector, one count of creating a false identity, and one count of aggravated stalking.

The famous sports wife had plans to leave Texas and return to her hometown of Boston, but her pending arraignment will prevent that.

CHAPTER FIFTY-THREE

THE DALLAS LONESTARS CHEERLEADER

~ FEBRUARY 3, 2025 ~

Shaunette accompanies Nikki to Jentry Rae's apartment on a chilly winter morning. Months have passed since that day at The Depot, but it still doesn't seem real.

Nikki uses the key Sonny gave her to open the unit, and they step inside. A group photo of the Dallas Lonestars Cheerleaders on a wall greets them. Locking eyes with her former squad mates makes Shaunette shiver. Or maybe the apartment's icy temperature is making her cold.

At any rate, corkscrew-crooked deeds are lingering in the air.

So many people in this scenario have done wrong.

"I'm sorry, girl," Shaunette mouths to Jentry Rae's face in the photo. The apology is a start in dispelling the bad blood between them.

"Nice place. But yikes—" Nikki tucks the apartment key into her pocket.

"Yeah. Jentry Rae always was messy."

"No kidding. Finding anything in here will be hard. At least Sonny suggested a few spots for us to look for the missing diary pages. Places he didn't have time to check. I want to prove to him that Royce tore the entries out and hid them. Anyway, first things first. Thanks for meeting me here."

They hug.

Nikki wipes a tear away.

So does Shaunette.

"You're crying. I'm not crying," Nikki jokes.

"I missed you, too." Shaunette laughs.

"*Erm*, how are you holding up? Sorry again about your mom."

"Thanks." Shaunette swallows hard. "Losing her was tough. But she isn't suffering anymore." She pauses. "And your dad is good, right? You told me that things are better with him when you and I FaceTimed last."

"Yeah. He's great." Nikki nods. "So, give me some updates. Where has life taken you lately?"

"In a whole new direction. I just enrolled in school to study psychology. I'd like to become a family therapist—to help young people strive for their goals instead of fulfilling their parents' dreams." Shaunette beams. "Using my brain instead of my looks will be refreshing. Student debt is another thing altogether but worth it, hopefully."

"New year, new you. You'll slay it." Nikki pauses. "So, no more professional cheerleading?"

"No." Does her expression adequately express her relief? "I met a guy, though."

"Fantastic!" The filmmaker tucks a chunk of dark hair behind her ear. "Um, while I was in California these past months, I thought of something, so, I'll just ask. If you're not too busy with college, will you co-produce the crime series with me? On the off chance that it's picked up by a streaming platform?"

Shaunette frowns. "I don't know the first thing about that."

"It's easy. And I have an inkling that money won't be a problem for you for long."

"What money?"

"I get these feelings." Nikki smiles. "Anyway, will you?"

"I'd love to." The prospect of steering her own ship fills Shaunette with excitement. But right now, she needs to get through being inside her dead friend's apartment. "All right. Let's show the world what Jentry Rae went through. To do that, we need her full story."

Nikki babbles out a recent update while they search for the diary pages. "I did a final interview with Chase Campbell. He's in the process of making amends with the family of the boy Royce killed with his ATV. He admitted that he shouldn't have covered up the incident. Legal repercussions are on the horizon, and Chase is willing to face them."

"Good for him. But he's still a prick." Shaunette rolls her eyes.

"Duke McCade's backhanded business tactics have been exposed to the police. Detectives found the proof on Jentry Rae's computer . . . she delved into the details herself. I hope McCade does jail time. Also, Piper Dupree deleted all her social media. No surprise there, right? She called and asked to be featured in the crime series—as a face for domestic violence survivors. She's professing that Royce was emotionally abusive behind the scenes."

"Which isn't impossible. Do you believe her?"

"I'm not sure," Nikki replies. "But I included her in the program anyway, in case the DV *did* happen. Secretly, I suspect she's looking for free press."

"Right. Okay. Well, this closet is a dead end. Where to now?" Shaunette asks.

Nikki points to Jentry Rae's powder room. "Sonny told me he didn't do a thorough search of it. He suggested we look behind the medicine cabinet."

As Shaunette passes the DLC group photo on the wall, she glances at her forehead scar in the glass reflection. The mark will remain deep, but she isn't fretting over it. It's a badge of courage.

Both women enter the small bathroom when Nikki turns the light on. She opens the mirrored cabinet door, removes ointments, cotton balls, sunscreen, and antiseptics, and after she lifts the shelving out, she extracts the cabinet insert with a crowbar Shaunette hands her.

Shaunette holds her breath. Taped to the back of it is a manila envelope. "Oh my God," she says quietly.

Hands shaking, Nikki slides out pages that were torn from Jentry Rae's journal. They're dated September 1, September 16, and October 12. As soon as she replaces the cabinet insert, she and Shaunette step out of the tiny powder room. "These pages must contain incriminating information. Hallelujah. Mission accomplished."

"Let's read them, but not here," Shaunette suggests.

They expel a breath.

"We turned out to be bad-asses, right?" Nikki smiles. "I'm feeling pretty proud. How about you?"

"I'm damned proud of us. How's your imposter syndrome?"

"Gone. I'm done self-editing and self-effacing. Detrimental habits. Anyway, we did what we set out to do. Now, there is only one thing left on our plate."

"What's that?"

"Returning to Vale View Farm."

A somber breeze rustles the pecan trees and the strawberry patches on Sonny Randall's property. Shaunette gets out of the equipment van and inhales the country air while Nikki remains in the driver's seat.

"This is something you need to do on your own," Nikki encourages her.

Nodding, Shaunette grasps her handbag closely as she trudges up the hill to Jentry Rae's grave. Butterflies tumble in her stomach when she reaches the top. The family plots are encircled by a low fence, and she enters the burial yard by stepping through a rickety gate. Thank heaven she is clear-headed today. Her lung and her arm have completely healed, too.

In the still morning, a haunting breeze rushes over the head-stones, as if the spirits below ground are blowing out a breath. The moment heightens Shaunette's senses. Or maybe she is feel-ing things so acutely because she hasn't had a drink in months. She doesn't miss it.

"Hey, Jentry Rae." She runs her fingertips over her friends' headstone. Leaves from a nearby tree fall on the marker, and she wipes them away.

"There is so much I want to tell you because so much has happened. First off, I should have been there for you. You were dealing with a lot, but I was deaf, dumb, and blind to your problems. You knew full well that I was texting back and forth with Royce, and I let you believe he was attracted to me—even though he and I were just friends.

"I apologize for lying about that. And I hate that I was your bestie disguised as your worst enemy. If I had valued myself, I wouldn't have treated you like a competitor. We were on the same team, for heaven's sake! You entrusted me with your deepest secrets, and what did I do? I secretly envied you."

Shaunette hesitates. "Incredibly, you were able to see what *I* needed. You told me to stand up to my mama, and I should have . . . long ago. Everybody needs to live their own life on their own terms, right? I hope you're glad to hear me say that."

Another soft breeze ruffles her hair. Jentry Rae might be answering her.

"But I was right about something you got wrong. You should've reported Royce to the higher-ups. Luckily, he can't hurt anybody anymore. I shot that son of a bitch. And when I did, I took back my power." Pride pings through Shaunette.

A warm, golden sun peeks through the cloud cover. Amid the unearthly hush, she withdraws Jentry Rae's DLC pinkie ring and diary from her bag. Nikki picked the ring up at the dance studio before the police arrived, and as she handed it to Shaunette, she explained that it fell out of Royce's pocket when he landed dead.

"Jentry Rae, your daddy wanted me to set these on your gravestone. But assuming robbers will take them, I'll—" She kneels down, paws at the dirt with her fingers, and then stuffs the objects deep in the earth. "There. Your prized possessions are with you forever."

Her eyes shift to Sonny's headstone. "Thank you for entrusting your farm to me and Nikki, Sonny. You'll be seeing us around here a lot. After all, you taught us that a person's heart should always be in the right place, and that doggedness is okay when it comes from the heart. Nikki and I didn't expect to *inherit* your farm, but we're grateful for it. And since you stipulated in your will that you want us to sell it, that's what we'll do.

"I'm done talking about me now. Because—what was it you said once? Complaining is as worthless as chewing gum on a boot heel.

"I really hope you're at the pearly gates with your wife and daughter. Have a nice rest, cowboy."

Epilogue

Good morning, Lonestars fans.
Don't fret. Another football season
is on the horizon.

SEPTEMBER 9, 2025

Nikki is at a Hollywood sound studio, about to be filmed for the "Director's Footnote" portion of the crime series. The seven-part limited show has been picked up by Hulu—and the subscription hub is asking for a personal touch. Sitting on a stool, Nikki shoos away the makeup artist who's been fussing over her. Then she takes a sip of water.

"Four-three-two-one. Rolling," Vince says.

"I hope you have enjoyed watching *Murder in the Lonestar State*. It was an honor for me to highlight what happened to Jentry Rae Randall—the magnanimous star of the Dallas Lonestars Cheerleaders. She lived a big, bright, beautiful life, but her death couldn't have been darker.

"In 2024, I was originally hired to put together a sports documentary about the comeback of the Dallas Lonestars football team. Jentry Raé was at the pinnacle of her beauty then, and considering her talent, leadership ability, and generous nature, she didn't deserve to die. However, one positive has surfaced from her passing. Her loss shined a spotlight on a certain quarterback's greed and selfishness.

"A famous head coach once said, 'Texas is to football what religion is to a priest.' Which is why I wanted to do right by the suited-and-booted global fan base of the Dallas Lonestars. Production of this series took nearly a year from start to release, due to my insistence that it include legal updates. Royce Holt, if he hadn't died, would have faced second-degree murder charges for the murder of Jentry Rae Randall. Dante Marconi, the former chief security guard at the Lonestars Stadium, is serving time for harassment and for taking bribes from Piper Dupree, Royce Holt's wife. Duke McCade has been forced to forfeit a large portion of his assets to reconcile illegal business dealings. And as portrayed in the show, Piper Dupree has been indicted for serious crimes, too. She is serving a five-year prison sentence while her parents care for her children.

"All of this is shocking news, but the harsh truth is scandal isn't unique to the Federation Football League. It has survived drug possessions, changes in controversial team names, bounty scandals, and labor disputes. However, it's safe to say that the game of football will remain an American institution.

"Part of that picture includes the Dallas Lonestars Cheerleaders. The dancers might operate at the intersection of everyday happy and hidden malfunction, but there is nothing wrong with women being alluring. If females want to celebrate their appeal on a worldwide stage, let them. Trouble only creeps in when we compare ourselves to standards we *believe* are impossible.

"In the end, being a revered professional cheerleader amplified Jentry Rae's voice. On that note, she embodied a universal, inspiring truth. That people are their most beautiful when they do what makes them *feel* beautiful. I personally believe anybody with passion, independence, and confidence is an irresistible force of nature.

"That being said, glorious Jentry Rae Randall might have dazzled the world, captured fans' hearts, and danced like nobody was watching, but she wasn't perfect. And maybe that is her greatest message. If you could be perfect, would you want to be?

"Thank you for exploring the effects of greed, jealousy, and betrayal with me. May all of us strive to do better. Goodnight."

Nikki moves out of the frame and hugs her father. He is wearing the spiffy new shirt she bought him. He is also enjoying the three-thousand-square foot home she purchased for him in LA.

Vince turns the camera off saying, "That's a wrap."

Nikki thanks everybody, including Shaunette.

Shaunette glows with approval. "Amazing job, Nikki. But I wish you could add my DLC teammate Ashleigh to your list of crooks. Yesterday, she was thrown off the squad for allegedly planting banned substances in other dancers' lockers. The Lonestars are keeping the incident on the down-low while they investigate it. Ashleigh issued a statement of regret for trying to sabotage me with the rat and for framing Priya, but nobody has accepted her apology."

"The whole thing is unbelievable." Nikki shakes her head.

"Next year there will be a new team of thirty-six squad members," Shaunette reminds her. "I hope this project is a cautionary tale for them."

"Right, because we know what can happen when you don't follow the rules," Nikki half-jokes.

Together, she and Shaunette have endured something life-changing. And now, their resilient friendship feels like a rubber band that can stretch but will never break . . . a bright spot in a sometimes-difficult world.

Which is what Jentry Rae was.

Something dawns on Nikki.

She pivots around. "Vince, can you please turn the camera back on? I want to make one more comment."

"You got it."

Standing erect, she looks straight into the lens and adds, "Wherever you are, Jentry Rae, I wish you 'Cheers and God-speed.' And with utmost respect, I also want to say, 'Bless your heart.'"

THE END

ACKNOWLEDGEMENTS

Being a former Dallas Cowboys Cheerleader isn't a subject that comes up in everyday conversation. But when my literary agent found out I used to be one, she said, "Wouldn't it be cool if you wrote a murder mystery in the world of pro football?" DEATH OF A CHEERLEADER was born, thanks to her.

Heartfelt gratitude goes to everybody who made this book possible. After all, an idea is nothing if it can't be pulled off.

Audrey Linton at Hodder and Stoughton in the U.K., you are wise, fun, and wonderful.

Jessica Case at Pegasus Books U.S., you are simply incredible.

The crackerjack teams at Hodder and Stoughton and at Pegasus Books U.S., I am speechless over your tremendous efforts on this book. Thanks to everybody involved—down to the art departments, the publicity squads, and the copy editors.

Acknowledgements

Kristina Pérez at PLE, you are intelligent, caring, and so easy to work with. Thank you for believing in me from the beginning. Like I said, you came up with the idea for this book, and then you patiently helped me construct it. It was a blast tossing football metaphors back and forth.

Isabel Lineberry at PLE, you lent your keen eye and fresh viewpoint to this story and influenced it greatly. In fact, it turned into something I never thought it could be because of your superb guidance. How lovely that we have a Phoenix connection.

Nick, *grazie* and hugs for encouraging me to do my thing.

Alexa and Gianna, your faith in me is a constant boost. I am the luckiest mom on earth and will always strive to make you proud. Alexa, you're an awesome beta reader. Gianna, I learn so much from your perspective. I love both of you beyond words.

My sister Lisa and my parents, you have always been my still point in a turning world—to paraphrase T.S. Eliot. I love you.

Cathy McDavid, Pamela Tracy, Tina Wheeler, and Libby Banks, better known as the Savvy Scribes, thank you for being outstanding critique partners and close friends.

Bookstagrammers, librarians, BookTok, and reviewers, I adore you. I'm also grateful to my fellow thriller authors who've welcomed me into the literary community with open arms.

The Dallas Cowboys Cheerleaders organization, my time on the squad was an enormous honor...a highlight of my life. It will stay with me forever.

Acknowledgements

Last but not least, I want to thank you, readers. My dream of publication spans decades, so I appreciate your picking up my debut thriller more than you know.

RAISING READERS
Books Build Bright Futures

Dear Reader,

We'd love your attention for one more page to tell you about the crisis in children's reading, and what we can all do.

Studies have shown that reading for fun is the **single biggest predictor of a child's future life chances** – more than family circumstance, parents' educational background or income. It improves academic results, mental health, wealth, communication skills, ambition and happiness.[1]

The number of children reading for fun is in rapid decline. Young people have a lot of competition for their time. In 2024, 1 in 10 children and young people in the UK aged 5 to 18 did not own a single book at home.[2]

Hachette works extensively with schools, libraries and literacy charities, but here are some ways we can all raise more readers:

- Reading to children for just 10 minutes a day makes a difference
- Don't give up if children aren't regular readers – there will be books for them!
- Visit bookshops and libraries to get recommendations
- Encourage them to listen to audiobooks
- Support school libraries
- Give books as gifts

There's a lot more information about how to encourage children to read on our website: **www.RaisingReaders.co.uk**

Thank you for reading.

---

[1] National Literacy Trust, Book Ownership in 2024, November 2024
https://nlt.cdn.ngo/media/documents/Book_ownership_in_2024

[2] OECD. 2021. 21st-century readers: developing literacy skills in a digital world. Paris, France: OECD Publishing.
https://www.oecd.org/en/publications/21st-century-readers_a83d84cb-en.html